THE END

ALPHA

AARON RYAN

Award-winning author of the bestselling post-apocalyptic alien invasion 6-book saga *Dissonance*, the Christian dystopian fiction saga *The End,* the sci-fi thriller *Forecast, God is Not Santa, The Christian Kids Values, Identity & Affirmation Picture Book Series* and many more.

Published in 2025, Edition 1.

Paperback ISBN # 9781965372180 · Hardcover ISBN # 9781965372197 · eBook ISBN # 9781965372173.

Edited by Denouement Editing. Published independently.

Cover art by CM LLC. Man by muratkalenderoglu on Pixabay.

This is a work of fiction. Any similarities to persons living or dead, or actual events is purely coincidental.

For Sweeps, Bren & AJ:
my true loves.

Thank you for being part of my beginning.

CHAPTERS

"Satan likes to hide wolves in sheep's clothing, but that's alright. God hides lions inside of lambs."

- LatterDayHelp

"Fool me once, shame on you.
Fool me twice, shame on *me*."

- Unknown

"The prayer of a Christian is not an attempt to force God's hand, but a humble acknowledgment of helplessness and dependence."

- J.I. Packer

"The dead cannot cry out for justice. It is a duty of the living to do so for them."

- Lois McMaster Bujold

"Judgment without mercy will be shown to anyone who has not been merciful. Mercy triumphs over judgment."

- James 2:13

NOTE ON AI

We live in an age of AI. Every day, more and more services spring up promising revolutionary and innovative results using artificial intelligence. The authoring industry is not immune to this.

I want every one of my readers to know that not once did I employ, nor will I *ever* employ, the use of AI to sculpt any part of any of my stories. Those who know me know that I am staunchly and adamantly opposed to such cheats.

I'm very proud to be a verified human. The ability to create is a gift that I was endowed by my Creator, and I will never forfeit that nor set it aside to propagate something synthetic and imitative.

Everything you've read by me in this saga, and in all my other works, is 100% entirely created by me, the genuine article. I'm a verified human, and always will be.

To my fellow authors, I urge you to preserve the sacred gift of human creation and never stoop to such lows. Always cherish this gift you've been given. If you encounter writer's block, take a break. Don't cop out. Don't take the road more traveled by. Don't cheat. Toe the line for all of us, and keep creation – *true* unadulterated creation – alive.

Long live humanity.

Sincerely,

Aaron Ryan,
Verified Human

CHAPTER 1
Sage

1 . 1 . 2113
Maple Park, IL

Ξ   Ξ   Ξ

Some people are just wolves in sheep's clothing; we all know that now.

All that glitters is not gold, and so on and so forth. We all learned the hard way, and now, all of us were living in raw, cold fear.

We were running from Nero 24/7.

When he burst onto the scene in the Senate in 2095, most of us didn't really know who he was. I was too young anyway. That wasn't his name then, of course: it was *Constantine Jedidiah Goodfellow*. But history has always been rewritten by those in power as they see fit; it's happening even now, certainly. There will be no mention of forced edicts, or worship… or even the Guardians. But we know they exist. I definitely do. My whole family knew they existed just before they were shot down and deprived of life, right after dad hid me.

We should have seen it coming. With a name like his, you might think that such a person *was* all good. Constantine means *steadfast*. Jedidiah means *beloved of the Lord*. Goodfellow means, well, *good fellow*.

That's why no one saw it coming.

I wish the stupid virus had never happened. That unquestionably set the stage for Nero to do what he did, and we, in our foolish blindness and extreme naiveté, trusted him. But all such wishing is futile, right? You can't go back. None of us can. You can't go home again. Forward is the only option, even if forward is through grinding metal and scorching flames, and all of us depending on the guy next to us to toe the line and hold firm in the faith.

No one even really knew how the virus happened. Unfortunately, there was a lot of supposition that Christians had spread it. There was nothing empirical ever presented for that accusation, but Nero ran with it, using it as grounds for further dissent. And then you had the wackos, the nationalists, and the crazies who whipped a lot of people up into a frenzy with scare tactics and polarizing viewpoints that galvanized people into negative action. You had Christians committing assassination attempts, thinking Nero was the antichrist. You had Christian preachers going *crazy* and stirring up dissension against him. The simple, pure message of the gospel itself got swallowed up in message dilution. People erroneously relinquished the gospel in favor of something far more aggressive.

That's when the riots happened. A bunch of hotheads cried out for justice, pleading with others to take back our capitol, take back our country, take back our world for Christ. Their intentions were honorable; their execution sucked. That just added more fuel to the anti-Christian fire and spawned a *lot* of negative sentiment toward those who called Jesus Lord. It ended up being far too much to recover from reputationally, which gave Nero far too much license to stamp out Christianity for good. A lot of us did it to ourselves, frankly.

And then, no one was strong enough to oppose him. Before we knew what hit us, he and his military tech were empowered beyond measure. Beyond restraint. And where you have empowerment without oversight, you have a god complex.

Christianity itself, once the bedrock of our country's democratic and ethical principles, became the scourge of the world: of ill repute, undesirable, and a government-labeled 'unholy threat.' All because Nero was at the helm.

And then came *The Cleansing*.

I was lost in thought, shaking my head at the memory and the horror of all of it.

"Sage, you still alive over there, buddy?"

His question jerked me out of my reveries. My eyes were released from the mesmerizing amber licks of the fire. I turned to Hunter, my best friend. His brow was furrowed as he watched me, his face framed by the fake flames coming from the artificial fireplace in front of us.

But not just the flames. From the back of his neck came the amber glow. *The glow from the mark.*

Same as me. Same as nearly everyone in here.

I nodded. "Just thinking. About time to hit the hay anyway," I replied in a melancholy drone.

"Man, you said it. I'm worn out."

"Me too. I've done three years' worth of Remembrance in just one night."

He chuckled and nodded solemnly.

Remembrance. That's what Swifty called it. It was like what the Vietnamese and other cultures did. The Kinh people believed that the incense they lit would lead those who had died to safe passage. They believed it would guide them home as well. They did it in remembrance, and they were very intentional about it.

I guess when over half of the world's population has been wiped out by a virus, and a malevolent, paranoid delusional, Machiavellian psychopath now occupies the highest throne on the planet, it's good to do a little bit of *Remembrance.*

Even if it's only ever filled with pain.

On this New Year's Day – which was now little more than just another day – there was no celebrating; there was only remembering.

Maranatha. Come, Lord.

Ξ   Ξ   Ξ

We'd been at Maple Park for three days now. The flight from Dekalb had been terrifying; we lost four on the way. The Guardians were definitely getting faster. Whether that was through software or hardware upgrades, or they may have even been new models, was anyone's guess. They had some kind of new scanners that could pick up if we were branded, whether they could see our necks clearly or not. Awful. Awful and unfair. All we had now were our collective prayers for strength to patiently endure.

There was a nun here – the only one left at this church – and her name was Sister Theresa. Saint Mary of the Assumption Catholic Church had lost everyone except for Sister Theresa, who silently kept up the grounds like a ghostly warden, providing shelter and praying for souls. She did it at great risk to herself. Half the church had been bombed right during a service. It was amazing that any of it was still standing, though it was now a blackened, bombed-out husk of its former brick glory. All of the religious institutions like this one had, of course, been mapped out, and the Guardians may have some thermal imaging available to them; we weren't sure. Thank God someone in their right mind had the prescience to build a bomb shelter below it. That's where we now lived and worked out of.

I guess Nero regarded a blackened and charred half-structure like this church – like all the churches – as *fait accompli* because he moved on and didn't have them check here again. For that, we were grateful.

Swifty sent us ahead of him, and then he and six other guys held off Nero's Guardians until they could regroup and make a break for it. That's when we high-tailed it home, sticking to the crops and fields. For whatever reason, Guardians weren't good at picking out organic against organic. If you were stuck somewhere in the metro, they had you. All that signal bounced off the aluminum and metal, and they would zero you like you were in a 3D grid, and then they'd lock and load. That's why we steered clear of the big cities. Chicago was uncomfortably close, at only an hour and a quarter away by car. We were safer in the country.

When the eight of us finally made it back to Maple Park, our mouths were dry and our lungs were burning.

The goal was a bit far-fetched, if you ask me: to get to DeKalb Taylor Airport and see if we might be able to catch a flight further out west. Maybe to Seattle, and then off to Hawaii. Many said that was pointless: Nero's arm had grown long indeed, and his reach was greater than any of us had ever known. Others thought we should fly north and make for Canada. The prime minister was either dead or in hiding, but maybe there would be some stout souls that would be willing to stand up to Nero, enforce whatever remained of international extradition policies, and provide us asylum, at least for a while. Most everyone shook their head no matter the suggestion. The Guardians were everywhere. It didn't really matter where you went; the Guardians were watching, which meant that Nero was watching.

Hunter saved me.

Hunter Preston was my best friend. I'd known him since I was eleven. Or twelve? There's no more clear record since we've been on the move so much. I have his back, and he has mine, and that's the way of it. I looked over at him now, sound asleep, twitching. I stifled a chuckle, watching him; he's always had that nervous tick, and it even comes out when he sleeps.

Hunter's family was killed in a blast, just as mine was. Except for Heather. I heaved a sigh and thought back, shaking my head. I didn't want to, but I had to. Trying to picture them in my mind was the only way to keep them alive, to keep me going. I knew where mom and dad were; I knew where Heather was. I knew. They were with Jesus now. With Jesus, basking in His warmth, while Hunter and I continued to fight it out down here in the dark and cold, Guardians always tailing us.

I closed my eyes and remembered.

Ξ   Ξ   Ξ

11 . 4 . 2099 · Des Moines, IA

"Keep up, Sage, honey, we're almost there."

"I'm hu-ungry," I whined through my mask.

"I know, I know. Almost there, sweet boy," Mommy encouraged me again, and I went back to my FidgetBot, abandoning the notion of food for the moment.

My little feet trudged along next to her, holding her hand, as she carried Heather. Daddy was feverishly filling out the form on the tablet he had been given. For something called a 'census,' though I had no idea what that meant. All I knew was that so many people around us had died, and somebody called President Goodfellow had made a lot of promises that made Mommy and Daddy so very happy.

We lost Auntie Leah and Uncle Ethan to the sickness. They died. Daddy said they went to heaven. A few of my classmates too, but I don't know if they went to heaven or not. Then they cancelled school altogether, starting with the youngest. My preschool was one of the first to go. They said something about little kids being 'cesspools,' and I didn't know what that meant. Mommy and Daddy didn't talk about the virus with us much; every time the word came up, they just seemed to look at each other and take a big sigh while their eyes went wide, and they'd tell me it would be okay.

We were almost there. It was nighttime, and a cold wind was wafting across the parking lot, with the occasional gust and chill. There were a *lot* of people with us, all wearing masks, filtering in and around us into the school auditorium, which was where I would have had my first assembly. I barely remembered it from the few times we went to see Heather in a school musical performance. I was too distracted to care, and it was too loud for me in there. I remember really having to pee during one of those performances, and Daddy got kind of mad that I couldn't hold it. He had to take me to the potty and was telling me to hurry; he didn't want to miss Heather singing. That's all I remember.

We walked right past the bathroom where Daddy had taken me to potty, and he took a big sigh and told Mommy "okay, I think I got it."

"Yeah?" Mommy asked him back. I looked up and watched them both talk quickly.

"Yep, basic stuff," Daddy said, "address, DOB, social security, all that. They asked about religion, too, which I thought was weird, but whatever. I listed us as Christian." I remember he dropped his volume on the last line.

"Proud of it, baby," Mommy said, smiling. I glanced up at her quickly, remembering something she had said a few weeks ago about being careful who we tell that to. As I did so, my big sister raised her weary head off Mommy's shoulder and yawned, looking around blearily and rubbing her eyes as she came to.

"Daddy, what's *religion* mean?" I interrupted, not pulling my eyes away from my FidgetBot.

"Oh, it just means who we worship, who we pray to, that kind of thing, kiddo."

"You mean Jesus?" I asked him.

Daddy smiled and answered me almost before I said His name. "Shhh, yes, punkin,' that's right," he said, scooping me up and looking around cautiously. "Thank you for being so patient. We're gonna head right home after this and get you a snack. I know it's late."

"Late is right," Mommy said. "Why they needed this so urgently is beyond me. Such a long drive."

"Yeah, I don't know," Daddy said. "But it's November, ya know, turn of the century. They've got a lot to get back up and running, and I bet they just wanna get all the info they can as quickly as they can in order to take care of everyone as best they can." They looked at each other just then. "You have to remember this is the second major calamity of this century after the alien invasions in the forties, sweetheart."

"*Aliens?*" I asked in surprise, looking up, my mouth agape.

"That's right, kiddo. Scary. Tell ya another time."

"You're right, I know," Mom said, almost cheerily. "God forbid we need a third. Everybody thought *that* was Armageddon. Next it'll be locusts or something," Mommy snorted.

"With women's hair!" Daddy teased back.

"Stop it," she protested with a smile. "This isn't Revelation come to life, you know."

"Mommy, what's *relevation*?" I asked her while still playing on my FidgetBot.

"*Re-ve-la-tion*," she corrected, glancing down at me. "It's the last book in the Bible, punkin. It's about the end times."

"That's right," Daddy replied. "Anyway, they're just trying to keep people safe."

"From the sickness?" I asked him, still not taking my eyes off my toy.

He kissed the side of my head, and I wiped it off.

"Yep, kiddo, from the sickness."

I looked at him to say something, but then Daddy acknowledged someone who was talking to him and directing us over to a line. Daddy nodded back and pointed at ourselves questioningly. The man who was looking at him had a dark outfit on and a cap. He blew a whistle and nodded, apparently instructing us to move over into the line. It was getting colder.

Daddy carried me over into the line and lightly bobbed with me in his arms. "Almost done, punkin.' Almost done. You're doin' great."

"I want macaroni," Heather breathed through a yawn.

"Me too," I said coolly, back to my toy.

Before too long we went all the way through the line, following a bunch of other people. It took way too long. Daddy stopped with me in his arms before a woman who was seated at a table surrounded by other seated workers all around her assisting other families in line. Beside each of them lay a long black device with a handle at the bottom and a translucent reddish cap on the end. I remember I couldn't help but think it was some kind of space gun.

"Hi folks. Name?"

"Uh, Maddox? Mark and Tracy Maddox."

I watched the woman scan through her list. "Here it is. Hailing from Cedar Rapids?" she asked warmly, smiling.

Daddy nodded. "Yes."

"Hey, Cedar Rapids is where you grew up, Daddy!" I exclaimed joyfully. "What does hailing mean?"

The woman looked up at me with twinkling eyes and smiled. "That's right, little one, good for you. Is it just the four of you then?" she asked, dismissing my question. Daddy nodded again and Mommy said *yes*. "And these are Sage and Heather; they're your children?" she asked.

"Correct," Daddy replied, and then squeezed me tighter to him, whispering, "It just means where you come from."

"Daddy, I'm hungry again. Can we *pleeease* go back to the car? I want a snack! And what's that?" I asked, pointing.

"Shhh, just a second, punkin," he said.

I growled at him, and I won't forget that, because he looked at me angrily. "Not now, kiddo. Just wait, please."

"Hmm, oh, this?" asked the woman with a rasp in her voice. "This helps us to check if you're all clear." She didn't look at me; she just kept tapping on the tablet Daddy had been using, and then turned and grabbed some kind of packet of information and handed it to him and Mommy.

"Okay, got it. Thanks for your patience, folks," she said with a sidelong glance, "I know it's cold, and it sounds like these cuties want some food. It'll be just one more second. Let's start with Daddy, okay?"

She stood up, creaking at the knees, and with a slight grunt, she lifted up the device that was sitting next to her on the table. "It'll feel hot for just a quick second, but I promise you no lasting damage will be done. It's just to check for the virus."

I gasped. "You mean the sickness?"

"Uh-huh, that's right, sweetheart," the elderly woman nodded and assured me. "The virus gets into our brain stem and stays there, and it's a bad one. This little gizmo helps us see if it's in there or not. To see if Daddy's a carrier. Here, hon, turn around please," she said to Daddy.

Daddy did so and showed her his neck. She aimed the device at the base of his skull as I watched, curiously. I glanced over at Mommy and Heather; they were watching too. "Okay, Daddy's clear, say *yay*, kids!"

"Yay!" Heather and I cheered. "No sickness for Daddy!"

"That's right! Okay, and now Mommy's next," the woman said, directing her smile to my mother.

It took my mom the same amount of time. She set Heather down, whirled around and pulled the back of her coat down, raising her snow hat at the same time, while the old woman raised her device.

"Guess what, looks like Mommy's clear too!" said the woman, happily. "Congratulations, folks."

"Yay, Mommy!" I said, as my stomach growled. I remember feeling a sigh of relief for both my parents as they were cleared. I felt it again when both Heather and I were found to be clear as well. The old lady said it would be 'just a little zap.' Come to think of it, I don't remember *anyone* in there being 'found' with the virus. Everyone, seemingly, was clear. I guess that was good news for all of us, although my neck itched and felt hot following my little 'zap.'

By now I was famished and was about to throw my FidgetBot. I needed a snack and was about to scream.

The lady put down her device and smiled at me, and I didn't return the smile. "These are your clearance papers; you're in what's now known as 'Sector 8.' Food vouchers, government stimulus claim form, and medical referral paperwork are all included. New job onboarding materials are in there as well." The mention of food made me scowl at her, but she didn't notice. "You'll receive a call in two weeks from a case worker for both vaccine intake and ramp-up to the new health system. Any questions?"

"Uh, no, that's great, thanks," Daddy said. "Okay, punkin,' guess what?"

"What? And my name's not *punkin*," I growled.

"We're going back to the car and going home! You want a snack now?"

I felt the heat in my face dissipate as a smile took over. "Yay! Yes, please, yes, please, yes, please, yes, please," I replied in a sing-song, while teeter-tottering my head in excitement.

"Alright, folks, you're all set," the lady said with cheeks knotted into a warm smile. "Nice to meet you and have a good night. Next?" She turned to the people just behind us in line.

"Bye, lady. By the way, this is my FidgetBot," I said, waving its arm toward her in goodbye.

"Bye, FidgetBot!" she said with a huge smile, leaning toward me as we walked through and then arced back toward the van.

Bye, FidgetBot.

Bye, lady.

We ended up saying goodbye to so many others.

Ξ   Ξ   Ξ

1.1.2113 · Maple Park IL

My eyes flashed open, and I sat up, scrutinizing the clock.

1:13 am.

I felt haggard and rubbed my eyes, sighing in discontent and lying back down with a yawn.

But the yawn wasn't from fatigue; it was from nerves, just like a dog licks its lips and yawns when it's nervous.

Nerves afire from treacherous memories.

Hunter yawned across from me in his bunk.

"Hey, you still up too?"

"Yep," I confirmed. "Memories. You know how it is."

He nodded silently through the dark, thinking to himself. "Well, like Swifty says, it's better if we remember together, right? 'Wherever two or more are gathered in His name, there He is in the midst of them,' right?"

I sighed. "Right. Okay, let's do it." I stuck a knuckle in my eye and sat up, yawning. The concrete floor was icy cold for my bare feet. I moved back toward the wall so my feet could elevate beyond the ledge of the bed. Hunter came over and sat next to me.

"That whole census had been one big setup," I began. "No one ever told me until a few years later, after the sentries came, after the churches had been blown up or smashed into, after everyone had been scattered, and I had been in more hideouts than you could shake a stick at."

Hunter nodded. His story was much of the same.

"The *perfect* setup," he agreed. "They told me later that President Goodfellow had held a press conference about the church bombings. He denounced these 'dastardly acts' and said that they would not go unpunished. They told me that he even wept, if you can believe it.

"But then I learned the real truth," he continued, "when they told me a few years later. Goodfellow had been unmasked; it was all at his direction: *all* of it. But by then he had quashed all opposition, and it was too late.

"Nero called it Directive 666, and they scoffed at the number and what it implied. They questioned his motive. The census had been nothing more than to locate all Christians. Identify them and their families. Find out where they lived. And then hunt them down," he finished sadly.

"And then hunt them down," I echoed grimly. "*The Cleansing.*"

"Yep. The Cleansing," he repeated. "What a joke."

"It had been launched to exterminate those whose religious views were *unfavorable and non-conducive to world peace,*" -here I employed my best tone of sardonic mockery- "so the leaflets said. And my mom and dad, like so many, they walked blindly into it, and boom, I was an orphan a few months later."

"Me too."

"Dad had the good sense to hide me in the crawlspace of our home. Heather wasn't so lucky, as they looked in our attic and shot her onsite. The branding on her neck told the Guardians everything they needed to know."

"I barely remember my parents now," Hunter said sadly, staring off into space. I turned to him. He had that thousand-yard stare. It caused me to don the same. My brow furrowed, and I frowned.

"Me neither," I said with a difficult lung-clearing.

We spoke no words for several minutes.

Hunter finally broke the silence. "That branding," he said, shaking his head and scoffing. "It only took a few weeks for that indelible glowing mark to show up. Dad noticed it on mom first, fresh out of the shower. And then she checked him and saw the same thing. They ran to me and checked me, and there was a lot of sobbing. To their horror, it was then that they realized that they had been duped. We all had."

"Yep," I agreed. "A total con. We hadn't been scanned for VZV2 at all," I said, rattling off the new variant of the Varicella-Zoster Virus. "We were being branded like cattle without even knowing it." I looked around. All the sleeping figures around us glowed amber at the backs of their necks. The marks burnt into them had a latent nascency: eventually, they all revealed their hosts' religion with a dim amber light, and the grim truth was simultaneously revealed.

I could practically hear him shaking his head in the dark. "All I remember seeing was the glint of titanium and tungsten in the night, and those cold, amber eyes. I remember hearing that whirr of the air through their rotors and the fast-moving treads crunching gravel and soot underneath as they wormed their way into our neighborhood – into *every* neighborhood, dude – and hunted down every man, woman, or child who professed the name of Jesus."

"I remember running," I told him. "After they killed Heather. I eventually found my way out of there and ran all the way across Indianola Avenue onto East Creston. I knew I had to keep quiet, but I was only four, and the tears erupted into bursting sobs of incredulity as my little heart quaked. I rounded a corner onto East Creston, and that's when I saw that teenage girl standing there, face to face with a Guardian. *Cassie*, I think they said her name was. It was the first time I heard one of those machines ask the question."

He scoffed again. We mockingly said the foreboding words together.

Citizen, this is your final warning. Do you recant?

"*Recant*," I breathed scornfully, shaking my head. "I didn't even know what the word meant then. But I knew what a bullet-riddled human looked and sounded like, and I witnessed it with my own eyes, as that girl shook her head and the machine fired away in a hammer-smash of bullets straight into her chest. A thudding cacophony, man. Blood sprayed everywhere, and she fell to her knees as the Guardian finished her off. She was a pile of meat. Others watching took off."

"Yeah, the Guardians were landlocked then, right? They weren't in the air, and that had been some saving grace. But it was really only a matter of time before Nero began to think three-dimensionally. I think it was 2105 when we saw them for the first time over The Windy City," he said.

"That's why some of us were reluctant to try the airport; the risk of interception was too great in the air."

He nodded, numbly scratching at an itch on his leg.

"Nero started deploying the AirGuard, and we found they could hover with some kind of advanced propulsion. That's when he started calling himself that stupid nickname."

"Prince of the Power of the Air," we both mocked.

"Yeah," Hunter agreed. "I guess that's what you get when you elect a delusional, psychopathic, techno-trillionaire into office who creates military-grade machinery and holds all the codes. To think he'd been building all of that to sell to the government. They were too afraid of him to not sign the contract with *NeroTech*."

"But back then?" I jumped back to my own story. "That little boy just crouched there, concealed in the bushes in a cloud of fear, staring out past the foliage at the dead girl. My little corduroys were steaming with pee. I trembled for my life, man, questioning every cracked twig around me. It was hours before I moved again, and I could only stumble over to the next house as they took me in. I passed that girl's corpse. She was turned on her side, and I could see the back of her neck. Her mark was fading, cooling, because her body was losing heat as she lay dying. She had professed the name of Christ, though. Probably the victim of an informant."

"*Informants,*" he hissed venomously.

"Hey," I said. "Forgiveness."

He rolled his eyes and sighed. "I know."

"Anyway, I was too young to understand any of it back then. I understand all of it now."

We didn't say anything for a while. I shook my head as I remembered that sweet elderly woman at the school during the census and 'virus scan.' That kind old woman had no idea she was part of it. None of them did. Nero used them like he had so many others. It was all part of his master plan. The woman wasn't scanning us for the virus in the elementary school. She was branding us with infrared, a mark that would eventually appear for all to see, and, in due course, be used to target us for elimination.

I took a deep breath. "Isn't it sick? That virus was the perfect cover for a branding operation. Those devices weren't scanning for viruses already present; they were *implanting* a virus in us via infrared laser. They were directly linked to the tablets that everyone filled out, my dad included. He had told them we were Christians. So, the device burnt an infrared mark into all four of us." I shook my head at the memory. "All because my dad selected 'Christian.' The scanner was linked to the tablet; the tablet was linked to our religion. My dad says we're *not* Christian? No mark for us. The family one aisle over at the census that said they were atheist? No mark for them, either, and they're most likely alive out there, presumably, subservient to Nero."

Good for them, I thought blandly.

Hunter was quiet for a while. At last he turned to me. "What would you say to him if you ever met him face to face?"

I smiled at my friend, but it felt fiendish. I thought of someday infiltrating his ranks, sneaking up to him, closer and closer. Like a jackal, gaining his trust and working my way in for the kill.

"You know what I'd say?"

"What?" Hunter asked me.

"I'd look him in the eye and say two things. 'There *is* a God, and you're not him.'"

Hunter laughed abruptly, but his laughter faded as he regarded my stoic expression. "But Hunt," I said, "the sad truth is that I might do a lot more than that before I could even calm down to speak to him."

My friend stared at me quizzically, but I knew that he knew what I meant. He'd expressed the same thing once or twice. We would never sit down to a nice coffee with Nero; we would kill him.

He was the man who was solely responsible for the annihilation of Christians and the eradication of Christianity.

The man hunting all of us down as we speak.

The man whose crusade had always been to blame the virus, and *all* the world's misfortunes since the dawn of time, on us.

The man who believed he truly was the Antichrist, and truly sought to usher in Armageddon. 'To call God out,' he had said. 'Where is your God now?' he challenged in his first address as Nero.

But Nero had no idea who God was, and he failed to recognize that God doesn't work on man's timeline. God works on *God's* timeline.

I slowly ripped off my choker and could see the wall splash in faint orange behind me in the dim light of the bunker. My mark was glowing, like all ours did. It helped the enemy to target us better, and I'd had it since I was four. I'd learned to live with it. And to cover it up.

I wondered if one day we would be equally as sinister in The Defiance. I wondered if we could be that cold and heartless as we struck back.

I wondered if I could be a sheep in a wolf's clothing.

CHAPTER 2
Maximillian

1 . 2 . 2113
Washington, DC

Ξ   Ξ   Ξ

It was so self-aggrandizing as to perhaps defy belief in the eyes of some, but defiance was the epitome of all that was Nero.

And I *loved* him for it.

The room was pungent with incense and bathed in the warm rays of the rising sun. The holes that had been punched through the roof of the Senate chamber allowed the sunlight to waft down in golden beams through the trailing wisps of incense. The shafts of light crisscrossed through a gaudy setup of multiple mirrors which facilitated a shameless light play, enveloping the overlarge throne at its center in a cerebral nucleus of worshipful, silent reverence.

It was, in a word, *righteous.*

Scantily clad women, interspersed around the perimeter of the room, lightly strummed on harps and sitars. A few slithered at Nero's feet, draped down either side of his high stairs in permissive and glorious decadence, their sweat shimmering through the swirling mist. His 'harem of great reward,' he called it. All of it was beautifully flamboyant and befitting the god-king.

One of them stood now behind him; her delicate fingers vigorously massaged his deltoids, trapezius, and neck as she swayed. Two others massaged his feet with their pierced tongues.

And ah, my lord! Emperor Nero, *His Eminence,* was beyond beautiful. Lavishly swathed in a multitude of paints draping his form in swirling circlets and a geometric rainbow of colors, the mere sight of him lifted one's spirits. There he was: enveloped in the purest of colored and scented oils, crowned with an ornate mitre that sparkled with precious gems set amidst swirling hues.

"Thank you, High Vassal," he said to me, graciously, as I refilled his chalice with more wine.

"Yes, your Grace," I breathed to him in reverent worship. "As the Divine Emperor commands." I smiled, grateful to simply bask in his presence.

His Grace bowed his head in reverence, and held up the ornate, sacrosanct vessel which contained his own tissue, fingernails, skin flakes, hair, and mucus: all sacred, all precious, all unique and wholly pure. *It was an offering*, he had said, *to one to whom he himself was but a servant.*

It was an offering to 'The Day Star,' as he called him.

"It is only a matter of time now, Maximillian, my faithful Vassal," he said to me, graciously.

"Yes, my lord Nero," I echoed.

"The time will soon come to upgrade to my new domain. To expand to new horizons, my servant. To take the throne that is rightfully mine, prophesied from the beginning."

"Success, my lord," I said, bowing.

"Success, Maximillian," he echoed, smiling, as he raised his glass to me. "The Day Star is pleased with us."

I felt his warmth radiate upon me. "Prepare for the orgy," he instructed as I rose to leave. "It will commence immediately following my nightly broadcast." Nero took a drink from his chalice, and the dark red dripped down his chin, which his concubines then licked his face free of.

Ξ   Ξ   Ξ

The lord Nero was being bathed, and I was dismissed for the time being to attend to his flock. I would be summoned once he was dressed and ready to address the masses.

I needed to see the Minister of Defense, Vassal Behmardi.

I found him in one of the southern offices. The Capitol building was not too much different from bygone years and administrations; it still retained its antiseptic plainness through the tapestries and carpets which were slowly being phased out in favor of Nero's new decorum and power aesthetic. I couldn't blame him; they were relics of a forgotten age that contained undesirable testaments to detestable members of that unholy religious sect, and they had no place here. Images of Mother Earth and the *true* religions, paganism and universalism, were all that were allowed here, and for good reason. They were unrestrictive, inclusive, and liberating in every respect. Flowering buds in earthen vessels adorned the hallways, allowed to grow freely out of their confinement and grace the halls with the glory that was all around us from earth to sky.

These halls, once abuzz with business, were now rightfully converted to a shrine of worship, and the statue of Nero stood high atop the peak of the rotunda, for all to see and be filled with amazement.

And everywhere you looked, lotus flowers grew: a symbol of spiritual growth rising above adversity and revered in many cultures.

Revered by Nero.

I felt as if I were gliding through the flowers, my fingertips neatly touching, not a trace of makeup running, and my tall capirote erect over my head. Lesser vassals bowed and smiled as I wafted by.

A tracing vine grew out of one such vessel, overarching the doorway of my favorite minister, Vassal Behmardi. He sat elegantly upright, meditating and gazing out upon the grounds beyond as the new day's sunlight streamed down upon the grass. Sitar music played on prerecorded media.

"And how are we today?" I asked Vassal Behmardi as I entered. He turned slowly to face me.

"Esteemed High Vassal Maximillian!" He rose and kissed my signet ring, which I extended proudly toward him. "To what do I owe the honor?"

"The lord wishes to have me assess the readiness of the machines for the continuing mission," I replied.

"Oh yes, of course. All is underway with the existing battalions. I was just watching the newest fleet of AirGuard overhead. They are mighty. They are glorious!" He clapped his hands with juvenile glee, practically hopping.

"Indeed they are. All hail Emperor Nero."

"All hail Emperor Nero," he agreed, bowing his head slightly and closing his eyes in reverence.

"And the third wave?"

"In production as we speak, and coming along nicely! Fifty thousand slated to be finished before March. They will all be autonomous and completely independent of the previous saboteur's programming."

"Have the new leaflets arrived?" I asked eagerly.

"Not yet, my good vassal, but they have been fully proofed, I assure you. All previous observations and holidays removed. Especially the two in question."

"The ones from the spring and December that we do not mention."

"The very ones," he smiled.

"And are there any reports of dissension or unrest?"

"There was one such report, my liege, out of Tampa. Mostly protestors of the new curfew. Nothing out of the ordinary. Incarcerated or eliminated as per protocol."

"And our *saboteur?*"

"The dissident known as Drexler, sir," he responded with distaste. I nodded in response, nearly wincing at the evil name. "Nothing so far. He has not yet been located, but information points to somewhere around Cincinnati."

"Hmm, all things in due time. And across the waters, international relations are always something of a question mark, or an exclamation mark where the UK is concerned. Hmm," -here I clicked my tongue in disapproval- "but we are making inroads with the Guardians and the new places of worship everywhere. The lord is pleased, and we are moving forward according to schedule. What is the final cleanse tally for 2112?" I asked, hopeful.

He smiled with great relish. "It pleases me to report to my lord that another 326,472 undesirables have been eliminated. We are counting fetuses in pregnant women now," he flicked his eyebrows up, beaming.

A thrill ran through me, and I clasped my hands together. "Oh, what joy. What unspeakable joy! His Eminence will be so pleased, *so* pleased to hear this, Vassal Behmardi. I shall report the good news to him post-haste. That should leave us with little more than ten million left to eradicate, since the virus unfortunately did not wipe them out first. His Eminence will be overjoyed."

"Indeed, he will be," the minister said, his voice rising into a gleeful adolescent squeak. He clapped his hands once more. "The less-than-humans are going the way of the earth, as the lord Nero foresaw. Justice is being served, is it not? They were the ones to spread the accursed virus in the first place. His Eminence is holy, and he has triumphed."

"He has, and he shall," I agreed. "And what of the new techniques and our recent captures?"

"Oh yes, we have a few candidates below who are being worked on as we speak, High Vassal. Nothing has been divulged yet. No one is immediately connected to the treacherous Drexler, but some worthy candidates may be in possession of valuable intel."

"Yet, nothing extracted? No usable information to find and exterminate our opposition?" I asked with suspicion, looking at him sidelong. There was no reason to suspect Vassal Behmardi of deception. I, however, was answerable to his Eminence, and his Eminence would require a favorable report that indicated progress.

"Unfortunately, nothing so far, High Vassal Maximillian. I promise to keep you fully informed once we have a breakthrough."

"Thank you, Vassal Behmardi. I take my leave of you." I extended my signet ring.

"Thank *you*, High Vassal Maximillion," he said as his neck slithered, and he tilted in admiration, kissing my ring once more, just as I was about to do with lord Nero. "Thank *you*."

"No. All thanks be to His Eminence, and all thanks be to Satan for paving his way. All hail Emperor Nero."

"All hail Emperor Nero," he practically sang as I walked out, and he turned to watch the AirGuard once more as the lotus flowers adorned my exit.

I took in a deep breath of assured air, reveling in this latest news. What a triumphant year! The Cleansing was nearly complete. Gold-emblazoned moldings with His Eminence's portrait stared out proudly at me as I turned on my heels to find my lord after his bath. The beauty of his image smote my heart as I gasped in admiration once more. I had seen them a thousand times, and a thousand more would not be enough.

All of the trappings contained in this sacred place were all so narcissistic as to perhaps strain credulity for some, but worship was the deserved reward for all that was Nero.

CHAPTER 3
Sage

1 . 3 . 2113
Maple Park, IL

Ξ   Ξ   Ξ

We waited, and we listened. I was doing it intently with them.

"Stay down," whispered Swifty, his plate of food on the floor near him, his AR-18 at the ready.

The whirring of the Guardians outside in the parking lots to our north and south could still be heard clearly. I guessed there to be at least five or six of them. They were communicating with each other in that strange, guttural electronic language of theirs.

Hunter crouched low beside me. It was early morning, and I had just finished breakfast when they were picked up on radar heading this way. Someone radioed the coordinates to the bunker, and then notified Swifty. I licked my tongue over my teeth, picking out the cereal flakes that remained, watching intently as I clutched my XM6 rifle.

To our west lay the fields and then Union Ditch Number 2. We could make a run for it if need be, keeping under the cover of the trees to our northwest, but we all knew that it was better to stay inside. We had sympathizers in most of the surrounding buildings.

Hunter let out a nigh-undetectable sigh next to me, his rifle muzzle pointed in the same direction as mine: the ceiling hatch. Not that it would make much difference if they found us here. They wouldn't come in; they'd just bomb it again. Exposed, out there where they could see you and they could see your mark, the Guardians were to be most feared.

The whirring continued. I swallowed.

Swifty motioned to Hunter and me to stay as he cautiously approached the covered-over window. He passed Asher and Emma Amari up ahead, each holding their own rifles. Asher was eighteen and Emma seventeen.

Asher was an incredibly scrappy kid, and if you ticked him off, he'd make a face you wouldn't want to see twice, glaring at you under his eyebrows. I thought it comical the first time, until he let me know with a left hook that it wasn't. His pride was his fist, and his vulnerability was his girl, Anja. He was one of the only people I knew who had actually tried to cut out his mark. The big, blackened gash and scarring across the back of his neck attested to his intrepid resolve. It didn't matter anyway; in doing so, you were automatically guilty before the Guardians. There would be no other reason to have a gash in the back of your neck other than to cut out your mark. His neck didn't glow anymore, but there remained a big, gaping, and ugly scar.

A scar there *meant you were a Christian.*

That left us all with only two choices. Cut out the mark and deal with a giant, uncomfortable scar until the end of your days, or keep the mark and wear your choker like you've been told.

The chokers. God bless whoever made them. The reinforced aluminum and glass plate positioned at the back would conceal your mark as you wrapped the choker around your neck. Thankfully, they didn't come full circle around your Adam's apple, or someone would see them. They could be easily concealed under a turtleneck or button-up shirt. Their signatures were small, and, thankfully, discreet.

Someone was an ingenious lab rat to come up with those. I'm sure they've saved a lot of lives so far, or at the very least kept people from being detected. They also allowed us to move around and blend in, but God forbid those things should examine us up close. In the wintertime, when we were bundled up tightly, it was better. Ultimately, however, you couldn't wait to tear it off yourself at the end of the day when you were back in hiding. They were hot and itchy, the plates needed to be continually checked for integrity, and the fabric needed to be washed.

Swifty, bold and fearless, ascended the small, folding ladder placed permanently below the window for just such a time as this.

Emma was not cut from the same cloth as her brother Asher, and her body racked with the shakes anytime the Guardians approached. She *remembered* what happened when the Guardians came. Asher had been away, and it was only her parents, her older brother Trent, and Emma. They had been hiding in their laundry room when the Guardians found them several months later. Her parents were dead in an instant as they tried to defend their children. The Guardians then asked Trent only once. Trent would not deny his faith. Emma swears she can still see his blood splatter on her shoulder.

I watched her closely as we waited. Emma didn't have the mark; she and Trent had converted to Christ later in an evening underground church service. Only Asher and their parents had the mark. Emma was then asked the *other* question by the Guardian; the one that they ask those without the mark who are found in the company of those who are marked.

Citizen, do you profess that Jesus is the Christ?

Emma denied Jesus. That's why they spared her.

It's something she still cries about. She trembles, both from fear and shame, haunted by the prospect of having to answer that wretched question again. I get it. We all get it. We might have done the same once. But at the end of the day, she's alive; she's forgiven.

As I watched her, my heart went out to her with pity.

As for Asher, he would have no pity. When he returned from staying at a friend's house, he flew into a rage, swearing to Emma that he would keep her safe and vowing revenge against the Guardians. Against Nero.

Against *all* who had taken their family.

The sound of gunfire jerked all of us back to consciousness. A few more bursts, and I thought I heard a muffled scream far off in the distance. I couldn't be sure. All of us bowed our heads in prayer. Some swore. We had other believers in hiding nearby, in the neighborhood houses between Elm and Willow. My heart sank. They must have been found.

The quiet descended on us once more. Every joint creaked loudly in that room as people shifted their weight and waited. That's what life had become, after all: waiting.

My thoughts went back to our friends as I looked back over at them. The scrappy incision on the back of Asher's neck was entirely visible, and he would flaunt it whenever he could, considering it a battle scar worthy of medals.

Then there was Luca, and Swifty's daughter Anja. Luca was 17, tough as nails, silent, and brooding as a winter snow. Anja was acrobatic, fast, and a natural leader. Asher was hard-pressed to keep up with his girlfriend. He talked a tough game, but he was a gentleman with Swifty's daughter. Swifty kept watch but was pretty adept at seeing the good in people.

Besides, Asher was a fighter, and in a world of conflict, perhaps he thought Anja would be safer with him than with a peacemaker.

Lastly, there was Charlotte. 'Charlie,' as she liked to be called, and I liked calling her that. She was my age – a few months older than me – and I knew I wanted her from the very moment I laid eyes on her.

She shifted her weight, though her head was bowed, with her Glock to her temple. She was praying. She preferred a handgun.

"Less weight to lug around, and easier to bullseye a dope," she had said. That's what she called the Guardians, though she said she hadn't made it up. Apparently a lot of people from her old neighborhood called them that: they were terrifying but dumb. Operating on singular software that only programmed them to kill. All they did was roll around in search of something to shoot. That's why we learned to be faster than them. Prey eluding the predator.

I had met Charlie a few years after Hunt. Her dirty blonde hair and captivatingly huge, immersive brown eyes drew me in, even in the dark of the house we had sought refuge in. She had a quiet resolve about her, and her eyes spoke more to me in the silence than our first few verbal exchanges did. You could get lost in those eyes. I sure did.

Hunter and I vied for her attention at first. He wasn't a bad-looking guy, but, thanks be to God, I got the vibes from Charlie that she was more interested in me. No harm, no foul. *Sorry, Hunt,* I had thought to myself. He blew it off. She liked the rugged type. I was, thankfully, the rugged type. Hunt was more clean-cut and gregarious.

Charlie looked over at me slowly, her eyes twinkling in the dark. She smiled, and the warmth traveled over to me. I nodded to her, giving her a thumbs up with my eyebrows raised, sending her a silent *You okay?* She nodded back and mouthed, *I'm okay.*

More gunfire outside.

My heart thudded within my chest. My throat felt goopy and mucus-laden, thick from the milk in my cereal.

His AR-18 slung over his back, Swifty was now carefully watching through the peephole over the boarded and curtained window. I had looked through there once. It didn't provide much of a view, but it was at least something. Our view was west, however, not north.

Swifty raised his right hand and whirled his index finger around twice. *AirGuard.* He thrust his finger forward west as if casting a stone. That meant some distance westward. He paused and flashed his fingers, counting to seven. Seven *AirGuard* units out there.

"Freakin' eh," I said quietly to myself. "That's a lot of 'em." Hunter looked at me and nodded, his eyes wide. I looked back down at Charlie, who was watching Swifty. My eyes traced back up to him at the window. He rolled his fists over each other rapidly like he was boxing against a hanging speed bag, but low to his stomach. *Guardians.* He held up his hand and paused, then pointed west and held up three fingers. So, there were at least three that he could see. He pointed north and waved his palm up and down for a moment, gesturing that he was uncertain about any more of them in the northern parking lot or beyond.

The good thing about Guardians is that they didn't cover the earth…*yet.* They couldn't be everywhere. They came and went in waves. People could go about their business and their lives without much fear of bumping into them.

That was good, because they were terrifying. Unfeeling, unsentimental assembly-line machines that were programmed to do one thing: kill off all those identifying with Jesus Christ. They were military-grade drones and effective killing machines designed to infiltrate and terminate without respect to age or class.

If they zeroed anyone with a mark, all hell broke loose; those not in the crosshairs knew to clear the area double-time, to duck, or to get to safety. They had gunned down the previous president and reduced a crying toddler to hamburger while others watched. Both were marked. The toddler couldn't even answer the *recant* question.

I shook my head.

It was a sullen assembly after that, once the machines rolled on. It didn't matter if it was your family or someone else's; the pain was felt – and shared – by all. *All* mourned. *All* helped with the cleanup.

And then the leaflets would drop from a passing AirGuard, and the engines would shake your home, your foundations, your very soul, to the core. A spine-altering, thundering reminder that they could strike at any minute, they could drop their propaganda and then roar out of there.

I actually found and read one once.

NOTICE OF VIOLATION

Citizens of the local populace, all hail Emperor Nero!

Dissidents were recently discovered in this area, and they have been dealt with accordingly. Undesirables and their treasonous behavior will always be dealt with swiftly to preserve the sacred state of worship for His Eminence, the god-king Nero.

The Guardians who have meted out justice here need not be feared. They are your friends. They are your protectors, and operate in the name of the god-king. Please regard them as his emissaries and know that they are simply operating on programming setup both for your protection and for the betterment of the new world.

We hope that you live a long and fruitful life.

If any of you have knowledge of any treachery or are in contact with undesirables who claim the name of Jesus as savior and are therefore engaging in terrorist plots against His Eminence, please report it at once to any member of your local Guardian battalion. Your reporting will be richly rewarded, and you will have lasting favor from the god-king, along with immeasurable financial reward.

Please distribute this leaflet to your neighbors, family and friends. Together, we will have a safer and more prosperous world under the god-king.

Remember, it is a crime punishable by death to pronounce any name as holy other than the god-king, His Eminence Himself, Lord Nero.

Thank you for your attention to this matter.
ALL HAIL EMPEROR NERO!

The leaflet made me want to vomit. I crumpled it up and ran.

The very memory unnerved me. I shook my head in revulsion. I tore myself out of my thoughts and drew my eyes up to Swifty. He had slowly turned around and was staring down upon all of us again. He was clad in an A-shirt and cargo pants as always, and badly in need of a shave. Didn't look one bit like our leader, but we knew he was. He'd survived this long and saved many others, and that's why we followed him.

He slowly descended the ladder and folded it back up against the wall with a sigh, removing his AR-18 and placing it on a rack that was mounted to the wall near the entrance. He patted it for good luck and returned to us, giving Anja a quick hug. To all whose eyes met his, he clasped his hands in suggestion of prayer.

Swifty was part military commander, part teacher, and part theologian-level youth pastor. At least, that's how he felt. He actually had a rank, attributed to him by all of us, young and old, and that was commander. 'Commander Gregory Hudson' was his official name, but we just called him Swifty, and there was a reason for that, of course. The dude was lithe, well-knit, and *fast*. If we were ever escaping Guardians, this was the number one rule:

Keep up with Swifty.

If you didn't, you were probably going to meet Jesus that night. Which wasn't a bad thing, of course; it's just that we were all still needed down here. As much as we ached to be away from the body and present with the Lord like 2 Corinthians 5:8 tells us, we were needed here to fight the good fight of faith. Nero had to be stopped, and no one knew how just yet. Until that time, we were all God's soldiers on the front lines.

And Swifty was the commander of the soldiers. At least in Sector 8. He now sat back down in a big huff with his knees folded up, bowing his head and arms over his knees and prayed. We scooted closer to join him.

"Abba Father," he began, "we're in danger every day and every night. We live in a world controlled by a man who wants all of your precious children dead. Around me even now are a bunch of those precious children. I know how I feel about my own daughter. I love her, Lord. We know how you feel about your kids. You love us, and you've always loved us with an everlasting love. Would you cover us and allow us to take refuge under your wings? Cover us with your feathers, and under your wings may we find refuge as Psalm 91 teaches us. Protect us, Lord, and protect those out there less fortunate than us so that they too may find shelter. Maranatha. In Jesus' Name, Amen."

Amen, we all agreed in unison. Even Asher over there with his gritty face and his grim-set jaw ready for action agreed, though it may have come out slightly in a hiss through his teeth.

I looked up at Charlie, who was walking over toward me. I felt a pat on my shoulder as Hunt looked at me with a smile, flicking his eyebrows up. I elbowed him. He grunted, smiled, got up and made room for Charlie.

"Hey, Char," he said, passing her on the way to get more cereal, presumably. Charlie sat down in between Swifty and me.

"Well, that was an adventure," she breathed, and she laid her Glock down behind her so that it wouldn't be stepped on by anyone around her and accidentally discharge. "Never a dull moment, right?"

"Not until Jesus returns," I said, smiling thinly. She grinned. "Seems like that's getting a lot closer. How you doin,' Charlie?"

"I'm okay. Just tired." She yawned, then proceeded to loll her head and lay it on my shoulder. The smell of her hair sent my senses into overdrive. "Been a long few days. That whole attempt on the airport," she ended lamely, shaking her head. "My quads still feel like rubber."

"No one could outrun Asher."

"Except Swifty."

We both glanced over at Asher. He was huddled together with Anja, his sister Emma, and Luca.

"That was crazy," she murmured sleepily. "I hope we don't have any other suicide missions soon."

I scoffed. "They're not suicide missions, Charlie. They're all important attempts to gain back a little ground, right?"

She didn't answer.

"The more little battles we win, the more chance we have of winning the war, right?" I squeezed her arm.

"Uh-huh," she said, blinking.

"Are you seriously gonna go to sleep on my shoulder?" I asked her. "No drooling," I said, with a playful flick to her forehead.

"Hey! No, I'm not sleepy, just tired. Waiting with every muscle flexed, ready to run again at a moment's notice, kinda wears ya out. Just need to recharge for a few minutes."

Ξ   Ξ   Ξ

Eighty-three minutes later, Nicholas was lifting her up and placing her on a couch in the far, dark corner of the bunker. I had just become accustomed to her quiet snoring. My butt cheeks were buzzing from inactivity, and there was a kink in my neck. I don't know when she dropped off, but it was right when I was getting ready to ask her if she was excited for her birthday. She was turning 19 in March. I would turn 19 after her in May.

She didn't even flinch or stir. Nicholas was a big, burly guy with tree trunks for legs and bowling balls between his shoulders and elbows. I would not dare to tangle with him. He was one of the few older adults that would usher us into planning meetings and include us in the briefings; he was smiling and kind, but quiet. He always had his hat pulled down low just above his eyes.

Charlie was asleep. I got up and stretched, feeling the blood return to neglected parts of my body. The tingling subsided.

"You make a nice pillow?" Swifty asked me, grinning with a knowing look. "Sage is *so* cozy," he jested, while loading magazines, stuffing round after round into magazine after magazine.

"Oh, can it," I said with a playful sneer.

"Citizen, do you profess that Sage is the pillow?" Anja teased while seated next to Swifty.

"Haha, very funny," I sneered again, frowning at her. Swifty laughed at his daughter's ingenuity. She was as acrobatic with the jokes as she was in the field. Real sneaky sense of humor. "I couldn't move. Didn't want to wake Charlie." I paused. "And I *do* profess." I said with a grin.

Swifty nodded. "All good, *Capitán Love*."

I punched him in the shoulder – hard – and he winced and laughed. "Okay, okay, ow! Good one, kid." He held his shoulder and rotated his arm, smiling with a slight wince. I hoped Asher had seen that one and deemed it a worthy hit.

"You ready for class today?" Swifty asked.

I nodded. "Yep. Always. Knowledge is power, right?"

"Knowledge is power. Know your enemy."

"But Nero isn't our enemy, Swi-"

"I didn't say Nero, kid," he bit back, scowling. "*Satan* is our adversary. Everyone else has been deluded by him, including Nero."

"Yeah, well, it seems Nero does plenty of deluding himself, as well," I argued. "And I have no sympathy toward him. The guy thinks he's the Antichrist and is doing everything he can to mimic him."

"Yes, he is. He has his reasons."

"So you think one day all will be revealed, and we'll understand why? How do we know he's *not* the antichrist?"

Swifty thought to himself for a moment. "Perhaps. I think so. Then again, we might not. We might get to Heaven and have no memory of this whole affair once the old order of things has passed away. But a big part of faith is chilling out, man. Chilling out and knowing that God's ways are higher than our ways, and we can't understand His ways fully. Once we get past that hurdle, we can unclench a bit more. Right?

"And we know he's not the antichrist, buddy. There's nothing supernatural about him. The Rapture hasn't happened. We don't have a mark on us that allows us to buy or sell. He's not a descendant of the tribe of Dan. He hasn't set up an image of himself in the Jewish temple, and it was destroyed long ago anyway. He has not fulfilled the Scriptures. There's a *lot* that needs to happen before the antichrist rises to power. Prophecies need to be fulfilled. Wars and rumors of wars. A lot hasn't happened yet."

"Seems like we've been in a war forever," I jeered. "But what if all those people dying *was* the Rapture?" I insisted.

Swifty frowned. "No way. That's not how the Bible says it will happen. And remember this: Nero is simply a man who has chosen to capitalize on the disappearance of so many around the world who would deny him his claim. In such a vacuum, resistance is lessened. Such a global crisis is an open door for opportunistic folks like Nero to position themselves to seize power."

I nodded in understanding.

"To be clear, God's ways are just a titch higher than Dad's and my ways," Anja added with flair, "and way, *way* higher than your ways, Sage." She grinned at me in mock empathy.

"Ask your dad how that hit felt. I'm sure he enjoyed it. I have more available if you're interested."

Swifty gave me a mock-threatening face to warn me that I'd have to go through him. But Anja giggled and jumped up, putting up her dukes.

"Yeah? Let's go ten rounds, man, here we go!" She dodged and weaved, ducked and shot a few jabs at me while I stood there, watching incredulously. Asher smiled at her approvingly. Eventually, however, the jabs stopped, and she giggled again, heading off to go sit and talk with Asher.

Birds of a scrappy feather flock together, I thought.

I shook my head and sat down next to Swifty.

"You sure have your hands full with her," I said.

"Always have, always will. That girl's my little wrecking ball, man. Wouldn't have it any other way," he said proudly, and then watched her plop down next to Asher and ram her shoulder into his as he grinned at her in slight aggression. "I'd hate to have her in my face. She's gonna do great things in this war."

"Yeah, if we ever get out of this bomb shelter."

Swifty looked back at me sidelong and smiled. "Perseverance produces character. Character produces hope. And hope does not disappoint us, because…?" he asked, leading me on.

"…because God's love has been poured out into our hearts through the Holy Spirit, who has been given to us," I completed, pounding my chest.

"Nicely done," he said, fist-bumping me. "Address?"

"Romans 3:3-5," I said. "I really love Romans. Every chapter is different. Every chapter is loaded with greatness."

Swifty nodded, finishing up with his magazines and handing me a few as backup for my pack. "It's one of the best. It equipped the Christian church in Rome. Got them ready before everything went down."

"Everything went down?"

"Before the first Nero's persecution of them. Before the fire," Swifty clarified.

I looked away from him, lost in thought for a moment. "All of that persecution and all those murders," I said. "I wonder which Nero was worse, that one or this one."

Swifty shook his head and frowned. "We may never know until we meet Jesus face to face and can ask him. But you know what He'll say."

I turned back to Swifty, confused.

"Both were lost, both were loved."

I stared at him for a moment. "I just have the hardest time with that, Swifty. I absolutely get that Jesus has unconditional love for all mankind and that God so loved the *whole* world, man. But to think that he would have any sympathy for the man who used to be Constantine Jedidiah Goodfellow…"

"He still *is* Jedidiah, Sage," Swifty said, stopping me. "*Loved by the Lord.* We're *all* Jedidiah. 'We all, like sheep, have gone astray; each of us has turned to our own way, and the Lord has laid on him the iniquity of us all. Isaiah 53:6, buddy. Nero is a lost sheep just like you and me. Jesus came *precisely* for people like Nero. We're *all* lost in our sin. We're *all* on the same trajectory as Nero is."

"Which is?"

Swifty stared at me solemnly. "Death."

I just looked at him, unsure what to say.

Ξ   Ξ   Ξ

We were all gathered at the far end of the bomb shelter now, seated in rows against the back wall, listening to Swifty and others teach. Sister Theresa had come down and provided lunch for all of us with the help of some of the adults. Charlie had come strolling back and plunked down right next to me. "Hey, Pillow," she quipped. "I heard you had a good convo with Anja about that." I jokingly told her not to remind me.

And now, class was in session.

"So, you have the fundamentalists, the nationalists, all of these different sects, right?" Swifty asked us. "And from that you have all kinds of activities that develop anti-Christian sentiment. Give me some of those examples, please. Yes, Luca?"

Luca had raised his hand, and we looked over at him. "The bombings in Tulsa in 2096?"

"Correct. And?" Swifty said, looking around. After writing '2096 bombings' on the whiteboard, he turned to us again. "Yes, Charlie?"

I hadn't noticed her raising her hand next to me.

"The Woke riots of 2099 all over the place. They were everywhere," she said glumly.

"Definitely one of them," Swifty said, adding '2099 riots' onto the board. "And?"

Asher spoke up without raising his hand. "The virus itself, man. It got politicized," he emphasized.

"And how did it get politicized?" Swifty asked. Asher shrugged and said no more.

"Didn't they say that it had come out of that group of labs owned by the Christian consortium?" Charlie asked.

Swifty nodded. "Low-hanging fruit," he said. "An easy thing to pin on Christians then, wasn't it? You have a Christian consortium of ministries in Austin, Texas, working together on cures for societal ills, physical ailments, degenerative diseases, et cetera, all in the wake of such travesty. Now, if those cures don't do what they're supposed to, but instead, a virus starts taking hold over mankind, it's an easy thing to blame those you had pinned your hopes to, isn't it?"

We nodded.

"But one thing didn't have anything to do with the other," Swifty clarified, holding up a waiting finger. "It's been proven conclusively now that though cases of VZV2, first documented around Austin, stemmed from dirty reservoirs that had never been fully cleaned following the war of the forties and the alien invasion. Everyone was still rebuilding after 2045, and there was a lot to do. A *lot* to clean.

"You guys are too young to remember the war in the forties, when the gorgons came," Swifty said. "Everyone thought *that* was the apocalypse. Many think the same about where we're at now. But you have to look closely at Scripture. Neither one had all the hallmarks of Revelation. And in any event, VZV2 was not a byproduct of Christian ministries working together on a cure for sicknesses. It was simply people banding together in the wake of tragedy trying to do their very best. When Protalaxifen didn't do what the Christian pharmaceutical companies, and more importantly the *populace* wanted, dissent grew. Frustration and anti-Christian sentiment grew. And who capitalized on all of that?"

"Nero," we all droned together.

"Precisely," Swifty said, and he began to draw a flowchart on the board, one thing leading to the next. "So, you have a crippled and rebuilding society compounded by preexisting anti-Christian sentiment compounded by a tainted environment compounded by a failed cure compounded by anti-Christian figurehead Nero, which leads us to where we are today," he finished. "Protalaxifen was just the proverbial straw that broke the camel's back."

"But didn't Protalaxifen have a net positive effect?" Luca asked. "We still take it, and we're fine."

"Yes, it did, Luca, but who controls the flow of media?"

"Nero," he said.

"And if the flow of media prevents such net positive effect news from reaching the masses, and the masses are dying, no one finds out about it."

He turned to face all of us. "What has Protalaxifen accomplished? Does anyone know?"

Anja raised her hand. "Mitigated the spread of viruses."

Hunter was next. "Reduced tumors for people with cancer."

Emma piped up. "Improvement of mood and energy levels."

"All correct," Swifty said. "But the only ones who know their benefits are the people who take it, specifically, Christians. Everyone else – deluded by Nero, that is – believes that it *causes* VZV2. And yet nothing could be further from the truth."

"Hey, Swifty?" asked Asher. Swifty motioned to him. "So, like, why did so many people die, and so many didn't?"

"That's a great question, Ash. And the answer is, 'Who knows'? Some people are genetically predisposed to resist the VZV2 strain. Others weren't so fortunate. We know now that it was a highly contagious respiratory virus, transmitted through person-to-person contact with infected respiratory tract secretions, and that it was virally airborne. And we know that we were contagious well before we showed symptoms. It was that aggressive. So, before we all had a chance to even know what was going on, the virus was making its way around the world, resulting in gliomas or tumors on the brain stem caused by the virus. Those with neurofibromatosis type 1 were most susceptible."

"Too bad Nero was immune to it," Asher concluded with a sneer.

"Yes, too bad," Swifty said. "However, the super-rich are sometimes able to circumvent natural calamity through extra protections. He's got the money to buy the best. So he might not exactly have been immune; he may have just bought his way around it. However, we know he's paranoid. Probably OCD with multiple phobias. But there may even be another possibility."

We leaned in, waiting for him to continue.

"Nero is a psychopath at his core. He's delusional. Yet those two things do not preclude high function. Some of the world's most notorious criminals were, on the surface, completely normal, unsuspecting people you'd have *no clue* were psychotic. Ted Bundy. BTK. Jeffrey Dahmer. Jean Graham. Jack the Ripper. Gary Ridgway. Some of these names you'll never know. But I like history," he said with a grin.

"Anyway, Nero has delusions of grandeur. Now, to be fair, he's a techno-trillionaire who was militarily brilliant: a creative wunderkind who blew everyone away with his tech. Before he was 12 years old, he won the National

Robotics Challenge, National Science Bowl, International Mathematical Olympiad, and more. Whatever contests they were able to resurrect, he won them. The guy's a genius. But a *cursed* genius. We all saw the surface: Constantine Jedidiah Goodfellow. But, brimming underneath, was probably a lot of things: things that we've heard from early defectors and from Colonel Thomas Drexler, his former partner. Things like schizophrenia, delusional disorder, and psychosis. Underneath…was *Nero*. Remember the story of Jekyll & Hyde?"

I nodded. One of my favorites.

"All it took was something to transform him. That something was, unfortunately, unbridled power. *Power tends to corrupt, and absolute power corrupts absolutely.* Lord Acton said that in the 19th century. Nero is absolutely corrupt because he has absolute power. No one can stop him. He literally thinks that he is the Antichrist from Revelation, and that it's his job to bring out the tribulation. Except?"

"God," several of us sounded simultaneously.

"Except God. That's why we pray for him. Continually. No one is irredeemable. As repulsive as it is, we pray for our enemy. What do we pray for?"

"Justice," I said, nearly immediately.

Swifty looked at me. "Yes, Sage, you're right – but justice is the purview of God, and God alone. First, we pray for…?" He held up his index finger again.

"Repentance," Charlie said next to me.

"Repentance," Swifty agreed quietly, then lowered his finger. "We pray for his soul, and we pray for him to repent. Jesus said it himself in John 6:44. *No one can come to me unless the Father who sent me draws them, and I will raise them up at the last day."*

"So you think Nero is actually savable?" I asked.

Swifty turned back to me. "In God's book, there's no one who isn't. So we pray that the Father draws him. Just like Ezekiel 33:11 says: *As surely as I live, declares the Sovereign Lord, I take no pleasure in the death of the wicked, but rather that they turn from their ways and live."*

I swallowed hard. That was a difficult truth to accept. Always had been.

I felt others looking at me. They knew my story, which wasn't all that different from theirs. Nero's Guardians had turned my big sister into raw meat right in front of me. They had taken away my whole family.

"But saving can take on many forms," Swifty added. "Sometimes God can use third parties to save people from themselves. That's where Colonel Thomas Drexler comes in. He is out there, somewhere, preparing." Swifty sighed.

"Let's take a moment now to wait, and listen, and see what the Lord might be telling you about how to pray for Nero, who is, just like us: a fallen human in need of repentance."

They waited, and they listened. But I couldn't.

CHAPTER 4
Drexler

1 . 6 . 2113
Hyde Park, OH

Ξ   Ξ   Ξ

All was clear on the northern front… for now.

Here we were, holing up in Hyde Park just outside Cincy. The Guardians were out in full force, and at night, they were a spectacular and eerie sight, especially through binoculars. Their preternatural, amber eyes lit up the ground around Cincinnati like fireflies over a swamp, and the AirGuard's searchlights made the ground blaze forth like beacons.

My brother-in-arms, Lieutenant Colonel Kent Cannon, accompanied me. In truth, no such rank was ever formerly bestowed upon him. Yet he was as indispensable as oxygen.

And here I was, watching it all from afar, safely and unbeknownst to his vile forces: unlocated.

Occasionally an AirGuard unit would accelerate and veer off course, hunting down an 'undesirable,' as Nero called them, riddling yet another soul with bullets, increasing God's kingdom with one more saint. The ground would erupt a geyser of fire, and then the latent boom would roll over the ground toward us.

Just below Cincinnati, south of the Ohio River and into Kentucky, had been killing fields. Lots of good people were put to the test, as Hebrews 11:37 says. We couldn't save them and had to pull out.

There I stood, in the dim light of a living room, staring through a former resident's blinds far off into the distance, watching the very equipment and forces I once commanded. My removal from them brought an unfamiliar and distasteful yearning. If only I had such munitions at my disposal, The Defiance would be further along in this war.

When I broke off from Nero, I did it knowing full well what kind of mark it would place on me. Though I wasn't branded like the rest of them, I *was* branded a turncoat and an infidel. More specifically, an 'undesirable,' along with the rest of God's flock. I was labeled a traitor and at the top of Nero's Most Wanted for nine years running.

The very thought made me smile with glee. *It's nice to be wanted.*

Suffering for righteousness. 1 Peter 3:8-17 said it all: *Finally, all of you, be like-minded, be sympathetic, love one another, be compassionate and humble. Do not repay evil with evil or insult with insult. On the contrary, repay evil with blessing, because to this you were called so that you may inherit a blessing. For 'Whoever would love life and see good days must keep their tongue from evil and their lips from deceitful speech. They must turn from evil and do good; they must seek peace and pursue it. For the eyes of the Lord are on the righteous, and his ears are attentive to their prayer, but the face of the Lord is against those who do evil.' Who is going to harm you if you are eager to do good? But even if you should suffer for what is right, you are blessed. 'Do not fear their threats; do not be frightened.' But in your hearts revere Christ as Lord. Always be prepared to give an answer to everyone who asks you to give the reason for the hope that you have. But do this with gentleness and respect, keeping a clear conscience, so that those who speak maliciously against your good behavior in Christ may be ashamed of their slander. For it is better, if it is God's will, to suffer for doing good than for doing evil.*

Amen, I whispered to the darkness around me.

Those had become paramount verses for me in these later years, running and hiding, being driven out of holes, being smoked out of nests, being ratted out by those I once called friends.

If Nero even had a clue how many people he pushed to Christianity through his ruthless crusades, his relentless persecution, and his filthy and obvious propaganda, he might have the good sense to abandon his campaign.

But Nero doesn't have a clue, and that is the sad truth of the matter, I thought. *He only knows vengeance, and oppression, and decadence. He stopped listening to me or anyone else a long time ago.*

I thought back to those early days, seeing him rise, the euphoria I had in being so quickly promoted and given whatever I wanted. I had thrilled at being on the cusp of multimillionaire status from *NeroTech.* The leeway and vast oversight I had in developing his machinery was unlimited.

The shock and dread I felt after he revealed who he thought he really was. The horror of betrayal.

The houses and neighborhoods of Hyde Park were a veritable maze. Streets and cul-de-sacs, offshoots and drive-arounds intricately and cleverly interwoven together. There were nearly seventy-five hundred housing units here, not that they were all occupied anymore; the virus, and then Nero's Guardians, had done their work all too well. Consequently, survivors, both Christian and non-Christian alike, shared their extra resources *and* looted the abandoned homes.

There were sympathizers across all religions, and there were all religions present here. We had fully scouted out this area and found a good place to hole up. It also helped that the back of my neck didn't glow like a firefly anywhere I went. I pitied all those to whom fate – to whom *Nero* – had not been kinder.

Watching all of the fiery devastation and unflinching hunting take place before my very eyes, from the comfort of this house that was removed by several miles, I flinched uncomfortably. Who was I, Lord, to be placed in such a position? Why were so many relying on me? What could I even do in this world?

To think that I had been evacuated while others were left to fend off the impending assault. That I was whisked to safety while they remained to die on the battlefield. It was too humbling to digest and too appalling to accept.

Nero was looking for me. For Cannon. For everyone. *But mostly for me,* I thought.

He knew that I knew his system and his equipment. He knew that I alone held the power to disable them. After all, I helped him create them at *NeroTech.* And that back door proved useful when we needed it. But a day would come when I would have to disable all of it… or turn his own turrets against Nero himself.

But would that solve anything? Would simply killing him off end the war? He had indoctrinated so many; his reach was broad, and his message was compelling.

O Lord, may your vindication and deliverance not be far away.

All was clear on the northern front… for now.

CHAPTER 5
Maximillian

1 . 6 . 2113
Washington, DC

Ξ   Ξ   Ξ

The lord Nero had need of me.

I abandoned what I was doing and headed to his chambers. My lord's private chambers were in the Hall of the House of Representatives, and the entirety of the chamber had been transformed into a lavish and opulent tribute to him. Great fountains gushed water silently down through majestic tributaries flowing into an undisturbed pool on which lotus flowers floated. The ceiling twinkled with artificial light beams and stars, a colosseum of the majesty of all the universe bending toward him in reverent adoration.

And there, enshrined in the center, reachable only by a small ferry, interlaced with gold and utterly dazzling with encrusted jewels according to my lord's pleasure, was a pedestal covered in the finest red Indian carpet. And on that red many-staired pedestal, high above the crystalline lake below that mirrored the twinkling ceiling above, was a bed. And on that bed, lay Nero.

It was always truly a wondrous spectacle to behold. The cost had been more than he had anticipated, and my lord grew angry with me when I reported the cost overrun years ago. But he had calmed, and I had apologized and apologized until the very words 'forgive me' flowed like honey from my lips into his ears, and the beating ceased.

I must confess that I was taken aback by the severity of the discipline. But my lord is just, and his ways are higher than my ways. I was wrong to question the length or severity of it, and I know that now. In that moment, I had failed to realize that I had *so* erred; and now, praise be to him, my eyes were opened to my own shortcomings. I had now attained wisdom.

This evening, I strolled through our hallowed halls to meet with my lord once more. It was dark and calm, and the sitars were playing softly, ushering all within this sacred building a blessed and pleasant repose.

Vassal Richards, my lord's personal bodyguard, met me outside his chambers, bowing politely. "High Vassal Maximillian."

"Greetings, Vassal Richards. Our lord calls for me."

"Indeed, you are welcome," he said, and he stepped aside and pulled open the chamber door.

I caught the glint of metal outside the high windows to our left. Guardians swarmed in full force, protecting our holy shrine with complete fidelity. The AirGuard soared overhead in endless sentinel vigilance. Parked outside on the grass was one of our newest and finest fleet members: an AirGuard *Epsilon*, an elite model ready at a moment's notice to whisk the Emperor or any of his trusted confidants away should we come under attack.

"All hail Emperor Nero," said Vassal Richards.

"All hail Emperor Nero," I echoed in reverent delight. "Oh, Vassal Richards, did you *see* his broadcast this evening?

Wonderful as always, yes?" I felt my lipstick stretch as I smiled in ecstasy.

"Indeed," he nodded and breathed calmly. "Our lord is wise and benevolent. The new recruiting program is genius, and the conscripts are enlisting in record numbers. They will serve him faithfully. And all of his wisdom on making our world a more peace-filled place without detractors. Oh my. Touching!"

"Verily. Thank you, Vassal Richards!"

"Thank *you*, High Vassal Maximillian."

I drifted past him and instantly caught the sound of the fountains mingling into the scent of pistachio, my lord's favorite. It was ice cream time, amidst the beautiful twinkle of many-noted waterworks.

My lord sat high atop the bed, facing me.

He was completely naked!

I gasped and bowed my head low, stretching out my arms and averting my eyes. Who was I to look upon my lord's nakedness? Surely the penalty for such an affront was nothing less than savage death: to see my lord in his uncovered glory. Surely no one could look upon his unclothed holiness and live!

But my fears were allayed. The god-king abounds in mercy. "Rise, my beloved Maximillian," he purred; his voice reverberated as a sweet music throughout the chamber, mingling with the trill of fountain droplets. "You have done nothing wrong but to behold me as I am. I would never harm you, my dearest Maximillian. I trust you know that."

"Yes, my liege," I whispered, still reluctant to look up. "Hail, Emperor Nero." Out of the corner of my eye, the boat drifted into view around the protective moat. As I glanced westward, I noted the ferryman's eyes also cast downward out of respect and reverence. Indeed, he too was shielding his brow.

"Gaze upon me, High Vassal Maximillian."

"Yes, my lord," I uttered automatically, pulling my arms back into my chest as I slowly raised my head, nervously.

Nero was now clothed in a near-translucent nightgown that traced the stairs delicately behind him as he descended the dais. The train of his robe twinkled with rubies, sapphire, and onyx. Glorious light shone about him as he approached.

"I know the hour is late. I ask your forgiveness."

I gasped again. "Who am I, lord, to grant forgiveness to you? Indeed, there is only one who can grant forgiveness, and I am in grave need of it for beholding you unclothed."

He shook his head and smiled. "I was simply in repose, my good vassal. Remember it often and think fondly on it. For not many will experience the wonder that you have witnessed tonight."

"Let it be so, my lord," I agreed, bowing lightly and closing my eyes.

"I need to speak with you about Vassal Behmardi. Do you think he is exceeding expectations with my fleets?"

The lord Nero had now reached the bottom step, and the ferryman slowed the boat to a halt, bowing before Nero and dropping to his hands and knees in front of him as a footman to provide a further step up onto the deck. Without looking at him, Nero took his hand and boarded the boat, walking at a leisurely pace to the other side. The ferryman scurried up and met my lord on the other side, once more bowing low and falling to his hands and knees before him. Nero once again stepped onto the small of the ferryman's back and disembarked the vessel. I extended my hand to escort him off the ferry.

The Emperor echoed the movement, taking my hand while offering me his signet ring. I kissed it worshipfully.

"Oh yes, sire, I do. I think he knows your fleet well, and is readying them for dispatch once more," I said, as His Grace passed me and descended the lower dais onto the hall floor. "The undesirables have been significantly reduced across the populace. Informants are increasing. Indeed, we've just received a turncoat from their so-called Defiance under the treacherous Drexler. He arrived last night, and we are verifying the information he has provided. The number of new conscripts and informants grows daily, my lord."

"They do indeed," he breathed, walking over to one of the fountains and grabbing a silver ewer perched atop a marble pedestal on the fountain's periphery. "Would you care for a drink, Maximillian?"

"Certainly, your grace, if it pleases you," I responded, delighted to enjoy the awe-inspiring privilege of a drink with my lord.

Nero dipped the ewer into the running stream and pulled it out. The sound was like tinkling pools of rainwater. He poured two goblets of sparkling water as his robe shimmered before me. His strong muscular frame shone beneath, and the wisps of his wavy black hair at the base of his neck traced up into the laurel wreath adorning his head.

"There is one thing that I would like to make clear to you and Vassal Behmardi, High Vassal Maximillian," he said to me after taking a drink and exhaling slowly, his voice becoming sharp. He did not turn to look at me, and I dared not approach for him to hand me the water until called for. "Should you and Behmardi fail me, you will not live to see the fulfillment of the ages." He turned slowly to me, holding both glasses of water.

A thrill of fear ran through me. "Of course, my lord," I said, bowing low.

"Both the manufacture and the massing of the fleets have taken far too long for my liking, and Vassal Behmardi is treading on thin ice. As are you, as his superior. You, High Vassal Maximillian, are singly responsible for all the vassals under your watch, and you are responsible for their action… or inaction. Their success…or failure," he finished.

"Of course, my lord," I replied slowly, feeling a tremble over my flesh. "I will not disappoint you. Vassal Behmardi is answerable to me. I will ensure his success."

"Just as you are answerable to me, and I will ensure yours," he said quickly.

I smiled at him, briefly closing my eyes and nodding.

He held my gaze for a moment.

"Good. Then we understand each other. Drink, my good vassal." He raised both our goblets high and then put my goblet to his lips, spitting heavily into it and swirling the contents around. He presented it to me, beaming.

I squealed with delight. "Success, my lord Nero," I said, taking the goblet from him and drinking deeply of the anointed fluid. My trembling subsided somewhat.

"Success, Maximillian."

I will always have need of my lord Nero.

CHAPTER 6
Sage

1 . 7 . 2113
Maple Park, IL

Ξ   Ξ   Ξ

We were no longer safe. It was time to move out.

There was a possible informant, and the church was not secure anymore. Charlie and Swifty had both grabbed AR-18s, while I chose my trusty XM6 as well as a Glock, the kind of handgun Charlie always carried. I've never used a Glock, but I figured it handled mostly similar to a Beretta, and I liked those. I loaded it right before we left and was fairly confident I had done it correctly.

We had never all-out assaulted a squad of Guardians or AirGuard. Not yet. We'd been fortunate. Oh, they'd been hot on our tail, but Swifty trusted me to scramble everyone and keep them out of harm's way. It wasn't like we were going to run into a lot of people anyway. Survivors knew that we were out there, somewhere, and they didn't like to tangle with us or get wrapped up in our affairs.

Usually, they'd just shake their heads and let us pass by. Many had the good sense to not turn us in, believing that there was in fact *no* reward for doing so; it was simply a ploy by Nero. But others had no such reservations.

Colonel Drexler was featured on 'Wanted' posters. We were fortunate that none of us were. There were a lot of 'undesirable' Christians still out there, but we were the grunts, not the 'top dog' as he was. For Nero, Drexler was Public Enemy Number One. The rest of us were Christians running around out there in the shadows still – forced to move around in the night.

We grabbed our things. It was 1:15 in the afternoon, which meant better visibility *and* great ability to blend in. It was January *and* cold, after all, so it was normal for us to be walking around bundled up against the weather. Our marks glared in the night: a bunch of amber will-o'-the-wisps bouncing around, providing an easy target for Guardians. If we could run around in the daytime, wear our chokers, and look inconspicuous, so much the better. You bungle around at night, and you risk someone worrying about a prowler and informing on you.

Informants – man, forgiving them was a tall order and a hard ask. Thankfully, we hadn't had any in our band, but I had definitely heard of them. Loved ones ratting out their family members to save their own skin. Brother turning in brother for a few thousand credits. Despicable. When Nero 'cleansed' the world of Christians, he was also dwindling the number of those out there with a true sense of honor. Hopefully, that would be his undoing someday.

Only time would tell.

Ξ   Ξ   Ξ

We were outside the church now, mingling south among the few other people along West Country Line Road. A scout had reported back to Swifty: we had some brothers and sisters at the remains of the Northern Illinois Ag Center building south of Ashton. They confirmed it with Scripture. That was the only way you could really confirm someone's intentions and fidelity; that and the mark. But if they had the mark, they could have since renounced their faith, and then the only way you could confirm them would be through Scripture. Various Bible verses. Truths from the Word that only you and they would know. That's why we memorized as much as we could.

As for the others, Deniers just rubbed everyone the wrong way. How could you turn away from Jesus knowing what He offers you? How could you do that? How could you renounce faith in Christ just because you're afraid? I don't know, maybe I hadn't been put to the test yet. When the rubber meets the road, maybe I would fail too. I'd heard of torture methods employed by Nero that would turn your skin white and make your blood run cold just hearing about them. Some reported how Christians had been put to the test. Grisly. Barbaric. But to deny Christ in that torturous moment and then to *continue* to deny Him? I didn't get that.

On top of that, you had Denier-Informants. D.I.'s, we called them. Those who had once tasted of the heavenly gift and had called Christ 'Lord,' then spat Him out and turned on their brothers and sisters, reporting them. *Despicable.* Some of them even turned in their own families for a few measly thousand credits. What was the going price for a Christian soul? It was just like a D.I. to give up a life in exchange for food.

Anyway, here we were, filtering out in groups. That's the only way we could do it, by keeping to small numbers. Some of us would go straight down West County Line Road. Others would venture farther east on Main Street, then double back down South Broadway, through the neighborhoods onto Willow Lane, then Ashton, and finally join us on West County Line Road. And still others would cut across country southwest to cross over Union Ditch Number 2, approaching the Ag building from the west.

That way, if any one of us were assailed, we wouldn't lose all twenty of us. Many of them were adults I didn't know all that well. Our group had a bit of a revolving door, sadly. The cold hard truth was that Nero's forces killed them.

So far, so good. I was in Swifty's group, and we were the ones heading straight south. Anja, Leona, Andréa, Fritz and Luca were heading in the other group led by Nicholas.

Charlie was to my left, and Hunter was to my right. We also had Asher and Emma. I checked my choker to make sure it was fastened securely. It was under my hood, but it felt like it had shifted.

My XM6 was strapped to my back, as was my Glock. It was the only way to prevent the Guardians from seeing our weapons.

The worst part was pretending. Walking and talking jovially like nothing was amiss. Pretending it all was okay. We all had to be actors in that sense. I hated that.

I scanned the sky as we walked. No AirGuard, at least not now. We were passing West Dekalb Drive and had about twelve hundred feet to go…when I heard them.

The familiar whirring and treads. Suddenly they loomed into view, coming up West County Line Road from

Ashton. Four of them, dead ahead! *Four* Guardians, coming right at us!

Our destination was a few hundred feet beyond West Ashton Drive. I could feel the heat of my heart racing through my thick coat. All of our eyes must be on the Guardians because we all slowed simultaneously.

"Easy, take it easy," Swifty said, and then he smiled theatrically. "You guys are nuts back there. You didn't even bring your hats!"

"It's not that cold," Asher protested, acting it out with style and aplomb. "I can take it."

"Whatever, man," Swifty retorted. "Suit yourself!" He pulled a bottle out of his jacket and started drinking out of it like a giddy drunk. Looked like water to me.

The Guardians continued toward us, rolling north along West County Line Road. An impending sense of dread welled up inside me, and I fought the urge to run. I could faintly hear Charlie catch her breath beside me.

"No sudden moves. Act normal," I urged, flicking my eyes to the dopes and back. They were coming right at us. Their guns were always jutting out from their black titanium flanks in an ever-threatening greeting.

We did the only thing we could do, the most despicable thing we could do: what *any* of us would do in such circumstances.

Swifty waved to the Guardians and pulled off to the side to let them pass, putting his hand over his heart and bowing his head. We all followed suit on either side of the sidewalk, repeating the mandated greeting as sincerely as we could, choking back the contempt.

All hail Emperor Nero.

The words sluiced out of my mouth like slow-rolling mud. I meant none of it. My mouth felt repulsively treacherous. Pretty sure all of ours did.

The Guardians passed right between us and continued their northward march. My hair stood up on end as they moved less than ten inches from me in the center of the sidewalk as we held steady on each of their flanks. The chill wind beat at us from their turbines as they moved through our midst. We didn't dare breathe.

Finally, the four Guardians passed us by and then split up, fanning out onto West Dekalb Drive on the west and Dekalb Drive on the east. We pulled our eyes from them and turned to resume our southern procession...

...when my gun fell out of my holster. It clattered to the ground with an unholy report, the sound of metal clinking against concrete. I heard a separate sound, higher-pitched but no less loud: the sound of the chambered round slipping out and tinking against the metal and the concrete sidewalk. Both sounds would be unmistakable to Guardians! In a frenzy, I spasmed and reached down for the gun, quickly holstering it. Charlie grabbed the bullet and slipped it into her pocket.

I didn't need a mirror to hear the Guardians stop, come whirring back around the corner, zero us, and then reapproach us, swiftly. I'm sure they saw my sudden movement.

"Stop, Citizen. You are ordered to stop." The electronic pitch-adjusted voices drew closer. Those voices were always unnerving. Robotic and inhuman. As they approached, I could better make out the encircled and gaudy *NT* logo on their chest plate.

Act normal, I told myself, looking around clumsily and pointing to myself as if to ask, 'Me?' The others did the same. I could feel Swifty behind me assessing the situation.

"What did you drop?" the foremost unit asked me.

"Drop? I didn't drop anything."

Its guns stared me down threateningly. "Open your jacket at once."

"Yeah, okay," I said, unzipping my coat and showing them my pants. I was careful to keep my scarf on and keep the nape of my jacket pressed closely against my neck. One wrong move and I would expose my choker.

My heart was pounding like a winepress.

Right now Swifty was probably calculating how much time it would take for him to rip off his jacket and whip out his AR-18, firing away madly as he pushed us out of their way and dove for cover.

"Slowly," the unit commanded, and it suddenly lurched one of its arms out toward me. The many turrets of its right appendage were inches from my face, full of bullets ready to fire and snuff out my life. The others were watching the rest of our team, silently assessing them up and down, lines of code running through their CPUs as they presumably ran threat assessments. Hopefully, all our chokers were on tightly, and none of our weapons were poking out from underneath our jackets.

The Guardian remained motionless, but I sensed it scanning me up and down and assessing every movement from its unfeeling irises. There was a cluster of them on its head. It looked fiendishly like some sort of metallic spider. When I was finished, I kept my hands raised in the air and wondered if it could sense my body heat rising and my blood pressure pounding.

"What is that in your pocket?" the dope asked me.

I looked down. "What, this?" I extracted the only thing in my pocket. "Oh, this! Sorry, I dropped this. It's my lip balm. Cherry Chapstick. It's the best. You want some?" I asked sarcastically, holding it out toward the Guardian.

The machine did not respond. It regarded me, silently, perhaps computing an alternate route through the conversation now that its initial line of questioning had come to a resolution. "What is your purpose here?" it asked me.

"Oh," I said, zipping up my jacket once more as I half-turned and thumbed behind me down the road. "Richie's. The pizza takeout? Right down the road here. We were just hungry and wanted to grab a few slices. You wanna join us?" I held my arms out. The ridiculous nature of the invitation made some of my compatriots giggle.

"Identification, please."

I gulped hard, trying to conceal my fear and keep my cool, but it all came down to this. If I were on some sort of terrorist registry, this is where it would all end. The psalms were buzzing through my mind as I lifted my left arm in salute, the underside of my wrist facing them.

I held my breath and waited as they scanned my wrist ID, coded under my skin as part of a global measure instituted at birth to prevent identity theft. It was the same with all of us. Many years ago, licenses and ID cards were actually printed and carried in a wallet; now they were laser-etched under our epidermis. Probably the same technology used to brand all of us. My eyes flickered to the left as I felt Hunter stir. Swifty moved slightly, silently, behind me. I waited.

There came no reply from the cold mechanisms. Asher snickered to my right. One of the units whipped its head over to him. His smile faded into disdain.

"Proceed," the unit finally said after a pause that seemed long enough to thaw ice. "All hail Emperor Nero."

"You got it," I said. Swifty nudged me from behind. I nearly rolled my eyes. "All hail Emperor Nero," I said, obligatorily. The machines retreated slowly, rotating one hundred eighty degrees with their bodies while their heads stayed trained on me. They resumed their northward sentry once again, their titanium brainless heads finally swiveling around, facing north. We pivoted and headed back south.

I wasn't sure what I was more upset over: nearly costing us our lives or the fact that we weren't actually going for pizza at all, but just past it to our new hiding spot.

Charlie leaned into me. "Next time let *me* load your Glock, goofball."

I smiled at her, but my throat caught from my nervousness, and my stomach felt nauseous.

Hunter sidled up next to me and put his arm around me after casting a nervous glance back north. "You okay, bro? That was quite the encounter." His shaggy red hair poked out from under his hat.

I kept walking. "Let's just get inside, man. I'm hungry, and pizza sounds good, but I swear after that I'll probably just throw it right up." Indeed, a wave of nausea passed over me again, and I had to clutch my stomach.

As if from out of nowhere, an AirGuard soared into view from the south, blasting the wind all around us as we looked up. Glaring light shone down, momentarily blinding us. Presently, the light switched off, the wind abated, and the AirGuard proceeded north as well. Scanning. Searching.

My knees buckled.

Without warning, a gargantuan and soul-stopping *boom* sounded behind us. We all whipped around. A fireball rose to the heavens, slowly fusing black and orange in a scalding billow of smoke. It was coming from Saint Mary of the Assumption Catholic Church.

The church we had just left. My heart was heavy for Sister Theresa.

My knees buckled once more as we turned back around and continued south. Thought I was going to faint.

"Whoa, whoa, steady there, bud," said Swifty. "We're almost there." He put his arm around me to steady me. I appreciated that; my mind was racing.

"Okay. Okay. Okay," was all I could repeat. My head was throbbing. That was the closest I'd ever come to an interrogation, and I wanted no more of them. Ever.

"Surely He will save you from the fowler's snare, and from the deadly pestilence. That's Psalm 91, baby. 'Course, offering them lip balm and pizza was an interesting touch."

I nodded, in no mood for jokes.

The thick, black smoke rose to the heavens behind us. At this point, the Guardians were probably combing the grounds. I wondered if Sister Theresa was still inside.

No. I knew in my heart she was dead now.

We passed Richie's Pizza on the right. The lights were on. The scent of warm pizza wafted through the air and hit me. A frustrating combination of yearning and loathing battled for mastery as I trudged through the street toward the beat-up Ag building. Swifty cast one wary glance back north in case the Guardians decided to watch us and ensure that we had in fact gone in for pizza.

The other teams would be along. We had made it, though I was sure I was going to throw up any minute. I had heard rumors that they had facial recognition technology. How we weren't identified or stopped is beyond me.

We were safe, for now. It was time to settle in.

CHAPTER 7
Drexler

1 . 8 . 2113
Lunken Field, OH

Ξ　Ξ · Ξ

Always on the move. Never a dull moment.

Rumors grew of an informant somewhere in the network, so we were on the move once more. Cincinnati Municipal Airport was not a safe place to be near, according to logic. But I had enough military experience under my belt – and wits in my head – to know that sometimes the closer you are to danger, the safer you are from harm. The enemy was searching far and wide, not close and narrow. This airport was a staging ground for more Guardians and more supplies for local recruiting offices, and I could keep them under my watchful eye here, from close by.

That was the advantage of being able to hack Nero's servers and gain intel: I knew where all his units were stationed. Prior to my departure, I had installed surveillance, which only helped matters.

So, now I was on the outskirts of the airfield, watching their every move. My trusty compatriot Kent Cannon was with me as usual, scanning the airfield and talking with our contacts in the area.

The bounty on my head was now 10,000,000 credits. A hefty sum. Who might turn me in, I wondered? That was enough to feed a family of four for at least a few years.

Tempting. There were plenty families of four in our network that could benefit from that.

Cannon walked in to my room briskly. "Sir."

"Yes, Cannon, what is it?"

"Contact. Wishes to meet with you. Alms Park has plenty of cover. It's Lieutenant Mathieson, sir. I could arrange it if you wanted to step out for a breath of fresh air. Masks are ready."

"Sounds good, Kent. Thank you. He's coming from Evanston?"

"Yessir. Standing by, sir."

"Good man."

Ξ   Ξ   Ξ

The meeting was set for 1800 hours. I enjoyed stealing away at night and rendezvousing with any troops in the area. It was good for morale. Helped them to know that leadership was alive, well, and that we were continually plotting Nero's demise.

The Defiance was massing. Dissent was growing. Sympathy for Christians was increasing, which I knew Nero did not want in the slightest. It gave me great joy to know that he was probably squirming. After all, you can't kill off 326,472 Christians in a single year, justify your campaign under the mantle of labeling them 'undesirables,' and expect the rest of the world to stand idly by. He was playing a risky game: the same risky game he had played in trusting me to carry out his insidious plot.

Soon, I deemed, both would cause his unraveling.

The forest was quiet from the recent snow. The ground crunched softly under my boots as I made my way slowly toward Stone Slide playground. The rendezvous point was just beyond it in the thick forest cover beyond Alms Park Circle. It was 1756 hours.

It was stuffy inside my mask. Their 3D printing perfectly conformed to my face like the plaster cast monster masks of the Hollywood movies of old. This one suited me well. Instead of a 50's-ish graying German American, I was now essentially a pony-tailed 30's-ish Dutchman. No one would recognize me. I had a reprogrammed wrist ID to match.

Besides, Nero's forces kept switching on the facial recognition, and we just kept switching it off through our back door. How many lives that had saved I couldn't know, but it was a valuable countermove. Nonetheless, I couldn't take a chance on being spotted. I was Public Enemy Number One as far as Nero was concerned. Thus, the mask.

The smell of cigarette smoke hit me first. I smiled.

"Mathieson," I said, as he emerged from behind a tree up ahead. "Good to see you, old friend."

"Good to see you too, Chief," he said, walking closer and embracing me with a warm grin. I could practically feel the heat of the mark on his neck under his choker. I couldn't see it, but it was there.

I took him by the shoulders. "Been too long. Thank you for all you're doing. How is the family?"

"Good. This is a nice look for you. You look like an elf, for goodness' sake." He took a hefty drag on his smoke.

I shrugged. "Makes sense that I would be walking around in the woods then, no?" He chuckled, but he appeared stressed. I continued, "I wish I could pry this mask off. Hot under here. But they're getting better and better. Do I have you to thank for this?"

Chris Mathieson nodded. "That's how I know who to look for. Get the masks to you ahead of time, coordinate with Kent who you'll 'be' at our meeting, and then we have the rendezvous. It helps that I don't have to factor in a choker."

I shook my head. "Those chokers. They've certainly provided forward momentum, haven't they?"

"They have, indeed. But we're working on something less conspicuous, my friend. And that's what I wanted to talk with you about. I only just received word that you were in the area; I'm glad we could meet to discuss it."

"Tell me."

"I will." His face clouded over. "But first, there's one more thing. It's," -here he paused, looking into my eyes as if searching for something- "it's Sanchez, sir." Another long drag on his cigarette. He was quite obviously stressed.

"Sanchez?" I tilted my head, feigning surprise. "He's the informant, isn't he?"

Mathieson nodded once more. "It's been confirmed, sir. The enemy knows you're somewhere in this area. He may know you're in these woods even now."

"Well, smoking a cigarette is certainly a good way to stay undercover and keep us hidden," I said, and Mathieson looked confused. I laughed. "Don't worry," I admonished him, waving a finger. "Nero isn't that smart. He's not omniscient. And we must always remember, my friend, Nero himself is not the enemy. He's a grave foe, to be sure, but he's not the enemy. Our enemy is the devil."

"Certainly, Colonel Drexler, I just mean that Sanchez has intel on you that he could have easily delivered to Nero by now."

"Intel such as?"

"Your location, for one. They have never stopped hunting for you. And secondly, your family. If they find your family, sir, they could use them as leverage for you to surrender yourself."

Mathieson finished his cigarette and dropped it to the ground, extinguishing it with his boot. He exhaled loudly.

"Relax, my friend. All of these concerns have been taken into account already. Nero doesn't know the location of my family, neither does Mario Sanchez. Furthermore, *I* don't even know the location of my family. My wife and son have been hiding in undisclosed locations under constant guard; they are regularly relocated, for their own protection – and for mine."

"Yessir. But Sanchez was with you before Cannon. He knows far too much for his own good. If Sanchez were to divulge certain codes that you've maintained for the operation of Nero's armada and fleet, Nero could cut you out and patch the back door you've been able to maintain."

I couldn't help but smile. "And do you think that I would have been so foolish as to trust Sanchez with the actual codes?"

He stared at me, and then it hit him.

"Sanchez has *incorrect* codes. You knew he'd inform." His face was a study in surprise.

I smiled.

"Has he never tried them then?"

"Not to my knowledge. I am the only one with the codes, my friend, and I won't part with them until my dying breath. That's the way it needs to be."

"But if Sanchez gives up your location, or even your general whereabouts, Nero will be on this place like bees on honey," Mathieson insisted.

"Then I shall have to be the murder hornet lying in wait within the honey," I replied. "Nero has to catch me first, Christopher. I am all too happy to take out his fleet if they dare come too close."

Mathieson smiled, seemingly relieved. "How did you know about Sanchez?"

I looked around, taking in the ambience of the park around us and the chilly night air. "Something he said to me in one of our last meetings before I dispatched him to Dayton. We were discussing The Cleansing. He made an odd comment when I had observed that there had been such a great loss. He said 'Well, *everyone* has experienced loss. Even Nero.' The empathy for Nero was unmistakable. He revealed himself inadvertently. He slipped, and then tried to reverse course and stutter his way into a lame defense, but it was too late; he had already outed himself. From then on, I changed the access codes and used new encryption."

"I'm guessing he fled straight to Nero from there."

I nodded. "Sadly, that seems to have been the case. Now, let's talk about those new chokers, eh?"

"Ah yes," Christopher said with excitement. "Sir, they're even better than the last ones. We're going to need a new name for them! They're basically an appendage. Latex over aluminum, but foldable as well, conforming to the contours of the neck – *any* neck – and waterproof. You wouldn't need to take them off. They blend right in. Once applied, they wouldn't come off, and they're guaranteed to repel a scan. You didn't notice, did you?"

"Notice?"

Mathieson pulled his collar away from his neck. He wasn't wearing a choker, yet there was no amber glow emanating from the back of his neck. My eyes widened, and he let me examine it. "What is this? Some sort of a patch? This is fantastic, my friend!"

"A patch. That's precisely what we're calling it, though it seems too simple."

"Excellent, my friend. Most excellent! Well done. When can they be ready?"

"We should have the first shipments going out in three days. I have ten for you right now." He handed me a small package.

"Excellent. Of course, we have our work cut out for us in terms of dissemination, but I leave it in your capable hands."

"Thank you, sir," Mathieson said.

"We're making progress, Chris," I assured him, sidling up to him and laying my arm across his shoulders. "I believe we'll see the end of this war in less than five years. I'd like you to be around to see it."

He tilted his head.

"You're important to The Defiance, Christopher. Let's pray for the day when you quit smoking. There are less expensive and more healthy avenues to stress-free peace." I looked at him under my eyebrows, smiling.

He chuckled, turning slightly red. "Yessir. I appreciate it, Colonel Drexler."

"Stay safe, Chris. I will pray for you."

"You too, sir. Thank you, Thomas."

Mathieson turned away and headed out. So did the 'Dutchman.'

We were always on the move. Never a dull moment with us.

CHAPTER 8
Sage

1 . 12 . 2113
Maple Park, IL

Ξ   Ξ   Ξ

This place was wearing on me.

Too little comfort could be found in a basement also populated by rats. Somewhere, there was a hole, and somehow, they were getting through. It was a nuisance, and a dangerous one.

Hunter and I were eating dinner when Charlie came over with Luca and Anja. Luca didn't greet us, as was his wont, silent and brooding. Anja gave a sing-songy 'sup' and sat down hard on the bench in a huff, making the whole picnic table vibrate.

"Everything okay?" Hunter asked her.

"She's just mad because Swifty wouldn't let her go for pizza with Andréa," Charlie said.

Andréa was a sweet lady. Very maternal toward all of us, and she always took great pains to make sure I was taken care of and had my needs met. I couldn't shake the feeling that she somehow favored me.

"*Pizza,*" Hunter moaned in distaste. "I never thought I'd get tired of it," he said, eyeing his piece with disdain. "It's every kid's dream, right? Pizza all… the… time." He sighed. "But jeez, I guess that's what we get when we're right next to a pizza joint: pizza for breakfast, lunch and dinner. Never thought I'd actually get tired of it." He ground his red-toed boots into the ground. I loved to tease him about those things. They were black, except for the tips of each boot, which were a fiery red.

"I didn't care about the pizza," Anja protested. "I just wanted to get *out* of here. Going stir crazy. I wish something would happen to get us into gear. Asher and I are itching for a fight."

Hunter rolled his eyes. "You know what they say, Anja. *Be careful what you wish for; you just might get it.*"

"Who's *they*?" she demanded.

Hunter frowned. "I dunno. *They.* Uh…*them.* Ya know, people before us."

"Yeah, well, I'm guessing *they* had more things to eat than pizza all the time."

"Oh, relax," I said, laughing. "We're getting breadsticks and salad as well. Picky, picky."

Anja threw me a dirty look and sunk her head down into her arms on the table. Charlie rubbed her back briefly in sympathy.

"Eventually we'll get something else. Don't worry," I reassured her.

"We better. I'm getting acid reflux. No more pizza for me," said a voice, and we all looked over in amazement. The mumbled voice belonged to Luca. It had taken me some time to identify it; he just didn't talk much.

"I hear you, buddy," I said. "Hopefully soon. Get some water, yeah?" I offered him. He nodded and then trudged off. I could see Nicholas and Miles off conspiring with Leona and Fritz in a far corner of the basement, poring over some paperwork with Swifty. Luca made his way over to them.

Charlie looked at me mournfully. "I'm getting it too." She frowned. "Too many tomatoes, all that pizza sauce." I put my arm around her. "What I wouldn't give for a real cheeseburger, *ugh,*" she moaned.

"Without the ketchup, though, right?"

She looked at me and smiled. "Yeah. No ketchup. I'm gonna get some water too, I think." She stood and walked over to the corner in Nicholas' direction.

A thundering cacophony blasted through the building, and dust sprinkled down on us from the ceiling. Hairline cracks splintered across the ceiling. The floor caved in by the stairs, and concrete collapsed in broken fragments. One of them struck Leona. She fell to the ground and lay motionless.

My eyes went wild and fearful, full of alarm. The blast threw Charlie backward toward us.

AirGuard! Someone had informed on us!

"Move! Move!" cried Swifty. "Grab your guns, let's go, let's go, let's go!" he cried, clapping his hands. His voice was laden with urgency, his eyes were fiery, and his head was bleeding.

Suddenly, all hell had descended upon us. Everyone was growling and yelling. We all sprang into action, our hearts thundering in our chests. Another horrendous detonation sounded above, and the wall next to where we were sitting buckled. Fragments went flying everywhere. I heard crying. All that could, ran.

Just before the attack, Asher had been resting against the wall opposite us. At the bombing, he leapt into action a hair too late. A flying piece of shrapnel from the wall transformed into a sharp projectile, shooting across the room and embedding itself into his right clavicle. He yelped in pain, sucked in his breath and winced. Asher tore it right out of his shoulder, staring at it momentarily before spitting on the offending material and casting it aside.

I thought of those poor people in what remained of the Ag building above us. It wasn't clear if they were still alive.

All of us bolted in every direction, mostly toward the armament positioned by the stairs. They were broken and tattered, but still usable. Navigating up them would take caution. Light peeked in from the moonlight above us, until suddenly, wheeling and turning in the night sky, a shadow obscured our vision.

"Look out!" Swifty cried, thrusting me aside. He had grabbed a rocket launcher from the wall. He turned, took aim, and fired.

Whoosh. The RPG whistled out of his turret and spun toward the heavens. The AirGuard probably wasn't anticipating such a quick response. It swerved to avoid it, but too late. Perfect hit. The rocket-propelled grenade struck just aft of its target's starboard wing, splintering it into fragments. The AirGuard plummeted to the earth.

In a few seconds, the ground rocked around us from the crash. A fireball erupted toward the heavens once more.

Swifty was back up and continuing to hand us rifles and artillery. We were in various stages of dress. Those fortunate enough to have been fully clothed at the time of the attack slapped on a jacket and proceeded up the stairs. Fritz handed out chokers as we went. We needed those; they could *not* be left behind. We applied them and stuffed additional ones into our pockets.

Dust poured into the basement from something that had toppled upstairs and spilled down onto us through the blown-open aperture, leaving us all coughing.

"Hunt! Charlie?" I yelled. Dust swept into my lungs on the intake, and I spasmed and retched.

"Here, bro, here!"

"Right here! Where are you?" Charlie screamed.

"I'm here, over here," I shouted. "Swifty!"

"Come on, kids, let's go! All of you! Nicholas, Fritz, let's go! It's too late for Leona. Luca! Where's Luca?"

We couldn't find him! He was nowhere to be found. *Luca is dead,* I thought in horror. *I didn't even know his last name.*

"There's no time, we'll have to come back and look later! Go!" Swifty yelled. "Sage, you lead them! Use those awesome ears, buddy. Charlie, you got medic! Hurry! Protect each other! Miles, Reina, you got the others, go!"

"Roger," I cried out instinctively, slipping into military talk. I threaded my way up the stairs. Leona's dead body spilled over a gap where the stairs had been blown apart. The plywood buckled and bowed dangerously. "Up this way, follow me!"

I had established a reputation for having dog-like hearing. It's something that aided me ever since I was a young kid, threading my way through neighborhoods and abandoned cars on my way to safer hideouts. You had to listen for that whirring.

"We're coming!" Hunter breathed amidst coughs. Someone gagged and threw up from the dust and the sight of Leona. I think it was Emma.

"Luca!" Swifty called one last time. *Nothing.* It was almost as if he had entirely vanished. There was no time to search under the pile of rubble in the corner where the cave-in had occurred. Luca was most likely buried underneath.

We filtered out of the basement as best as we could. The heat from the downed AirGuard seared the cold winter night. Snow fell lightly all around us.

Andréa came running back from Richie's pizza. She was armed. She had no pizzas in her hands. *You got your wish, Luca,* I thought sadly to myself, choking back tears. *No more pizzas.*

And then the anger took me. I stared down into that basement through the blown-out hole; small fires burned in pockets, scattered all around us. Distant imagery wavered and swayed through the flames. Hunter shoved against me, pressed by the remaining evacuees. Charlie did the same. She had her med bag slung over her shoulder and chest as they both brandished their weapons.

"Come on. This way," I yelled to them, and headed southeast for the road. Five figures fled after me: Hunter, Charlie, Anja, Asher and Emma. Asher was nursing his shoulder. Behind them at some distance came Fritz and Nicholas. Both had grabbed extra munitions and slung them over their back in green canvas bags. I couldn't see Swifty.

We headed southeast toward Lincoln Highway.

Something whizzed past my head! Another! And then another! We whipped around in a reflex to face the noise. There, barreling toward us on West County Line Road, were two Guardians, firing a volley of deadly bullets.

"Get down!" I cried.

We hit the deck.

My anger erupted into rage as I screamed, knelt, and returned fire just as a Guardian bullet punctured Hunter's arm. He howled in agony.

The Guardians' preoccupation with us gave Swifty the opportunity he needed to strike. A trail of white, chalkish smoke shot out from the demolished Ag building. It blew both Guardians off their treads. One of them lay feebly twitching, batting its treads in the air sideways in order to right itself.

Asher approached, opening fire with one hand while holding his injured clavicle with the other.

"Asher, it's down, come *on!*" I urged him. He glanced back at me, briefly, turning once more to spit on the downed Guardian, then racing to regroup with us.

I heard Hunter moan. "Ow, man, I'm hit." Charlie ran over to him and extracted a bandage wrap from her shoulder bag, which was an impromptu medic kit. She was clad only in her clothes with no jacket. The chill wind was biting through my coat; she must have been colder than ice. She feverishly wrapped the bandage around Hunter as he looked around wildly and wailed. "More of them, three more of them, coming north by northwest!" he screeched.

Swifty reached us. We turned and saw the other Guardians barreling toward us, racing down Lincoln

Highway. More bullets whizzed past our heads. Hunter turned and took aim while Charlie wrapped him up, unleashing a volley of ammunition. Two of the machines splintered and sparked. The rest of us joined in, even as a hail of deadly projectiles raced past our ears.

God, please help us; we really need you now, I prayed silently.

The Guardians exploded as the nine of us unleashed our fury upon them.

And then, the sky lit up with searchlights.

Coming also from the northwest, speeding with all fury, was another AirGuard. It sliced through the wind with lights blazing, its deadly siren howling in pursuit.

"I can't load another one in time!" shouted Swifty.

"It's okay, *go!*" cried Fritz. "I've got the grenades. Just go! Take my bag and run, Greg!"

Swifty scoffed. "You can't take down an AirGuard with just a few grenades, Fritz. Come on!" he shouted, yanking on his jacket to flee.

Fritz turned to him in the cold of the evening. "You wanna bet? I still have my arm. *Go.*"

Fritz was a pretty good baseball pitcher in his time. He was nearing his seventies now, but when it was still somewhat safe to go out and throw the ball around, he was the one you didn't want to go up to bat against. At least that's what they said. And now would be his finest hour, pitching a shutout against AirGuards.

"Fritz…" Swifty pleaded as the tears came. "Brother…"

The AirGuard sped toward us.

"I'm not gonna tell you again, Greg. *Go.* I might get to meet Jesus today. Don't deny me that! Greater love has no man than this, that a man lay down his life for his friends." He smiled faintly, his eyes glistening.

John 15:13, I thought to myself.

Swifty bit his lip as we pulled him off of Fritz. I clutched Fritz' bag and threw it over my shoulder. Swifty grasped in vain at the older man's jacket. Fritz shook him off. With all the gentle fury he could muster, he screamed at Swifty. *"GO!"*

Andréa gave him a quick kiss and a hug and raced off after us.

We sprinted away, shredding through the night as if our feet were made of fiery wheels. We were scattered down Lincoln Highway in a thirty-foot spread. Anja was the fastest after Swifty. She tore up Lincoln with me just as I hazarded a look back.

Fritz hurled a grenade as the ground strafed around him. He pitched another. The one-two punch connected, and the AirGuard erupted into a concussion blast above him, plunging clumsily to the earth behind us as we bolted east down Lincoln.

But not before it launched.

The wounded ship dropped two incendiary bombs right at the intersection of Lincoln and West County Line Road. A roaring inferno tore through the night behind us, and the surrounding fields lit up in devilish orange. Off in the distance, more dots could be seen speeding our way. Lights flashed as they converged toward Fritz's final pitcher's mound.

For now, though, the old guy had done it. The AirGuard spun over and over off into the field south of the intersection to our right and behind us, crumpling in on itself. It erupted into a blazing ball of orange, adding to the mayhem of the incendiary bombs. Even if Fritz had tossed and bolted, there was no way he could have survived that triple blast.

Others were coming. Far off north and south, we could hear the faint sirens and see the glaring lights heading our way.

We ran, with everything that was in us.

We prayed that there were no Guardians on the highway ahead of us.

Our prayers failed. Up ahead, we could make out the faint whirring and the flashing lights of a single Guardian advancing toward us. It was far off, but it was coming.

"Off the road! Quick!" whispered Swifty. We split up and followed him down into the corn stalks on either side of Lincoln Highway. Our hearts thundered as it drew near, quietly surveilling the area and assessing the damage at the intersection beyond us.

Charlie was right next to me, and Hunter was on her other side. We watched it slowly pass by as seconds felt like the nightmarishly long minutes of an endless time. Our mouths formed open o's and our eyes were the only things that moved, tracing the Guardian's steady march, a stalking sentinel.

It had almost passed when Hunter winced and let out a sharp hiss as shattered bone grated against tissue. He bowed his head. My heart stopped. Charlie covered her mouth.

The Guardian slowed and then came to a stop. The dope's fully revolving head searched this way and that through the darkness, trying to pierce it. Trying to find us.

Breaking the silence, suddenly there was a deep voice. A quiet voice, but no less deep in pitch. "Hey!" it called out. I knew that voice. It barely ever spoke, but it was familiar to all. Charlie covered her mouth with both hands. Hunter looked at me with eyes wide.

The head whirred back around, facing west. There, staring it down not fifty feet up the road, was Luca. Ash-covered and bruised; his head was bleeding from the cave-in at the Ag building. He raised a sidearm and began to fire. Unloading hot bullets into the armor of the Guardian that faced him. He ran toward it, crying, even as the Guardian's double turrets fanned out from its body, lurched forward, and began to fire at him, thundering away.

His shirt became soaked. His expression flinched. He stumbled back to his feet only to discover that his ammunition was now expended. He winced at the pain and calmly lowered his head as he swooned, bending down to the ground in pain. His breathing slowed.

There, in the dim light of the fading moon, with his head bowed, an amber insignia glowed at the base of his neck. It was the mark that identified him as a son of God, baring all before the enemy.

The Guardian registered it instantly and proceeded, pausing its barrage of bullets, and instead firing off a single question in its chilly robotic multi-noted monotone.

Citizen, this is your final warning. Do you recant?

Luca raised his head. Sweat dripped from it.

He staggered to his feet, clutching his blood-soaked chest, and heaved a great sigh.

With every ounce of his being he shouted out from the well of his soul in a voice that thundered the air around us.

"Jesus Christ reigns! The Son of the Living God reigns!" And he laughed with proud and reckless abandon.

It took the Guardian less than a nanosecond to register his words. In flashes of lightning, it barraged him with destruction, sending bullet after bullet into his weakened torso. He fell to the ground in a pool of his own blood.

From our hiding place, many of us belted out *No!* I don't know if I did. It was hard to respond to anything through my swimming eyes and the heat flowing through me. But the Guardian didn't even have time to whip back around. Eight of us lurched out of the corn stalks and fired round after round, obliterating it.   We took full advantage of being too many targets for a single Guardian. Our reign of fury pulverized it as thick black smoke wafted into the air, its hull pierced from every side.

Our beloved and brave friend was dead in the street. We could do nothing for him.

Except run.

Luca had sacrificed himself, just like Fritz, to save us. Both had laid down their lives for their friends, and there was no greater love.

We had no idea where Miles and Reina's team was.

The roaring of the inferno faded. The crackling diminished into distant noise, soon fading into silence. The night was black all around us. The only sounds were the flapping of our feet on wet pavement competing with our desperate gasps for air. Emma was running next to me. I had been right; her wet shirt reeked of vomit.

At the next intersection of Lincoln Highway and Schrader Road, there was a long circular driveway leading into a well-manicured and spacious lawn. A row of red buckeye trees screened off the property from the street. The house was dead ahead, and to its right was a red barn with a few farm vehicles scattered around it.

We barreled toward the house and then raced up the front porch, knowing full well that we couldn't stay there. We had no idea if there were any occupants inside, but we needed to get out of sight, and fast.

Mercifully, the front door was unlocked.

All of us threw ourselves inside and down on the floor to catch our breaths, caught between panting, retching, and crying.

"My heart," breathed Andréa, clutching at her chest as she lay down gingerly. Nicholas attended to her.

I looked around. "Well, Anja, you and Asher were itching for a fight," I panted. "You got one."

Anja burst into tears. Several of them did. *What did I say?* I thought to myself, looking out into the cold of the night beyond the windows.

Luca. He never stood a chance one-on-one against a Guardian. He lived a lonely, quiet life on the run, and died with acid reflux in his esophagus. Probably didn't even get his water either.

And now he would be surrounded, for all eternity, by Christ's Living Water. He had gone down in thunderous glory, honoring his God, and rejecting the very notion of recanting.

And then there was Fritz, sacrificing himself as Luca had. Just like that: gone.

And Leona! I barely knew her, but she took care of all of us with food prep, partnering with Andréa. Her mortal life snuffed out on the stairs, just like that.

Three down.

For the Christian, death is another event we live through. They are guaranteed safety, but what of those left behind?

And what about Miles and Reina, and their team? They remained unaccounted for.

God, where are you? I thought numbly as I stared at the floor.

This war was wearing on us.

CHAPTER 9
Sage

1 . 12 . 2113
Virgil Township, IL

Ξ   Ξ   Ξ

She stared down the barrel of her shotgun right at our group. There was no love there; only fear.

The old woman had been frightened out of her wits at the sound of us storming into her house. Dressed in only her nightgown, she had been preparing to turn in when we arrived.

Those old legs whisked her into the great room when she heard us, and she had her shotgun loaded and cocked, aiming it right at Nicholas, since he was closest to her.

"Guns down!" she cried, and we complied. She inched the twin barrels of her shotgun right into Swifty's chest.

"Ma'am, we mean you no harm. I swear it," Nicholas said, holding his hands up in defense.

"That's right, *shhh*, it's okay. We're so sorry to burst in on you like this," Swifty agreed.

"Shut up and turn around!" she commanded. "All of you! Do it right now, slowly!"

We all complied, slowly revolving around with our hands up. I knew right away why she was asking that. Most of us had forgotten to don our chokers, or had lost them in the frenzied flight from the refuge.

"I *knew* it," she hissed. She clicked her tongue.

"Ma'am, I can explain," Swifty said, facing away from her. "Please let me explain."

There was silence. She cocked her rifle.

"You got sixty seconds."

Ξ   Ξ   Ξ

Swifty did his best to bring the old lady up to speed.
Saint Mary of the Assumption Catholic Church.
The bombing.
The Ag building.
The attack.
Leona.
Fritz.
Luca.
The others.

The old woman was silent for a long time when he finished. Finally, she sighed heavily. We couldn't see her, but something wooden tapped the floor, and then the creaking of knees sounded loudly. She gasped lightly. Then… rocking.

Out of curiosity, I turned around slowly and eyed her.

The old woman sat down in the rocking chair close to the kitchen counter, her shotgun perched on the floor beside her. She grasped the ends of the rocking chair arms while staring us down, dark, beady eyes set firmly under thick brows. Her silver hair was pulled tightly back into a ponytail, and her frail form was covered by a thin, floral-patterned nightgown.

"Always knew this day would come," she breathed. Swifty slowly dropped his hands and turned around to face her. The rest of us followed suit. "Good thing I hadn't initiated shutdown, or everything would have been locked and armed. Worked out well for you." She smiled thinly.

"Ma'am, again, we're so sorry, we-" Swifty started.

The woman held up her hand. "S'alright. Name's Iris. I heard the explosions and saw a bit of what went down up the road. Those accursed machines." She shook her head in disdain. "Did they get you?"

I nodded. "My friend here, he's hit in the arm, but he's bandaged. And my other friend," -here I pointed to Asher- "got hit in the upper chest by some shrapnel. We… lost three others."

Iris unleashed a groan as if the wind had been knocked out of her. "Oh, I'm so sorry. Those things just don't care, do they? Who's hurt now?"

"Me," said Hunter, and he feebly raised his arm. He shuddered with a nervous tick. I glanced over at him. He was looking white: pale from the loss of blood and the pain; exhausted from the run. Sweat had matted his shaggy, red hair to his scalp.

"And me," Asher mumbled angrily.

Iris rose slowly, looked Asher over briefly, and handed him some paper towels to staunch the bleeding. "It's not bad," she said. "Keep those pressed on it; I'll come back to you. Looks like you already pulled out whatever it was that got in there. Nice work," she said, and she winked at him. Iris walked over to Hunter. She tenderly evaluated his arm. "Bullet?"

"Yes, ma'am," he said quietly.

"Who wrapped this?"

"I did," Charlie spoke up. "I was serving as medic."

"Well, Charlie-serving-as-medic, nice work here. Let me improve upon it. Why don't all of you head upstairs. There's a rec room up there that we had for the grandkids. I don't see them much anymore since their father was taken. He converted," she said, sadly, glancing briefly up at Hunter.

He smiled empathetically at her. Her son had been taken away for confessing Christ. It was all over her face.

"Anyway, the rest of you head up there and stay. I'll initiate shutdown and re-bandage these two young men. Anyone else hurt? Who smells?"

Emma raised her hand.

"I can take care of that too. You're about my size. Come here, darlin.' You too, kiddo," she said to Hunter. "The rest of you, follow this young man upstairs." She motioned to me. "Head left, then right. Big room off the back wall. I'll be up with some food and drink in a minute. These ones will help me."

Hunter, Emma and Asher stayed with her. The rest of us did as she directed.

"HomeSafe, initiate shutdown," she instructed. A mechanical voice acknowledged. Over the next few seconds, locks whirred tight, lights shut off, and an alarm panel on the wall changed colors from green to red. Something shifted on the thermostat as well. This woman's house was a veritable Fort Knox. I wondered if her son had helped her bring it up to speed, installing these security measures before he was taken. I wondered if he knew his days were numbered, and he just wanted to protect his mother during his own absence.

We all headed upstairs.

Ξ   Ξ   Ξ

I thought we'd died and gone to heaven, but quickly felt convicted by the thought, as we literally had just lost three – and possibly more with Miles and Reina – to that very scenario. I choked back some guilt.

The 'rec room,' as Iris called it, was large, with an old game console, couches, beanbag chairs, and an exercise treadmill. There were toys and crafts, a small fridge, and even a small bathroom in the corner.

The room was warm and inviting as we all found a spot to recline upon. Charlie muttered something about the Ag building and how this was so much better. She must have primed a pump, because we were soon all sighing or weeping. The trauma caught up to us, and we were safe to now grieve.

Grieve Leona.

Grieve Fritz.

Grieve Luca.

Grieve this war.

Emma soon joined us in the rec room in a new shirt – Iris had put hers in the laundry – and though there were no words exchanged, she was soon bawling as well.

Anja was deeply convicted.

We were doing nothing more than sitting, eating and talking, when our lives were upended. The last thing she remembered doing was complaining about the overage of pizza. "Such minutiae," she groaned. "Such BS." She asked us why she was so ungrateful and how much more would Luca and Fritz and Leona like to be alive right now?

It was all we could do to try to console her.

About ten minutes later, Hunter, Asher and Iris emerged through the door. Hunt's arm was now set in a splint and bandaged up. Asher's clavicle was treated and bandaged. They were helping Iris bring in plates of food. The old woman was the last to enter, when she gasped, clicked her tongue, and shoved past them both.

"Oh, no, no. This won't do," she said. She scurried past him to close the blinds on the long window running the length of the rec room. "I don't wager you'll want to be seen tonight, right?"

Swifty thanked her.

"Are you okay, dear?" she said to Andréa.

"Better," Andréa replied. "I just get some occasional palpitations. All of that kerfuffle just worked me up, but I've settled. Thank you so much, Iris." Iris smiled sweetly and patted her on the shoulder.

Iris panned her view all around the room. Swifty and Nicholas took the plates from Hunter and Asher and proceeded to pass out the food. Charlie was sitting right next to me; and I could feel her shivering. Nicholas passed her some bread, meats, and cheese which she downed in a hurry. Swifty followed him with cups of water after that.

"Guess I'm a sympathizer now, eh?" Iris declared, tongue-in-cheek and with a wink. "Stupid machines. Stupid Nero. Mark my words: I'm no Christian, but I know good people and bad people when I see them, and if Constantine Jedidiah Goodfellow is a good man, then I'm a Smurf."

My nose crinkled. "What's a Smurf?"

Iris waved me away without looking at me. "Before your time, kiddo. Anyway," she said, glancing around the room, "I've had enough of all these drones and machines tearing up the countryside and blasting the dickens out of Christians. You poor folks," she said, frowning and regarding all of us. "Look at you. Hunted. And so young."

I gazed at her. She was smiling and kind, oozing empathy through her twinkling eyes. She looked down and seemed to remember something sad again. For the second time, I wondered if it was about her son.

"Those nightly broadcasts of his. Despicable. They're all propaganda, all one-sided: *his*. Why, dissent is not even allowed – why would it be? Everything is from his perspective, and his perspective only. Have you seen his pathetic broadcasts? Have you seen them?" she asked, motioning to Swifty, seeming to understand that he was our leader.

"I've seen them," replied Swifty. "It's been a while, but you're spot on, Iris. They're all about his new world order and propaganda. The things he's blamed all of us for… the virus, the assassination attempts, all of it. Those were just a few bad, confused elements among us."

Iris grunted. "I know. I know. You've had it bad from him. I'm so sorry, folks."

Charlie leaned in closer to me, and I put my arm around her. "Thanks for taking care of Hunt," I whispered to her. She smiled at me.

"Well, Iris," began Swifty, "he's a deluded man in need of saving grace. We were all that way once. Hopefully, he'll have his day. We pray for him, that he'll be converted, and turn, and God would heal him."

I ground my teeth together. I don't know why the very words and the very notion grated against me so. I wanted him dead, not converted. That's the honest truth.

"Well, it looks like that day is far off," Iris lamented. "He's gaining in strength. The man has been in power for far too long now, with no one to oppose him. People in power don't relinquish it lightly. Why would anyone ever willingly come down off their throne that they've spent years building off the suffering of their fellow man? That's exactly what he's been doing. *Sickening*."

"Because Nero doesn't see us as his 'fellow man.' We're called 'undesirables.' We've willingly named Jesus as Lord. He wants everyone to name *him* as lord. We can't do that, of course, so we're marked and hunted."

Iris held Swifty's gaze, and then she exhaled noisily. "How's the food?" she asked, changing the subject and pointing at the plates.

"It's great, ma'am – uh, Iris – thank you," Asher rasped, followed by a cough. "Sorry, lots of smoke out there."

"I don't doubt it. Those explosions were quite the noisemakers. Nearly scared Winston out of his skin."

"Winston?" Emma asked.

"My cat."

"You have a *cat?*" Emma exclaimed. "Can we- may we see him?"

Iris nodded. "Oh, certainly, if I can find him. He's probably hiding off in some corner. I don't doubt that he'll wander in at some point. Winnie likes people, just doesn't like loud noises. So, if you keep it down, His Royal Highness might make an appearance."

"It's been a long time since I've held a cat. We lost ours when-" Emma stopped short.

"When our house was bombed," Asher eventually finished for her. Iris turned to him. "When those punks took out our family and our home. When they tried to erase us. But we can't be erased just like that," he growled. "None of us can. We're survivors and fighters, and we're gonna survive and live on." His eyes were shining; his jaw was clenched.

"Hmm, I see you've got some fight in you," Iris breathed, regarding him gravely. "I respect that. How old are you? What's your name?"

"Asher. 17. Emma's my sister. 16."

"I was going to ask. You look like family."

"Where's your family?" Asher asked her.

Iris started, but she paused. Smiling, she let the air out of her lungs. "Gone. Arnold, my husband, died eleven years ago from the virus. I never got it. My son is named Jeffrey. He and his family survived the virus, but over time, well, he saw the same injustices that I saw. That you've all seen. Over time he just couldn't stomach it anymore, and he softened. Arnold was a believer. Jeffrey and I were not. Just never really was sold on the idea. Sorry. Maybe there's still time for me," she laughed softly.

My heart went out to her.

"There's always time for everyone," Swifty said quietly.

"Anyway," Iris said, moving right along, "Jeffrey called me one day and told me he had converted. He and his whole family. He knew that he would be in danger for doing so. I encouraged him to renounce. Would you believe that? I actually did. Heck, I was just scared. I didn't want to lose him too… or my grandkids. What's a grandma to do without her grandkids? Is she even a grandma anymore?" she asked, as her eyes welled over. "It's been so long since I've seen them, and I never will again. *Nero,*" she hissed.

We watched her recapture the pain of this past decade. Eventually she wiped her eyes and looked up again, drawing new breath for the strength to tell her story.

"He killed them just like he's killed so many of you. Or, at least, his wretched machines have. They're unfeeling, cold, imbued with evil, wholly inhumane."

"Yes, they are," Hunter grunted, massaging his arm through the makeshift splint.

"I never saw my son, my daughter-in-law, or my grandchildren again. I know they're gone. Since that time I've just tried to keep quiet and provide help in whatever way I can. I didn't mean to come at you with the shotgun. Just that I've seen some unsavory characters around here, sure enough. Seems like my house is right at a good waypoint for all kinds of naughty drifters," -here she looked at all of us in turn- "*and* decent refugees.

"Anyway," she concluded, "that's my story. Me and Winnie and Barney here. Just waiting for it all to blow over, I guess. Not that it will in my lifetime. Been going on too long now."

"Who's Barney?" Nicholas asked.

"My dog. He's older, but he's around the premises somewhere. Outside dog. Which makes me wonder: how did he let all of you just run right in without so much as a yelp or a bark? Maybe he knew you were no trouble and decided for himself. Who knows? Dogs have a sense about them, you know. Barney's got a good nose for friendlies."

She looked us all over again, and then suddenly rose. We were savoring the food she had prepared, immersed in our thoughts. "Why don't you all lie down and have some sleep? It's late. I'll deflect any questions should we have any visitors. The house is armed, and Barney will show anyone else the door. You can use the bathroom and walk around as you need to, just so long as you don't come into my bedroom while I'm sleeping. I'm quick to go for my shotgun these days," she said with a fiendish grin.

She smiled a knowing smile, and then her face clouded over as she glanced toward the window, listening.

"I would suggest you lay low; stay here tonight *and* tomorrow," cautioned Iris. "You can already hear that low hum; other Guardians are most likely out investigating what happened back northwest of here, and the muck you raked. Tomorrow night, they should have cleared out and taken off most likely, and then you can cut across the fields east. I've heard rumors – they're just *rumors*, mind you – of a gathering of Christians at the old high school. Kaneland. Off

Keslinger and Meredith, southeast of here. If I'm right, they're still there, and they can take you in. Pretty big complex for you to hole up in and find some fellow holdouts. If there are none there and that was just a concocted legend, keep moving east until you hit Elburn. Might find some there," she said, wistfully. "Just rumors, mind you, but they might work out in your favor."

"I've heard the rumors as well, but someone said they had moved on, so we weren't sure. Thanks for confirming. You've been most kind, Iris. We thank you with our lives," said Swifty. "All of us."

"It's no trouble, no trouble," she said, holding up her hands. We *sympathizers* do what we can. Sometimes sympathy is all you can give. That, and bread, meats and cheese. And heck, I must confess that every time I brush up against one of you, I feel something. Something different. Something that makes me wonder why Nero would want to 'cleanse' the world of such good folks. It must be your spirit. Or… something," she finished. "You're good folks. Barney and I think so," she finished with a nod.

Swifty shook his head. "Call it *the* spirit, and you'd be closer to the mark, Iris. It's the Holy Spirit in us." He smiled, and she smiled back at him. "May we pray for you?"

She eyed him for what seemed like an eternity, squinting her eyes. A war was raging within her: silent and concerted. At length, she let out a deep sigh, then slowly nodded. "Sure." She bowed her head.

Swifty smiled and then grabbed Nicholas' hand to his right and Andréa's hand to his left. The rest of us followed suit and took the hands of the people next to us. Charlie squeezed mine tight.

Hunter leaned back against the wall, while Emma lightly grasped the hand of his injured arm.

"Heavenly Father," Swifty began, "thank you for Iris. You tell us in Hebrews not to forget to show hospitality to strangers, for by so doing some have shown hospitality to angels without knowing it. I don't know if we're angels, but we know she is. Thank you for bringing us to her, and for her gracious refuge. We could have run into the wrong house, but you led us here. *Thank you,* Lord.

"Would you please fill her heart with a welling over of precious memories of her family, those she's lost? Would you please take away the sadness of losing them and the pain of isolation, and replace it with hope and cherished memory? Fill her heart and mind with peace, Lord. We are so grateful for her, and we pray for her peace and joy right now. Keep us and her safe, we pray in Jesus' Name. We thank you for her protecting us. We thank you for Fritz protecting us. And we thank you for Luca Harris protecting us," he finished, choking up. We all did. There were audible sniffles in the room. Swifty gathered himself once more. "Amen."

Amen, we echoed somberly.

Harris, I thought, learning his last name for the first time. *Harris. Lord,* thank you *for Luca Harris.*

"Amen," breathed Iris, raising her head. Her eyes were shining. "That was so kind of you. Thank you."

She smiled down at our group, no shotgun between us anymore. There was no more fear there; only love.

CHAPTER 10
Maximillian

1 . 13 . 2113
Washington, DC

Ξ　　Ξ　　Ξ

Three new reports had come in that were most promising!

The lord Nero would be exceedingly pleased with me.

I could see Vassal Richards standing guard outside the Senate chamber at the far end of the hall, erect and proud, awaiting my arrival. My heart leapt to see my lord! I could not wait to share the news with him.

The first: undesirables had been rooted out in the Maple Park suburb of Illinois, close to Chicago. Another Christian establishment was wiped off the face of Nero's earth – this one a Catholic church that we had apparently nearly leveled once before – and the rebels had been eliminated.

The second: Drexler's subordinate, an informant named Mario Davidé Sanchez, had come to us unbidden and provided information on the suspected whereabouts of the treacherous colonel's wife and son, which would prove to be most useful as leverage against him and his operatives.

And the third: Colonel Drexler himself had also most likely been located, and Vassal Behmardi and I were now coordinating an operation to destroy his headquarters. Our forces were arriving in the area and would be on him in two days' time. Drexler would soon be no more. While we held him at bay with the threat of his family's annihilation, we would move in with a stranglehold that would surround and destroy him. His love for them would be his undoing.

All of this would make my lord Nero *so* pleased with me. And with Vassal Behmardi. But mostly with me.

My cheeks hurt; I was so overcome by joy, and I-

Out stepped Vassal Dubois, Minister of New World Affairs. I was almost to my lord's portal when Dubois floated out of his office as if he knew I was coming. He blocked my path with his presence and that wry, saccharine smile. I did not care for Vassal Dubois, who always seemed to come off a bit too high and mighty, rather snakelike! A bit *snooty* for my taste. I was protective of His Eminence whenever I was in their mutual presence, wanting to keep my lord from being contaminated by the likes of Dubois.

His office was in the *Old* Senate chamber, on the way to my lord's throne room in the new Senate chamber. Dubois claimed that he needed so much space for his planning and execution of the Emperor's directives that he took the old Senate chamber for himself. Papers were scattered everywhere. It was an environment unbefitting a vassal, and I made no bones about voicing my strong disapproval.

However, the new world order was my lord's chief concern, so no amount of real estate seemed too much to relinquish to Vassal Dubois in order for him to be able to see it through. My own office was much smaller, however.

"Vassal Dubois," I said, exasperated. My eyebrows were raised with suspicion.

"Vassal Maximillian," he responded in that whispery, shrill, and whiny voice of his.

"*High* Vassal Maximillian," I corrected him.

He spread his arms out wide and bowed low. "Oh, forgive me, *High*" -here he over-emphasized *High*- "Vassal Maximillian. What a delight this is, running into you like this," he dripped. "To what do I owe the pleasure?" At the end of *pleasure,* his voice dipped and then rose annoyingly to a high, condescending pitch.

"To nothing," I replied, trying to keep my composure. "I was just on my way to see His Eminence, my lord. What may I quickly do for you?" I offered tentatively.

"For me? Oh, I am certainly fine, High Vassal. Thank you most kindly for your offer. I was just on my way to see him as well. May I accompany you?"

I started to protest, and then paused, attempting to conceal my disdain. "I think, my good Vassal Dubois, that we might be better served to hold different counsel with the Emperor. Perhaps it would aid us and provide better focus as we address him separately."

"Oh, is something amiss with your focus, my good High Vassal Maximillian? Do you need a draught perhaps?" he teased, reaching out for me with clawed fingertips. "Certainly you would not be implying that our *lord's* focus needs sharpening."

"No!" I said, a little too sharply, my eyes widening. "I mean, no *thank you*, my good vassal. And I wasn't implying anything. You misperceive me." I felt my blood pressure rising. "I just mean that you have your agenda of things you wish to discuss, and I have mine. I do not wish to overburden our lord with too much schema at once."

"I wasn't aware that the Supreme Emperor, our lord Nero, could in fact be overburdened," jested Dubois, pulling his hand to his chest and feigning dismay. He said that aggravatingly loudly. As he did so, he turned and looked toward Vassal Richards as if to recruit him to his side against me. "Can the Supreme Emperor not handle all of our needs? Is he not 'supreme' enough, perhaps?"

"*No*, my good vassal," I said firmly, but then I faltered as I felt a heat wave pass over me. "I mean, yes, of course he is!" I clicked my tongue and cleared my throat. I did not need to explain myself to this lowly servant. "It's just that presently I possess three notes of good news to share with our lord, and I wish to do it unencumbered by-"

"By what? By *me*? Oh my, dear Maximillian, I would not dare intrude upon your good news sharing with our lord. How intrusive and unbecoming of me! Please. Proceed unencumbered. Far be it from me to stand in your way with the wonderful revelations that you possess." He theatrically stretched out his arm, waving me toward the lord's chamber, bowing, and moved aside in tiny, shuffling footsteps.

I watched him as my body remained tense and focused forward. "Thank you, Vassal Dubois," I muttered. "*Most* kind of you. I shall alert you when I have finished counsel with our lord."

"I'm sure you will," he said, blinking rapidly at me and sneering sarcastically through his pointed teeth. He giggled something prepubescent and waved me off.

I wanted to say something again but thought better of it. Instead, I proceeded toward Vassal Richards with a roll of my eyes and a thick, hot exhale.

"Good day to you, High Vassal Maximillian," Richards greeted me. "All hail Emperor Nero."

"All hail Emperor Nero indeed," I said. "Thank you, Vassal Richards."

Richards pivoted and pulled the heavy Senate chamber door open for the two of us. "My lord, High Vassal Maximillian approaches," he announced.

"Ah, good Vassal Maximillian," the Emperor greeted me, turning toward me from high atop his throne, and I felt a swell of vindication in the greeting. I'm sure he has never greeted Vassal Dubois with such esteem. At least I hoped not.

I approached him, bowing low and extending my arms out. "My lord Emperor."

He descended and, at the foot of the dais to his throne, was greeted by a procession of his beautiful harem. They were gorgeous. He had allowed me to share them as I had such need, but usually I was too focused on serving and worshipping him to distract myself with such carnal pleasures. He required my all, and I gave it.

The Emperor dismissed them with a flick of his fingers. My lord extended his hand toward me, with his signet ring out.

"Why are you overdue?" he asked me.

I was in the middle of kissing his beloved ring when I stopped. My eyes rose to meet his. "Forgive me, my lord. I was stopped by Vassal Dubois en route to you."

My lord smiled. "Ah. And what did the good vassal wish with you? Was it perhaps to recruit your assistance with organizing his office again?" A smirk came over his lips, and I *loved* that he recognized Dubois' notoriously unkempt state of affairs. I felt vindicated.

Good vassal, I thought. *An overstatement, really.* However, I reproached myself for questioning my lord's choice of words, and cleared my head.

"I am sorry, sire, I do not know. I attempted to come straight to you, and he felt the need to interject his thoughts and delay me. It will not happen again."

"It is fine, good Maximillian. Tell me. What brings you here? I am told you have good news?" he asked, tilting his head and smiling at me. "Have we caught the treacherous colonel yet?"

I swallowed, cracking my fingers. "Unfortunately, no, sire, not yet."

The Emperor's smile faded. His eyes turned sullen.

Please do not beat me, I thought to myself.

"And why not?" His voice was monotone.

"Oh, plans are forming, sire, *good* plans. May I brief you on them?"

He did not reply. My lord took a breath, let it out by degrees, and then turned resolutely away from me. I watched him as he strode, his arms clasped about himself. The tension was unbearable. He cast one long, penetrating look at me on his way to one of two plush beds lying at the base of his throne mount. Gardens enshrined each, overflowing with lotus flowers while two concubines sprawled seductively across them.

My lord gracefully sat and then lay upon the bed, his eyes never leaving me. Both concubines began to run their hands over him. He put his arms behind his head and nodded.

"Tell me."

A euphoric thrill of arousal coursed through me, and I advanced closer to him.

"Thank you, my lord. First, we have demolished another stronghold outside Chicago, in a suburb of Illinois. A Catholic church, my lord," I said, frowning, the very words distasteful, "along with its custodian. There was an infidel, perhaps more than one, killed and trapped in the rubble below."

The Emperor said nothing.

"Uh, secondly, the traitor we seek had an informant that has arrived here. Mario Davidé Sanchez, my lord. He has provided us the location of Colonel Drexler's family, sire! We can use that as leverage, my lord."

Still, my lord Nero was unresponsive.

"Continue," he finally said, quietly and methodically.

"Yes, my lord," I continued. "We, uh, we also believe that Colonel Drexler's whereabouts have been determined. Somewhere in the Hyde Park region of Ohio. I have personally arranged his arrest with Vassal Behmardi, and we have coordinated an operation to destroy his headquarters. Your forces are en route there, sire. We are preparing to contact him and delay him under threat of pain to his family. While he is occupied with their safety, sire, we shall move in and exterminate him!" I said, with a certain glee, my arms outstretched in triumph. I had practiced this presentation. But once again, the Emperor did not seem pleased. His face was impenetrable.

I was confused. Why was my lord unresponsive and so hard to read? I did not know! I was so excited to present this good news to him! I was unsure why it did not seem to please him perfectly.

Nero stood suddenly and slowly advanced toward me.

"Is my lord dismayed?" I finally asked him. "Please forgive me if I have erred, sire. I sought only to please you, my lord." I tried to be proud and grateful, but I felt as though I was beginning to whimper. My mouth felt pasty.

At that moment, the doors to the chamber opened, and I whirled around in surprise. There, to my dismay, was Vassal Dubois, entering with Vassal Richards. I gnashed my teeth in vexation at the sight of the two intruders.

"My lord! Vassal Dubois seeks an audience with you as well," Richards declared.

My lord said nothing, but he then motioned for Richards to let Dubois in. The snarling snake approached both of us, bowing low.

"Most excellent lord Nero, all hail!" he greeted my lord as I studied him judgmentally. My jaw was sore from clenching. "Please forgive the interruption," he said, "and you as well, High Vassal Maximillian, forgive me," he said. I acknowledged him with a quick nod, though my lips were tight. He approached Nero and kissed his signet ring, and I felt a swell of jealousy arise in me. I tried to subdue it in my mind; to fully repent of it knowing Nero was my lord.

"Greetings, Your Eminence. I bring news from New World Affairs!"

"And what news do you bring?" Nero asked him quietly. "The news I have received is all of potentialities and possibilities, but it is apparently bereft of certainties. Do you bring certainties?"

Vassal Dubois rose, his eyes wide. "Oh, sire, I do! I do, indeed," he hissed with glee, rising to full height. "I have just been informed that Emperor Nakamoto of Japan has surrendered, pledging his undying loyalty to you. He plans to cede his title and cement his servitude this very hour in a general assembly before his people!"

Nero smiled, and there was at last a twinkle in his eye. I felt a surge of nausea wash over me. Why was my news any less valuable or exciting? Surely, he valued my offering no less than Vassal Dubois'? Surely, he was more pleased to know that we were closing in on his chief opposition? I knew full well that Japan surrendering was a victorious and glorious stroke, praise be to Nero! – leaving only the United Kingdom to bow the knee to him – but this interruption seemed too choreographed for my liking.

"That… is… *wonderful*, Vassal DuBois. I am most grateful," said Nero, parading toward him and embracing him by the shoulders.

Dubois bowed, and if I didn't know any better, he was trying to conjure up fake tears. Such a pathetic actor. I prayed my lord would see through his theatrics. I watched him with pursed lips, my eyes darting back and forth between him and my lord.

"I am most pleased with this news, Vassal Dubois. I have been thinking," he said, and then he turned to address me as well. "We are needing to step up our efforts. In order to see the final solution fulfilled, which is the eradication of the undesirables, we must truly think as *one*. And I, alone in my chamber here, need to know that everything is being handled according to my wishes and designs outside this hall." He rose up and began to declaim now, as if reciting a speech long prepared before a vast audience as we beheld him. His concubines began to purr with adoration.

"It is time to take my grand plan to the next level. This next level will require more closely coordinated efforts," he orated, drawing his arms out wide and then close in to himself as if in an embrace, "and I find myself in greater need of proficiency. I am therefore going to appoint *you*, Vassal Dubois, to be my third-in-command, equal only in rank to High Vassal Maximillian here. You are to be his equal, and he yours, and you shall both serve me!"

I froze in shock, and my jaw dropped. Dubois dropped to his knees before my lord and sobbed with glee, kissing the Emperor's ring, fawning at his knees, squealing with praises, reverence and Nero knows what else.

The Emperor slowly raised his head and brought his eyes to mine. I was speechless. *Flummoxed* was more the word. Frustrated, although I know I shouldn't be. My lord was supreme and perfect in every way. Infallible and inerrant. How could this be anything other than his divine providence and goodwill?

I collected myself. I had to. I was so conflicted! Seething with rage at Dubois, yet transported into worshipful reverence before my lord.

"Oh, Greatest, my liege, our savior, all hail Emperor Nero," I said, reverentially. "Your will is good and perfect. I humbly accept your will, my lord. I shall serve you in fidelity and worship with Vassal Dubois here." I just could not bring myself to address Dubois as 'high' vassal.

Nero raised a finger and bobbed it back and forth, tilting his head at me.

"*High* Vassal Dubois, Maximillian. *High* Vassal Dubois. Yes?"

"Yes! Oh yes, sire – my sincerest apologies," I exclaimed, nearly at the point of sobbing. "It's all so new. And… so… exciting! Forgive me, sire!" I tried to conceal my eyes welling over. "My lord is just and right in all he does. Thank you for this gracious decision and one that will surely demonstrate your power over the earth." I bowed to him. I couldn't decide if it was out of reverence, or to conceal the anger that was clouding my face.

"My good servant. Carry on. Keep me informed as to Sanchez and the location of the traitor."

Nero pivoted and returned to his concubines.

I slowly glanced up. Vassal Dubois was watching our lord retreat to his harem, and then he slowly moved his head toward mine to meet my eyes. Those icy orbs and that serpent's tongue twisted together into a sinister smile that gawked at me mockingly as he mouthed two words:

High Vassal.

And then he flaunted his snakelike, toothy grin.

My heart sank. I did not wish to share my position with this serpent. But my lord had decreed it! Surely, he could not be mistaken, could he? Surely not. It must be me! I must have erred somehow. Not been worthy enough? Not pleased him enough?

All I wanted to do was to serve my Emperor. Not to share my position with someone so undeserving! Vassal Behmardi and I had worked *so* hard on our upcoming operations. They were sure to be successes. Vassal – I *won't* call him 'high,' not in the slightest! – *Dubois* didn't even do anything to elicit obedience from the Japanese emperor. That was all my *lord's* doing. Yet Dubois was credited, and subsequently promoted to equal stature with me.

"Yes, my lord," I breathed to him, though my voice trembled, and my heart sank low in my chest. "We are commencing the operation tomorrow evening and will, of course, keep you apprised. Success," I said, but I stopped, needing to clear my throat. My emotions were getting the better of me. I tried again, though my croaking voice seemed to whisper through a squeak. "Success, my lord."

"Success, Maximillian," he echoed, though he did not turn to face me. "High Vassal Dubois, stay a moment please. I need your assistance on the speech for my next broadcast. Thank you, High Vassal Maximillian, that will be all."

I choked. *I* always helped my lord with his speeches. "My lord, I…," I trailed off. His Eminence turned to face me, and his expression was clouded by a frown. I did not wish to compound his unhappiness. This was surely for the best. "Nothing. Thank you, lord. All hail Emperor Nero!"

I spun on my heels and headed out. I wanted to flee from that chamber, to *run,* and just weep. I had not received a physical beating from my lord, but I had received an emotional beating from Dubois.

I would have preferred the former.

This new development was beyond vexing.

CHAPTER 11
Sage

1 . 14 . 2113
Virgil Township, IL

Ξ   Ξ   Ξ

Things were quiet now.

We were coming up on two full days here. If the rumors were true about the high school, then we needed to get there with our people and not jeopardize Iris' safety any longer. She had fed us and provided new clothes for us that would serve us well in this cold weather. Arnold, she said, would have approved.

An initial survey team had shown up to assess the damage of the downed AirGuard back at the intersection, as well as the destroyed Guardians. We could see some of it, peeking out through the rec room back northwest.

At one point a team of three young men came to the door, knocking loudly. Iris approached slowly and inquired who they were, gun in hand. They requested that she open the door. She did so, keeping the screen door closed. Barney was inside, barking his head off ferociously.

We were all clustered quietly in the rec room with the light off. Iris didn't let them in. She was unnerved when she came up afterward and reported what she saw. They were in uniforms that she hadn't seen before, complete with a hat and some kind of emblem sewn into the chest. And they were young: two of them younger than us! Early to middle teenage. When she described the emblem for us, it was clear: it was Nero's. Two diagonal slashes set over a thin circle with a small star hovering over all.

The young soldiers were conscripts, recruited into Nero's forces. They had even handed her a yellow flyer. Emblazoned across the top were the words *Friends of Nero*.

It unnerved Iris. She said it reminded her of stories that her great-grandfather used to tell her about Nazi Germany and indoctrination, although she couldn't recollect all the details. She had simply been too young. The flyers painted a rosy picture of a smiling Nero holding a baby, his arm around a young man with a uniform similar to what Iris described on the young conscripts that had visited.

I looked at it with disgust.

At any rate, Barney's barking would not abate as he pushed to get at them through the screen door. It was all part of Iris' plan, however: make the soldiers uncomfortable and nervous, sending them packing. If they didn't, she'd loose her dog on them.

The only things that Barney *wouldn't* be able to handle were the two titanium-tungsten mechanoids hovering silently in her driveway behind the soldiers, menacing arm-turrets at the ready. It was all too clear that Nero's forces were here, surveying the aftermath and searching for 'undesirables.'

Ξ   Ξ   Ξ

All was quiet now. It was almost 1900 hours. We needed to head out across country soon as Iris had said, to get to the high school. We had no idea if someone would even be there, if we'd run into friend or foe, or something even worse. Swifty kept praying Psalm 91 over the past few days. By now we had it memorized:

Whoever dwells in the shelter of the Most High will rest in the shadow of the Almighty. I will say of the LORD, 'He is my refuge and my fortress, my God, in whom I trust.' Surely he will save you from the fowler's snare and from the deadly pestilence. He will cover you with his feathers, and under his wings you will find refuge; his faithfulness will be your shield and rampart. You will not fear the terror of night, nor the arrow that flies by day, nor the pestilence that stalks in the darkness, nor the plague that destroys at midday. A thousand may fall at your side, ten thousand at your right hand, but it will not come near you. You will only observe with your eyes and see the punishment of the wicked. If you say, 'The LORD is my refuge,' and you make the Most High your dwelling, no harm will overtake you, no disaster will come near your tent. For he will command his angels concerning you to guard you in all your ways; they will lift you up in their hands, so that you will not strike your foot against a stone. You will tread on the lion and the cobra; you will trample the great lion and the serpent. 'Because he loves me,' says the LORD, 'I will rescue him; I will protect him, for he acknowledges my name. He will call on me, and I will answer him; I will be with him in trouble, I will deliver him and honor him. With long life I will satisfy him and show him my salvation.

Man *that's a good scripture,* I thought. Swifty had us memorize it over the past few days while helping around the house and building some shelving for Iris. She canned fruit and needed to be ready for the spring. Now she had some shelving to put all her jars on. We also reinforced Barney's doghouse. And through all of that, we'd pore over that scripture, again and again, quizzing each other until we felt we had it really down pat. God's Word is powerful, and we needed to draw upon that power.

If I could just get past that 'a thousand may fall at your side' part. It only served to remind me of Leona, Luca and Fritz, as well as Miles and Reina's team, whom we still hadn't heard from. We didn't want to lose anyone else. We didn't want to fear the terror of night, nor the pestilence that stalks in the darkness. *God, be with us…*

Charlie was unusually pensive and quiet over these past few days. Last night I asked her if something was bothering her. She told me that she wished we could have gone back for Luca and seen if he could have been tended to. She simply couldn't register the sheer, raw reality that he had been pulverized by bullets. No medical treatment would have saved him. But still, the gnawing regret ate at her.

It ate at Swifty as well. Uncertainty plagued him. I found him alone yesterday, crying. All had seemed well, and yet there he was, off in a quiet corner of Iris' house, weeping while staring out through the windows.

He was *tired*, he said: tired of this war, tired of losing people – we had, after all, lost eleven before I even joined up with the group – and tired of trying to lead when he felt like an incapable imposter.

I did my best to encourage him with the truth of his valuable leadership.

It was Swifty, after all, who had snapped us all into action after that first blast hit the Ag building.

It was Swifty who got us on the move again after Leona and Fritz. And it was Swifty who had the good sense to get us out of that church when he had heard rumor of an informant.

It was Swifty who had saved lives. That's what a leader does, I told him. I think it did some good for him to be reminded of the truth, but it was up to him to fully reconcile that to himself and accept the mantle that he had been given. Satan is, after all, the accuser of the brothers, and sometimes we struggle to see our beloved identity beyond the accusations.

I couldn't blame him for being weary. We all were.

Ξ   Ξ   Ξ

Swifty insisted on keeping up with our teaching times. *After all,* he said, *we're nothing without knowledge.* "Education is power," he said. "And where you have education, you have knowledge. The knowledge of good and evil is something mankind has forgotten – it's certainly something Nero has forgotten."

And then, he began to talk to us about Jesus and Judas. I had always regarded Judas as something of a lightning rod: a persona both misdirected and misunderstood.

"Judas wanted to bring about Jesus' reign in Israel, their deliverance from the Romans," Swifty said. "He was trying to force His hand. However, what Judas didn't realize is that wasn't even why Jesus came. He didn't come to liberate Israel. He came to liberate the human heart. To free us – *all* of us – from captivity to sin."

"But wasn't Judas cursed from the very beginning?" I asked him.

"Cursed?" Swifty asked. "Or predestined?"

I hadn't heard that term. "What does that mean?"

"Well," Swifty said, "was Judas predestined to betray Jesus? Was it his destiny to do so?"

"Yes," most of us said.

"But God could have used *anyone*, right?" I asked. "He's God. He could pick someone out of a crowd and use him because he needed *somebody* to betray Jesus."

"Correct, Sage, but he said that Judas was 'doomed to destruction.' When Jesus was praying to the Father in John 17, he said that he had lost none whom the Father had given him, except the one doomed to destruction. That's the argument that many make for predestination. Judas was predestined for destruction."

"But didn't Judas willingly *choose* to betray Jesus? It's not like he didn't have a choice; he *did* have a choice. I mean, wasn't it his own decision to turn Jesus in to the Pharisees in exchange for money?"

"Sure," Swifty said. "But, Sage, did God know all of that was going to happen? Like you said, 'He's God. He could pick someone out of a crowd and use him because he needed *somebody* to betray Jesus.'"

"So you're saying that God picked him out of a crowd because he needed him?"

I felt the others' faces ping-ponging between us as we went back and forth.

"Why not? Doesn't God have the freedom to appoint some for noble purposes and some for ignoble?" Swifty asked me.

"I guess?" I answered. "I just can't see how someone could be predestined to destruction. Judas helped bring about Jesus' death and resurrection, which ultimately benefited all of us, right?"

"That's one way to look at it," Swifty said. "But, again, God is God. Jesus is Jesus. If Jesus wanted to, he could have leveled those Romans with legions of angels. He had that power. He willingly chose to suppress his own power to win – to forsake it – in order that God's will might be fulfilled."

"So Judas could have suppressed his own power, and God could have brought about the same end result?" I asked.

Swifty nodded.

I thought to myself for a moment, quietly. God picks Judas… God uses Judas… Judas betrays Jesus… Jesus dies for all mankind. In my mind, Judas did what was required of him, so how could he be 'doomed to destruction' as Jesus said? It seemed like God *needed* Judas to betray Jesus. And it seemed like in Judas' heart, he *wanted* that.

"Sage?"

"Huh?" I looked up, snapped out of my line of thought. "Yeah, I guess that makes sense."

Swifty watched me for a moment, almost as if he sensed my equivocating. In my mind, Judas betrayed Jesus for redemption, ultimately. I couldn't help wondering if God would use someone to betray Nero for redemption as well.

Perhaps God would use me that way: to betray Nero and bring about redemption. In my heart, I *wanted* that.

Ξ   Ξ   Ξ

1900 hours. It was time to go. Under cover of darkness, the roads and skies were quiet.

We bade Iris goodbye inside the very front room where we had stormed in a few nights prior. Barney had taken to all of us, and his tail ceaselessly wagged in approval. I had not seen her cat Winston once, but such, I'm told, is the nature of cats: reclusive and avoidant. Emma thought she had seen him.

Iris cautioned us to keep to the fields and avoid the roads. She didn't know many of the neighbors around here; the few that were left didn't seem like they wanted to stay. Some had moved on. Some had been taken. Those remaining guarded their property and their possessions with their guns and their lives.

If we cut southeast through the cornfield, we would have a straight shot until we reached Watson Road. Iris cautioned us that the last exchange she'd had with Mr. Brewer off Watson Road had been very unpleasant, and so we should avoid going that way. Instead, when we come to the hedge surrounding his overly large property, we should turn south and proceed toward Keslinger. She still advised staying off the road, so we should cross as quickly as possible into the fields between Watson and Schrader. Big expansive field there, she said, and no one for a good few thousand feet in all directions. Then we could curve southeast again and navigate south of the suburbs until we once more reached the fields. We would then have an unmolested approach to the high school once we crossed over Keslinger again. Overall, it shouldn't take us more than two hours to get there if we maintained a stealthy pace.

"Iris, you've really been too kind. We thank you from our hearts, and with our lives," Swifty said. He had gathered and composed himself after what I reckoned was a good, cleansing cry. I've had those. They do help. It just made me appreciate him all the more as someone who was a truly well-rounded human, willing to be vulnerable.

"You're so welcome. All of you." And then she addressed us each by name. "Gregory, Andréa, Nicholas, Sage, Charlotte, Hunter, Asher, Emma, and Anja. I'm so sorry about those you've lost. I'm glad you came to me. Arnold would have loved meeting you. So would Jeffrey and my grands. I'm going to miss you. You're welcome back here anytime. And if things take a turn for the worse down by the high school, you have a place with me."

She smiled at us warmly. "I've also filled your packs with some snacks and bottled water. Part of my stores in case all hell breaks loose, and that idiot in DC raises the price of food again. Nicholas and Greg, I think you have enough ammunition in those bags, but I've supplemented it with what Arnold used to have. He was an avid hunter, my husband. I think you'll find that the ammunition I've supplied will work in your magazines. Let's pray you never have to use it on any of those young conscripts, and never have to use all those other wonderful toys I saw in your packs." She shuddered and clutched herself, frozen in thought over all our artillery.

"Go with my blessings," she finally said, and then we all hugged her in turn. "Hunter, take care of that arm. It's healing. Asher, same with your clavicle."

Hunter was the last to hug Iris, and then we all stepped out. Asher nodded in gratitude one final time. Barney wagged his tail.

The night air clawed at us, chilling our bones. We swaddled ourselves tightly in the clothing Iris had supplied, and we were off.

The skies were clear, and we listened intently. The gravel and snow crunching under our feet was annoyingly loud, but Barney accompanied us out to the road, and his panting obscured some of the noise. We reached Lincoln Highway once more. I turned back and noticed the old, frail form of our friend standing on the porch. She raised her hand high, waved, and then turned, vanishing into her house.

Like shadows, we crossed over Lincoln and took to the fields, rustling through the tall corn stalks and keeping as silent as we could. Small rodents fled before us. We couldn't afford to use flashlights or we'd be seen, and we had no night vision goggles or anything so extravagant. We had to make do with what we had.

Before long, Swifty stopped us. Thankfully, he had a compass, and he checked it, figuring that we were drawing near to the point Iris said we should avoid Mr. Brewer's land. We turned south and silently filtered single file down toward Keslinger. Eventually, a property loomed up before us, with dim amber light filtering out through some of the windows. A tall corn silo stood next to an old, dilapidated barn, with other outbuildings dotting their complex. We didn't want to arouse suspicion or get any other dogs barking, so we veered back west to avoid that property. That way we would not have to climb any fences either. We finally made it to the road.

I thought I heard something, and tut-tutted everyone. "Swifty," I whispered, and held up a fist, cautioning us to hold back. He paused, listening with me, and then motioned for us all to get down. Everyone hunched below and stayed concealed in the corn stalks.

Good thing. Just then a convoy of trucks appeared on the horizon, down the road west of us. Three Guardians led their way. We could barely make out another grouping farther down the road, flanking them.

"Lie down. Everyone," ordered Swifty.

Lower profile. Good thinking, I said to myself.

The rumbling drew nearer, and the sound of clutches mixed with the whirring of the machines was almost upon us. My heart started to race. I hugged my XM6 closer to me.

There they were. Looming into view and passing in a great cavalcade were seven convoy vehicles. A tank followed them, trailed immediately by three more Guardians at the rear. They slowly processed east, and for a moment I feared for the high school, wondering if the rumors were true and if they were about to be attacked. I prayed to the Lord for their protection.

The convoy passed by us. We waited until they were completely out of earshot before we thought about getting up again.

Finally, we were crossing over Keslinger and quickly blending into the tall corn stalks south of it. This was the 'big expansive field' Iris had spoken of, and I immediately felt safer in it.

We had traveled another few thousand feet when my ears pricked up again. Something was out there. I snapped my fingers and beckoned to our group and Swifty once again. I strained to listen, glancing up toward the sky. The dark silhouettes of the corn stalks towered over us, framed as darker spots against the thick black ink of the night sky.

"There's an AirGuard over us. High up. I can hear it, barely. It's there," I whispered.

The others looked up toward the heavens.

We watched and waited, silently, listening.

There it was. Some dark, vast shape was crossing the sky, blotting out the stars as it came, quietly running in some sort of stealth mode. It was high up and ultraquiet, but we could see its silhouette and feel its presence. I could practically feel everyone's eyes tracing it across the canvas of the night sky.

"Okay, it's moved on, heading north," I breathed. "Wow, they have some kind of stealth mode, I guess."

That made my flesh crawl. How could we fight something we couldn't see coming? This was a new development, and one that made me shiver. If Nero indeed had this new technology, it would lead to incredibly deadly sneak attacks on the holdouts.

In another twenty minutes we had reached Watson Road and threaded our way through low fields south of a small suburb. The fields weren't very tall here, which left us vulnerable to detection. But soon, mercifully, we reached Kaneville Township with its fields of thick, tall grass and plenty of distance all around us.

In another twenty or so minutes we were drawing once more north toward Keslinger. The dark shapes of a mass of buildings clustered together were silhouetted on the other side of the road.

We had finally reached the high school.

Swifty had us all pause and take a knee.

"Okay, gang, this is it. There are nine of us. I don't know about you, but I don't plan on losing any more. Keep your wits about you. Guns drawn. Be ready. The rumors *could* be true; Iris didn't know for sure, nor do we. So let's be careful, stick together, and if anything goes south, we double back into the fields and wait right here. Got it?"

We nodded. Some of us whispered 'yeah.' I looked at Hunter. He gripped his rifle and licked his lips in anticipation. Charlie, beyond him, did the same, tensing up. She eyed me as she took in a deep breath.

"God bless you guys," said Swifty. "Who wants to pray?"

Anja raised her hand.

"Okay, baby, you dial. I'll hang up."

Anja nodded. We set down our rifles and grabbed hands.

"Heavenly Father," she began. "We love you. We thank you for keeping us safe and keeping us alive so far. Would you please let there be Christians in the high school? Please let us gather in numbers and increase our Defiance. You say that wherever two or more are gathered in your name, there you are in the midst of them. Well, there are nine of us here, and so we pray that you're here in even greater power. And let there be *ninety*-nine in there so that you'll be here in even *greater* power, Lord. We love you and worship you. Maranatha, Lord. Amen."

"Maranatha, indeed," her dad continued. "Thank you for my daughter's sweet mathematical prayer." We giggled. "Yes, Lord. Increase exponentially in power wherever we are gathered in your Name. The Name of the Lord is a strong tower. The righteous run to it and are safe. Let it be so. In Jesus' Name. Amen."

Amen.

Ξ   Ξ   Ξ

As soon as we released hands in a chorus of 'Amens,' we each crossed cautiously over Keslinger. For a moment I thought back to Iris and wondered if she had told HomeSafe to initiate shutdown. The very words seemed so comical, but I wondered if the high school had any such similar security accommodations.

There were some non-functioning streetlights along Keslinger here; unfortunately the ones dotting the lane across from the high school were still on, exposing everything under them to harsh light in a broad swath. We would have to make a dash for it.

"Sage, you hear anything?" Swifty asked, gripping his AR-18 fiercely.

I closed my eyes to listen intently. There was nothing. I looked at him and shook my head.

"Okay, this is it. Ready, everyone?"

We all nodded.

Swifty led the way as we bolted from the fields up over Keslinger Road, and into what was arguably the main bus drop off and pickup lane to the west of the complex. The lights faded as we retreated further from the street, thankfully. In sixty seconds, we were now shielded from view and threading our way around the west side of the westernmost building of what was formerly Kaneland High School.

We circled around the back and through a drive lane. The school had security gates around it, but part of the gate had been broken. We slipped in through there, quickly and quietly.

Once inside, we were panting, taking up position undercover and against the wall.

"Andréa, how's your heart; you okay?" Nicholas asked. She panted, nodded, and held a thumbs up, indicating that she was okay.

"Kids, you okay?" Nicholas asked us.

We nodded back. I was desperate for water at this point and had to pee. Hopefully we'd find a bathroom somewhere.

My thoughts were cut short.

A tiny speaker mounted to the underside of the rain cover suddenly sprang to life, and a quiet voice sounded.

"Who are you? What do you want?"

We turned in alarm, facing it.

"Uh, we're, uh, just seeking refuge," Swifty said.

"Refuge from what?" the voice interrogated quickly. It was a youngish voice but was commanding nonetheless. There was gravitas in that speech.

"Refuge from… unsafe conditions," Swifty replied, looking to tread carefully.

"And what do you define as 'unsafe conditions'?"

Swifty looked around for a possible video camera that might be watching us. I could tell he was tired, and he longed to get inside. He wanted to get all of us inside, but he had to use caution.

"The unsafe conditions that have taken over our world, making it an undesirable place to live for those who are… undesirable," he finished.

The voice paused. We looked at each other.

Suddenly a door at the far end of the covered area opened up, leading into the corner building. Light streamed out of it, though there had been no light emanating through the windows at the top of the building we were perched against. They must have been boarded up from the inside.

My heart was thudding. This was a delicate game of calling one another's bluff.

A man, seemingly in his early twenties, wearing fatigues and a cap, peered out at us. He was holding some kind of rifle. He studied us briefly and then sighed, turning and voicing to someone within, "Jenkins, Foster. Visitors."

Two others joined him, and then all three began to advance toward us with their guns drawn. "Drop your weapons."

We did so. Swifty held up his hands.

I'll never forget the words that came out of the man's mouth. Words that we all knew, and that instantly put us at ease.

"For God so loved the world…" he started.

Swifty's eyebrows went up, and he took up the verse, "…that He gave His one and only Son, that whoever believes in Him should not perish…"

The young man smiled slowly, a twinkle in his eye as he watched Swifty, and then lowered his weapon. "…but have everlasting life." He craned his neck and pulled his jacket collar away from himself. The familiar amber glow of his mark illuminated his grip and the inside of his collar.

Swifty smiled in return. "Hello, brother," he greeted, showing off his own mark.

"Greetings, fellow undesirables," the man beamed to all of us. "There are sixty-four of us here. Now it looks like there are seventy-three. Good number. You're needed."

The Lord had answered Anja's mathematical prayer.

We all let out our collective breaths.

The thudding of my heart subsided.

Things were quieter now.

CHAPTER 12
Drexler

1 . 15 . 2113
Lunken Field, OH

Ξ   Ξ   Ξ

The message had been received.

Kent was certain it was legitimate. A trace concluded that the call had originated from the Capitol Building. No one friendly to The Defiance would be anywhere *near* the Capitol Building, much less inside it!

It was 1703 hours. The night was fast approaching.

Kent had his earpiece to his ear, and he was nodding, eyes widened while staring at me. "Confirmed. Thank you, Evan. Put it through; we'll let them eat static." He clicked off. His phone began to ring once again.

"Sir," he said, clearly nervous, "it's a verified trace. They're coming for you, sir. They say they have your wife and son."

I shook my head. "No. It's a bluff. *No one* knows where my family is. Not Sanchez, not even me."

"Yessir, I realize that, but what if it's true? What if it's not a bluff and they've found them somehow?"

I paused. "We'll have to take that chance, Kent, but this reeks of a trap. They obviously want to keep us here. Their objective is to stall us. Don't take that call."

"Roger that."

"Prep for evac."

I whisked off into the side room and gathered my things. Of all my possessions, the most critical and the most precious was my satchel, which I could sling over my shoulder in a hurry. Ultimately my life was in there, and all of our operations: my laptop, a Satcom interface, patches, a few masks, my Beretta and its magazines.

Since my clandestine meeting with Chris Mathieson at Alms Park exactly one week ago, there had been much activity at Lunken Field, and we had watched the shipments and convoys go rolling out. Soldiers could now be visibly seen on the field; young soldiers in uniforms. They were conscripts, no doubt, but I had never before seen such young ages enlisted in Nero's forces before. Through binoculars, some appeared to be as young as ten.

Then we saw the leaflets drop. These were new, yellow leaflets. Planes taking off from Lunken Field opened up their cargo bay and dumped thousands of them. Everywhere one looked, little flyers rained down and littered the air all over Ohio, and I daresay neighboring states. *Friends of Nero*, it boldly proclaimed at the top. The artwork and verbiage were sickening:

Young people of the world, all hail Emperor Nero!
This is your chance!
Nero needs you. Yes, YOU!
As you know, our beloved Emperor and his forces are committed to a full-scale and drawn-out conflict involving the undesirables, "Christians" as they call themselves – the very term sacrilegious to His Eminence – and you are needed in the fight! They will stop at nothing. They are dangerous

infidels! They strike without warning, injuring and sometimes killing women and children with no shame. Utterly despicable. We must stop them!

Conscripts are now being recruited all over the world, and young people are seeing the illuminatingly righteous light of His Eminence's just cause.

YOU, TOO, CAN BE PART OF THAT CAUSE!

If this world is to ever recover from the wretched virus that has plagued our nations – brought about by the undesirables themselves – we must restore order swiftly.

His Eminence, the god-king Nero, needs you in this fight. JOIN TODAY! The list of benefits is long and prosperous, full of lifelong favor from Nero and the new world order. You will be taken care of for life.

Please contact your local Guardian battalion to enlist. They are in your neighborhoods as we speak. Transit will be provided to Washington, DC at no expense to you, where you will receive proper training for the fight ahead. Friends of Nero enlistees will be richly rewarded and will have lasting favor with the god-king, along with immeasurable financial reward.

Please distribute this leaflet to your friends and social circles and over the NeroNet socials, if you have access. Together, we will have a safer and more prosperous world under the god-king with YOU in a position of command.

Remember, it is a crime punishable by death to pronounce any name as holy other than the god-king, His Eminence Himself, Lord Nero.

Thank you for your consideration, future Friends of Nero. ALL HAIL EMPEROR NERO!

We crumpled them up to use as crude toilet paper. Such usage is always fitting for refuse.

And now, those very soldiers were on Lunken Field's runways, presumably to fan out in search of me. After all, that 10,000,000 credits bounty was still on my head, and all of those youths no doubt had hungry families.

Sanchez was out there too, somewhere, and most likely had already sought asylum with Nero. If he had valuable intel in exchange for favor with Nero, he would supply it, no doubt about it.

The only things he couldn't provide Nero were the encryption codes to the backdoors I was using.

Ξ   Ξ   Ξ

Kent filtered down the steps, his mask form-fitted to his face. I did not recognize him.

Kent Cannon was a stocky thirty-two-year-old Russian immigrant with red hair. However, the man who greeted me now with Kent's voice was a roughly 55-year-old Mexican named Hector Vasquez.

I, on the other hand, was now a 35-year-old Frenchman named René Angelou. I enjoyed being younger again. If only my body would comply.

Our new identities were reprogrammed under our left wrists, matching the new masks.

And now we had another advantage.

We had the new chokers. These were called, simply, 'patches.' Chris Mathieson had made good on his promise from our previous rendezvous, and delivered forty of them to me on the 11th. I suspect that's when whoever informed on us became aware that I was in the area. I also suspected that surveillance must have run a trace on my face and couldn't place me anywhere, therefore ID'ing me as a potential saboteur and alerting Nero's forces to my general whereabouts.

The patches would help. Kent was now donning his, and I could neither see nor detect his mark with our equipment. His mask stretched seamlessly over the patch. I, of course, didn't need one.

"It's a little stuffy in here," he complained.

"You'll get used to it, *Hector.* Let's go," I countered. "And work on that accent."

"Yessir, René, sir," he jested.

Our plan was to make for the Ohio River Trail and head for Lumsden Street. There was a walkway leading down to a dock. A small motorboat would carry us across the Ohio River into Kentucky. From there, we would continue our monitoring and undermining of Nero's operations.

We filtered out of the building and walked calmly down Wilmer Avenue. There were several Guardians and patrol vehicles cruising around. I had my bag over my shoulder and my sidearm therein. Kent had an Uzi .22 caliber LR submachine gun under his heavy jacket, with plenty of magazines. A real classic weapon.

Wilmer curved south and would then arc southwest again. From there, it was a short walk up Ridge Avenue, and then Lumsden Street was one street over. We should be able to make it as long as we weren't detained or delayed.

The city was crawling with recruits and forces. A pack of Guardians clustered together on the tarmac just past the main entrance to the airport. Servicemen wearing *NeroTech* logos on their caps inspected them.

As we headed south, I looked to my left. There was a giant AirGuard, bigger and sleeker than the others, sitting on the tarmac. Same telltale spiky fin, same giveaway searchlights, same imposing nosecone, and threatening wingspan, but it was clearly an upgraded model. Enlistees and Guardians poured out of its open cargo bay. Off in the distance, another one of these sleek new AirGuards was coming in for a landing. It was obvious what it, too, contained.

The place was abuzz with Nero's wishes. His will was at work here, and all of these poor deluded soldiers were captive under his sway.

I wondered briefly what information Sanchez had given them.

A large group of enlistees suddenly broke into a run on the tarmac, and a yell went up. They were all heading northwest. Other civilians, like us outside the airport, turned our heads at the commotion, watching curiously and waiting to see what all the trouble was. Gunfire erupted into the air as they charged.

Our pace quickened.

Suddenly, a Guardian whirred right into our path near the intersection of Wilmer and Airport Road. Its neck extended, and it stared at us unfeelingly with its many eyes. Show time.

"Sacre bleu! What is zis? Why you stop me like zat? Je n'en crois pas mes yeux!" I was grateful I knew French.

"Citizen, what is your name? Identification." it responded coolly.

"My name? René Angelou. Just out for walking with my colleague and wish for no Guardian conflict!" I clicked my tongue and raised my left arm. It always felt oddly like a salute. Perhaps Nero intended it that way. My new fake license shone through in amber tones through the underside of my wrist. Amazing how it could be reprogrammed so simply with my alias. Nero hadn't thought of that.

Hector glanced nervously back at the airport commotion. "What's going on at the airport, my friend? Some kind of trouble?" he asked them.

"It is not your concern. Identification."

Hector raised his left arm in turn, and his alias glowed under his skin, identifying him as Hector Vasquez instead of Kent Cannon. The mechanoid examined him.

"What is your purpose out at night so close to curfew in a governmental area?" it asked both of us.

We looked at each other and played dumb.

"Governmental area?" I asked non-plussed. "I do not know anyzing about any governmental area, monsieur. My colleague and I work up off Dumont in the suburbs west of 'ere. Zis is no more zan a leisurely stroll, Monsieur Guardian."

"Is that the way of it?" the cold mechanoid asked Hector.

"Si señor," Hector agreed. "Leisurely stroll."

"Where are you from, originally, Mr. Vasquez?"

Hector sighed. "Oh man, that's a long way back. Well, I grew up in El Salvador, but we moved around a lot. Mi Mama, you know, she had the dementia, so it took a while for us to really make her see where we were, you know? Hard times, bro. Had to explain everything over and over again." The machine studied him coldly. "Mi Papa, he tried really hard. But Mama was going downhill, you know, they say like circling the drain, you know, man? That dementia, it gets you. She got the VZV2 virus, man. Hard luck. She got it and just went downhill *muy rapido* if you know what I mean. We just couldn't really-"

The Guardian interrupted him, deciding to forego any more data. "Final questions. Have you noticed any activity in the area from any undesirables known as Christians? And do you pledge eternal loyalty to Emperor Nero?"

We both nodded. "Oh, well, of course we do, Monsieur. But of course! Nero is our leader, oui, c'est la vérité. Zere is nussing better zan ze Emperor, mon ami," I said, fanning my arms out in theatrical adoration.

"Ain't no Christians here," Hector agreed. "Disgusting Christians." He spit on the ground near the Guardian's treads. It surveyed Hector's saliva, looked back up at him, and then turned to me.

At that moment, a large explosion sounded behind us. The two of us whipped around in surprise as the skyline lit up orange. The location was precisely where we had been staying. It seems we had only just gotten out in time before the soldiers at the airport charged our location and an AirGuard dropped a low-grade incendiary.

Metal claws on each of our shoulders whirled us back around. "You are dismissed. All hail Emperor Nero."

The Guardian veered to our left and sped around us, heading in the direction of the explosion. We shook our heads, played it cool, and then headed on to our destination.

"I'd say you nailed the accent, Kent, er- Hector," I said to him. I couldn't see him, but I think he smiled.

The boat was waiting for us.

"Colonel Drexler?" the driver whispered as we finally reached the shoreline and stepped aboard. "Welcome, sir. Glad to see you're still alive. We can't afford to lose you, Colonel."

"Thanks," interjected Kent, speaking up and getting in the face of the driver. "*We're* fine."

The driver looked at him in surprise as he ripped off his mask and let the cold night air breeze his face.

It was now 1746 hours. The boat sped across the Ohio River and into darkness beyond. I hoped Mathieson made it out of there. I hoped he and his cell were safe.

Nero knew where I was. This Emperor wanted me dead more than anyone else.

Message received.

CHAPTER 13
Maximillian

1 . 15 . 2113
Washington, DC

Ξ　　Ξ　　Ξ

It all came down to this.

The time was now 1712 hours. The call had gone through, but the contact was not picking up. My lord Nero was watching us, arms clasped around himself, engrossed in the video monitors.

We were set up in S-207, right outside my lord's great chamber, and Vassal Behmardi and I were eagerly coordinating with our technicians while he looked on. Dubois was watching as well and getting much too close to us. I had to constantly request that he step back and give us the room we needed to work.

Mario Sanchez was also here, watching. He was in shackles, and it appeared that he had suffered a black eye somehow. He looked on anxiously while my lord paced the floor. It was he who had arrived and provided the information on both the whereabouts of the traitor's family as well as the traitor himself. Perhaps more than one was helping Drexler. Now it was time to round them all up. My lord would be so pleased!

His Eminence was now in military attire: a dark gray uniform bedazzled with glorious medals that he had won for valor in battle. His shoulders were adorned with golden epaulettes; his cap was rightly embellished with shimmering insignias. I watched him as he paced, enamored by his beauty and the wonder of his presence. How deftly he could switch between various attires! His concubines and his Minister of Aesthetics, Vassal Vanitysium, were *so* adept at their craft. He always looked so dashing in uniform.

The call was not picked up. Why was Drexler not answering? The trace had been run, and we had a lock on their location, within at least one hundred feet. Surely the intermediary who put us through to Drexler had announced who was on the line waiting to speak with him.

I grew uneasy. This was an important moment that Vassal Behmardi and I had worked painstakingly to coordinate with my lord's forces in order to effect a killing stroke against our adversary and thus eliminate this thorn in his side. He was proving most undesirable and had fomented a Defiance in the wake of my lord's rise to power. He *must* be eradicated.

Multiple monitors from helmet cameras streamed into view before us. On one fixed screen we had an external view of the location where Sanchez had reported Drexler's family was hiding. It was a disgusting former General Mills factory on the outskirts of Minneapolis, abandoned for some time and dilapidated. They used to produce cereal and other goods there for citizens until the meal replacements came.

Sanchez watched nervously as our forces arrived in a convoy and began to deploy.

Nero smiled. I beheld him smiling! Oh, that brought joy to me! My heart leapt to see my lord so pleased! We were about to witness the downfall of the traitor, Colonel

Thomas Drexler! Vassal Dubois stood right behind my lord, biting his nails and looking on in disapproval. My joy faded as I regarded him, standing there so close to my lord and brimming with suspicion and cynicism. *Ugh.*

We watched and waited. The forces deployed. An AirGuard unit flew in and hovered over the factory. They had the area surrounded and were prepared to obliterate it. My lord had given the order to hold and make the call to Drexler.

It was 1720 hours.

On another screen opposite the first, we were seeing Lunken Field, Ohio, where Sanchez reported that Drexler had last been seen. Facial scans registered citizens who had not been previously cataloged, tracing them back to somewhere near a building adjacent to Lunken Field. Drexler had been secretly stationed there, monitoring our operations the entire time, unbeknownst to us!

Our new AirGuard ships were arriving at Lunken Field, deploying new enlistees and conscripts, as well as field equipment and vehicles. They now cheered and rushed toward Drexler's supposed hideout.

It was most quiet in S-207. My lord watched solemnly. Sanchez' eyes darted nervously back and forth between the large monitors and the various other streams. I, however, was filled with peace and calm, knowing this would vindicate Vassal Behmardi and me. A triumphant smile spread across my face.

Perhaps my lord would reconsider promoting Vassal Dubois and would leave me in peace to serve him singly, as I had faithfully done all these years. Oh, the anticipation was building. I nearly clapped my hands with glee; I suppressed it, however, not wanting to disturb the grand solemnity of the moment.

The convoys moved in. The call continued to ring. That was the only thing that vexed me: why were they not picking up? It ultimately mattered not, however. We had them all surrounded.

Sanchez stared unblinkingly at the main screen, no doubt anticipating his reward once Drexler and his family were eliminated.

"He is not answering the call," my lord growled. I turned to him as my smile faded. "The ruse is not working." He angled his body slowly over to me, and his expression was grave, full of displeasure, doubt, and slow-brimming anger. Behind him stood Vassal Dubois. I watched as he sighed, shaking his head at me patronizingly, as a disapproving parent might toward an erring child. It nearly sent me over the edge.

"Move the troops in on the woman and child," Nero commanded.

"It shall be so, my lord," Vassal Behmardi answered. "Teams, move in," he said, directing the troops in Minneapolis. Helmet cameras showed them searching silently. Guardians joined them, whirring and deploying, their arm turrets at the ready. But no one was there! The building was vacant, and looked to have been abandoned for some time.

We waited. The phone continued to ring for Drexler. Why was he not answering?

My lord Nero sighed and rolled his eyes. "Fine. Level the building at Lunken Field. Do it now. Make sure that there is no warning," the Emperor said coolly. I whirled toward him.

"But, my lord, Drexler may not be there," I gently whispered to him. "And there are civilians in that building. Our troops are in there, newly enlisted conscripts. Surely my lord does not wish to kill innocents as collateral damage?" I watched as his jaw clenched, and I knew then that I had displeased him.

His eyes grew wide and his chest puffed out as his face reddened. He started to speak, accelerating and rising swiftly in pitch and volume as he slowly turned to face me. "High Vassal Maximillian, target that building and level it to the ground! *Now!*" he screamed, and my blood crawled.

I stiffened and lost composure, nearly wetting myself. "Yes, my lord, right away!" I was wrong. Wrong to question my master. *What was I thinking?* "Behmardi, do it now, fire away!" I yelled.

"Lunken Field AirGuard, drop bombs. Repeat: drop bombs," he instructed them.

The AirGuard complied. Nero turned back to the screen and watched, breathing hard. I had truly upset him. Surely, I was going to pay for my insolence. I dreaded the aftermath of this meeting and this whole conflagration. I could not hold back my tears as I watched the AirGuard unit drop a high-powered incendiary that obliterated not only the traitor's reported whereabouts but also the surrounding buildings.

On the monitors, we could clearly see our troops – our newly-enlisted conscripts – on fire and running in terror through flames. Young children – *Friends of Nero* – dropped to the ground and rolled in their own flames as black smoke enveloped them. Children were burning to death amidst the sweltering heat and napalm. Small figures became blackened, smoldering husks that fell and lay still, burning into the night as flesh dripped to the pavement. A small cap blew off a tiny uniformed figure turned to ash.

As I watched, a single tear scrolled down my cheek.

Static bursts sounded, and the troops in Minneapolis reported over the com that the factory was completely clear. There was no trace of Drexler's wife… child… anyone. It was completely deserted.

A growing roar of agony emitted from my left. The voice was Nero's – anguish coupled with livid anger throbbing with misery and betrayal – and it rose in volume, cascading with a sound terrifying and agonizing to hear. It filled the whole room; my heart stopped with wide-eyed dread of his coming wrath.

The Emperor turned, pulled a dagger from a small scabbard at his belt, and walked briskly toward Sanchez, stabbing him in the throat. Sanchez gasped and gurgled. The Emperor struck again. And again. He stabbed Sanchez in the heart, the chest, the shoulder, the neck, the abdomen. He slashed and stabbed in his fury, blood spurting out and splashing my lord's rich military garb, tainting his medals. Dubois quickly ran to Nero and polished them off of him, dabbing at his uniform as Sanchez slumped down to his feet.

Sanchez's guttural grunts were too daunting to listen to. His half-formed words were unintelligible. I turned away in disgust. He had been powerless to defend himself there in shackles. I watched him slide to the floor as his life poured out of him. Nero breathed hard and clacked his teeth, snapping his fingers reflexively. He stared down at his victim, spat on him, and issued another order. "Level the factory!" The Emperor left the room in a rage, whipping his military cap off into the air. It landed in a corner of the room. For a moment I thought back to that tiny soldier's cap turned to ash.

I heard him leave. My vision swam. All I saw were the bodies of young children and teens burning, smoke rising to the heavens. It took the last of my breath as well. I was to kill off even more troops to satisfy his anger.

"Do it," I breathed silently to Behmardi, and I swallowed hard.

I heard no sound as the Minneapolis monitor lit up in white, and the factory was destroyed – along with all our troops inside and on the perimeter.

Surely, my lord was just in this decision. Surely, his anger rose like the dawn and was entirely justified. Wasn't he? Hadn't it?

Surely, it had. Surely, it was.

We watched, all of us, without a word. Except for Dubois. He sneered in disgust, shaking his head and uttering one word at Behmardi and me. 'Failure.' And then he left, presumably to fawn at the knees of my lord and attempt to console him, earning his favor!

I was now living on borrowed time. Surely, I would pay for this. Surely, I would be beaten.

Surely, what my lord did was right, wasn't it? Surely, it was just I who was wrong; I who had failed.

Surely, my lord might have mercy. I could appeal to his mercy. I *would* appeal to his mercy. I *had to* appeal to his mercy, and my life might be spared.

It would all come down to that.

CHAPTER 14
Sage

1 . 16 . 2113
Kaneville Township, IL

Ξ Ξ Ξ

There is power in numbers.

Anja's prayers had definitely been answered.

We had been here for two days. The guy who had met us at the door was named Tito Eldridge. His buddies were Mason Jenkins and Sarah Foster. There were indeed sixty-four of them, and they had all been here for quite some time. They called themselves 'The Camp.'

The sad truth was that The Camp members were rarely up top. The school had a boiler-slash-mechanical room below, as well as a basement: both under the gym and swimming pool. It was tight quarters packing sixty-four people in there, and even worse adding another nine. But it was necessary. The rest of the school needed to maintain the appearance of being abandoned. Thus, The Camp had to remain out of sight. The good news, however – with the mechanical room being right there – was that it was warm. That mattered a lot in the cold seasons.

The convoy that had rolled by the other night, the one that presumably had been searching for us after the altercation where we lost Luca – God rest his soul – had actually stopped by the school to fan out and search. The

Camp members had to disperse pretty quickly, or that would be the end of Kaneland High School.

Since the new 'curriculum' was in force and Nero's new education system was rolled out in the wake of the VZV2 death wave, children were only schooled at home, online via NeroNet. There were only a few sites available, and they were all monitored, 'until such a time as peace was achieved and more online exchange monitoring measures could be relaxed.' Such a joke. Thirteen years had passed since they had said that.

The sites were the official in-home education network, WTE, and then there were WNews and WChat. It was never clarified what the 'w' meant, though we all suspected it stood for 'world.' All controlled by Nero, governed by his new world. All information was prescreened before release, and all conversations and chats were supervised with AI monitoring in place to scan for any encrypted messages, any suspicious communications or patterns of suspected sedition.

Nero was guarding all the doors, and he was holding all the keys. Nothing passed through NeroNet without him knowing about it. *Boy, what I could do with that kind of power. The kind of good I could enable… the way I could freely spread the gospel!* I thought at one point.

So, what did all of that mean?

Kaneland High School itself was abandoned and crumbling, like the rest of the world. Either its former inhabitants were dead from the virus, taken for questioning, or killed. The structure was no longer needed.

Or worse, the students joined up as Friends of Nero.

So, here at Kaneland High School, in the dark basement below the gym and the pool, The Camp eked out their existence in the shadows.

Fifty-one of them had the mark. The rest were new converts that had been carefully surveilled and vetted before they were welcomed in. At times, there were heated arguments among Camp members as far as whom to trust and who to permit entrance to the inner sanctum. Tito was a good judge of character, they said, so he was assigned one of the final voices. Every new person was voted on. So far, they'd been fortunate, and God had protected them.

But the ultimate decision-makers, the *real* final voices, belonged to two people. Those who officially administered The Camp were a man and a woman affectionately known as Mother and Father. Their real names were Atticus Flansburg and Miranda Gable. Mother and Father held daily devotionals and prayer time. They organized times of group exercise in the pool with armed monitoring. They arranged for groups to be taken to the showers. There was plenty of booty leftover from the administration of the school, such as toiletries, gym clothes, wardrobes from the school theater department in all sizes. What they couldn't immediately use, they adapted for their community.

They had been here for nearly five years.

There was a sportsmen's club a little over two miles east of the school, just south of the Family Life Church Assembly of God. Thankfully, the manager was a Christian who had converted a few years before the initial cleansing. Jasper was his name. He had somehow survived. Elderly

African-American man with a kindly heart. Jasper had arranged for The Camp to make off with a large stock of weapons from the club in order to defend themselves. They made it look like a break-in, a smash-and-grab. Jasper lied his butt off to management about the stolen weaponry, and fortunately everyone bought the story. He even injured himself in the process and made it look like he had been assaulted.

Jasper struggled with guilt over 'lying in Jesus' Name,' but it had to be done. His ruse had worked, and The Camp was now equipped with arms to defend themselves. It wasn't a tremendous amount of firepower, but it was enough to provide a reasonable defense.

It was also enough for hunting.

White-tailed deer, squirrels, muskrats, chipmunks, coyotes, groundhogs, foxes, even mountain lions roamed more freely with the bulk of the populace killed off by the virus.

There were also geese, cranes, egrets, doves, wood ducks, turkey vultures, orioles, swallows, and more for hunting. No one paid any heed to the occasional shots fired; many people now hunted in order to provide for themselves and their family. It was not out of the ordinary to hear shots fired at random times across the countryside. Iris herself had provided food for us, which she had hunted. It was, frankly, delicious.

At the end of our first full day there, we underwent orientation. Amidst the flicker of candles and wall lights – they still had power – we learned of their plight and continuing struggle. It was amazing to behold.

Yet, through all of it, I couldn't help but think back to our old house. They lived in squalor here, scraping their underbellies on the ground as they snaked through the land in secrecy. Fading memories of the house we had, the toys we had, the food we enjoyed, the comfort, and the heat – all the things I took for granted when I was a little guy – came rushing back to me like a flood, and I wasn't sure why. After our recent losses and all the hiding and fleeing, stirring in me was a fomenting desire to see it all over with. I don't think I was alone in that. We all wanted the war to end. We all wanted to live without fear.

I missed the comforts of home. I missed my family.

I missed peace and quiet.

I missed life.

Ξ   Ξ   Ξ

"Atticus Flansburg," he said, extending his hand.

"Miranda Gable," she added, extending her hand in turn. I shook both of their hands. Dressed in plain clothes, just like the rest of us, they served the family of believers here in Kaneville Township tirelessly and with much grace.

"We're so glad to meet you, brother. And you, sister, Charlotte, was it? And Hunter?"

"*Charlie*," she corrected.

Hunter nodded his head.

We were enjoying our introductory dinner with Mother and Father. Someone had shot and served up goose for the occasion. I didn't know what the seasoning was, but it was delicious and finally quieted the rumbling of our stomachs. I thought back to that pizza a few nights ago. Before our world blew up and life became all about fleeing.

"These three are part of my group," Swifty said, putting his arm around me. "Sage here is as smart as they come, and he has great ears. Charlie is an exceptional medic, and Hunter is just a brute. Don't mess with him."

Hunter blushed and looked at his feet, smiling.

"That's good to hear. What happened to your arm, Hunter?" Atticus asked him.

"Oh, just a little run-in with some Guardians a few nights ago. A little bit of the bullet got in. The rest bounced off of me on account of my being a brute and all," Hunter said, grinning at Swifty.

"Well, we're always in need of great scouts and street-savvy sentries," Atticus said. "Parker is our best. He's the young man over there in the red sweater. And the rest of your bunch?"

"Well, that's my daughter Anja over there," Swifty said, pointing. "And over here are Emma and Asher, they're brother and sister. And here come Andréa and Nicholas."

Indeed, the two of them had come up to his right and now greeted Mother and Father with a firm handshake.

"We lost three on the way here a few days ago."

Miranda frowned. "Oh, my Lord, no. I'm so sorry," she groaned. "How old?"

"Luca, 17," I said. "He was a quiet guy but good in a fight. He went out protecting us. We bagged the Guardian that got him," I finished, squinting and clenching my jaw at the memory.

Miranda nodded, watching me intently.

"Fritz, one of our adults. I'm not really sure how old he was; I think early sixties," said Swifty. "A good arm and a great guy. Both helped us escape. We also lost a sweet woman, Leona. All were believers."

Atticus nodded and smiled. "Amen. Thank God for them. I'm sorry for your losses."

"How have you fared here?" Swifty asked, and I could tell by the tone of his voice he was asking if they had lost anyone themselves. I wasn't sure if he was curious or probing.

"We have been fortunate," Atticus replied. Miranda nodded enthusiastically, closing her eyes. "No one yet. And it's been five years. Must be some kind of stretch, right?" He smiled grimly. "I hate having to deploy our new converts outside this place, but out of necessity, that's what we have to do. The 'unmarked' generally fare better than we do out there, those of us who carry the branding."

"Yeah, well," Nicholas chimed in, "we have news on that front. We don't have many, but we do have extra of these," he said, fishing a choker out of a pack he was carrying. "They block the scanning signal, fit nicely around the side of the neck, and don't come around the front. Unless you're looking directly at the neck, or really searching for them, they're undetectable."

Both Mother and Father stared at them, eyes wide with surprise and admiration. "Impressive! I've heard of these!" Miranda exclaimed. "Never seen one in person. How long have you had them? Can you get more?"

"A little over a year now," Nicholas replied. "They're great tech. One of our former guys was a rover. They say he came from Colonel Drexler himself and was distributing these. He was unmarked. Easy for him to travel around and dispense them. We thank God for these little things."

"Definitely," Miranda replied. "We'd be grateful, certainly, if you have any extra." Nicholas nodded.

"What were your plans? Would you like to stay here with us, or are you still on the move?" asked Atticus.

Swifty frowned and shook his head. "Life has been different out there. It's been dangerous and we've had to stay constantly on the move. We seem to have been hunted more of late as we've been above ground. And all of us are marked, of course. Except Asher. Cut out his mark a few years back."

Miranda hissed. "Oh, that's awful," she winced, looking over at him. "Two of our own did that as well. Jenkins is one. I shudder to even think of it."

Swifty nodded. "Me too. But if you knew Asher, you'd know he's a scrappy kid." He attempted a meager smile.

"And how about you three?" Atticus said, turning to Hunter, Charlie and me. "Where do you hail from?"

I looked at Charlie and Hunter, gathering my breath. "Well, I'm originally from Des Moines, Iowa. I lost my family in the initial Cleansing." Atticus and Miranda looked at me gravely, nodding slightly. I knew that such an origin story was not uncommon to hear, but a wave of resentment washed over me again recounting it, and I briefly thought of Heather. I remembered neither my Mom's nor my Dad's face anymore.

"And you?" Atticus asked Hunter.

"Pretty much same as Sage," Hunt said. "Family killed in a Guardian blast when I was four. On the run since then. From Shorewood Hills, Wisconsin. Close to Madison."

They turned their eyes to Charlie. "And you, Charlotte?" Miranda asked.

"*Charlie,*" she said again, sheepishly this time, not wanting to be confrontational.

"Goodness - my mistake! Charlie," she agreed.

She waved it off. "I joined the group in 2109. Out of Aurora. We're practically heading to my hometown," she said playfully. "I wouldn't dare set foot there again, though. Too many memories," she finished sadly. I berated myself silently as I realized that I never even asked her the story of how she joined us.

There was a pause as we studied each other.

"Well, we're glad you're here. And glad you're safe. All of you. Praise God for that," Atticus said, smiling warmly.

Praise God, I thought, looking around and seeing the amber lights on the necks of so many here, bobbing around silently in the darkened room.

Ξ   Ξ   Ξ

It was time to turn in. Parker and the sentries were out up top on a rotating schedule. Tito, the guy who had met us at the door that first night, was also with them, patrolling. They listened for any kind of Guardian activity. They had a precious set of walkie-talkies, probably from that sportsmen's club they mentioned. Any report of AirGuard in the area, of convoys – of *anything* out of the ordinary – was to be relayed to the other sentries immediately. They kept under the eaves and close to the perimeter of the school walls, avoiding leaving any footprints in the snow. These guys meant business, and we felt safer being with them.

If only 'out of the ordinary' *truly* meant 'out of the ordinary,' I thought. Since Nero came to power, being on the lookout and serving as sentries was the *only* 'ordinary' we had ever really known.

Charlie and Hunter and I were clustered in one corner. Asher, Emma and Anja were a few feet away from us. I turned to Hunter.

"What do you think of our new digs, Hunt?"

He sneered. "As long as nobody breaks that glass and the pool decides to empty into here, it should be fine. It's toasty, but I'd rather be in here than outside."

"You got that right," said Charlie. "It's muggy, isn't it? Crazy how all these guys brave this every single night in here. Or maybe the heat puts you to sleep."

"Hunter's B.O. puts me to sleep. When's the last time you used deodorant, bud?"

He clicked his tongue. "Whatever."

"Just teasin' ya, buddy," I laughed, play-punching him in his good shoulder.

"Ow."

I put my arm around him. "How's your arm, man?"

"A lot better," he said. "I got two medics for the price of one," he said, winking at Charlie.

"Yeah, well, Iris has plenty of years on me, and that's a lot of experience that did you right. I'm glad," she replied.

"How long you guys figure we'll be in this place?" Hunter asked. He lay on his back with his free hand behind his head.

I looked around. "It's been a long time for The Camp here," I said pensively, watching them mill about and prepare for bed again. "But hey, if we don't have to go in and out with our necks all aglow because they have unmarked people who can do that instead, so much the better."

Hunter nodded and sighed. "Yeah."

"Looks like they all have a pretty sweet operation. I wouldn't want to foul that up," Charlie said. "Besides, I can't hunt to save my life. Just bring me the occasional deer, and I'll keep bandaging up arms as best as I can. Maybe I'll best Iris someday." She smirked.

I thought back again to not knowing her story. My guilt bubbled over.

"Hey, I didn't know you were from Aurora. Are we really headed that way?" I asked her. Hunter looked at me and seemed to furrow his brows. Whatever message he was trying to send, I wasn't receiving. I mouthed, 'What?' He merely darted his eyes back and forth between me and Charlie, shaking his head slightly.

She picked up on all of it. "Stop, ya boneheads," she said, elbowing both of us. "It's fine. I mean, we're supposed to do *Remembrance*, right? Takes an act of will. I wonder if they do that here at The Camp. It's how we keep them alive. At least that's what Swifty says, right?"

She gathered herself, taking a deep breath and holding it in so long I thought she'd overheat.

Charlie stared off into the distance.

"It was 2108. We were in hiding, pretty much like everybody else, right?" She smiled thinly. "We didn't live in Aurora at first; I'm actually from Ontarioville. But I don't remember it. The stupid Cleansing. Nobody our age will really remember all of what went down back then since we were only four or five or whatever. We were scrambling like everyone else. We moved there and lived in the attic of my aunt's house, and then we just stayed at my aunt's. That was in 2099. I was only five then."

Hunt and I glanced at each other.

"Anyway, we stayed at my aunt's house for like nine more years. It was June 2108. I had just turned fourteen a few months prior. I was upstairs having a nap. For whatever reason, I was beat tired that day. It was summertime, and so hot, man. We didn't have A/C in that house, and it was kinda sweltering. I had the fan running, so that was something, but it was just hot, hot, *hot*.

"Somebody knocked on the door. I assumed it was a neighbor. I had no idea it was Nero's people. There were Guardians outside. They just took my aunt out and held a knife to her throat. Asked where my parents and I were. They were yelling into the house, saying they would kill her if we didn't reveal ourselves." She shook her head. "So barbaric. Anyway, Dad wasn't about to let his sister get killed, so he and Mom came out of the attic with their hands up, and they headed downstairs."

Charlie sighed heavily, trying to free her lungs from the stress of the memory.

"I could hear them downstairs. They were asking my parents where I was. Mom and Dad told them that I had run away. Dad wasn't really a good liar. By that time, I had crawled out of the attic window and was scaling the backside of the roof. I don't even know how I wasn't noticed; I thought we were surrounded."

"Divine providence, right?" Hunter asked.

"Something like that. Maybe it was just the right moment. But they didn't see me."

"What happened, Charlie?" I asked her. Her eyes met mine.

"They checked and saw Mom's and Dad's marks. Shot Dad in the heart. Mom right afterwards. And then they killed my aunt for harboring us. Same way. Executed all of them right there. I only know because a few weeks after that I connected with a neighbor friend who was also in hiding. He had seen it all from across the way. Precious in the sight of the Lord is the death of his saints, right?" She smiled weakly at us, searching for comfort, and then her face crinkled, and she was lost to gathering tears. I wondered how long she had used that phrase to assuage the anguish. Losing someone you love never gets easier, no matter how many verses or cute phrases you throw at it.

Charlie was silent for a while, lost in thought. In the dim light of the mechanical room, the glow reflected off her wet cheeks. She rubbed them dry.

"Anyway, it wouldn't have been precious in my sight; I'm just glad I didn't see it myself. I jumped off the roof and dropped into the grass in the backyard. Thankfully I didn't break anything, ya know? I ran. And I ran and I ran," she said. "I heard the second and third shots as I was bolting. And then they just blew the whole house, thinking I was inside somewhere. I can still feel the heat and the percussion of it from a few hundred feet away. All of my things were in there. Everything. We were there for ten years, man. I had books and stuffed animals and a diary. My diary's all burnt up, I'm sure. Everything. Gone."

I didn't know what to say. Just like that, her family, too, had been snuffed out. Killed for their beliefs and for hiding from Nero. Just like that, her life changed. She had been on the run for a whole year until she finally found our group.

"Where did you go, Charlie?"

She looked up at me. "Anywhere. Anywhere I could, Sage. Hiding. Ya know," -here she snickered shyly, embarrassed at herself- "it's amazing to me that I'm still alive. I was in that house for nine years, dude. Why do you think I'm so pasty white? I look like a ghost."

"I'm glad you're not one," Hunter said.

She smiled. "Yeah, me too. Felt like Rapunzel, stuck up in that attic. Ya know how many times I prayed that some knight would come riding up and ask me to let down my hair? I even grew my hair long for that reason. Isn't that silly?" A tear escaped her eye and traced down her cheek. She quickly wiped it away and laughed nervously. "Mom figured out what I was doing, brought me back to earth, and gave me a haircut. Wanna know what she said to me? *Ain't no knights in this world, sweetheart.* I'll never forget that. Anyway, I met Swifty and you guys that night in Sycamore at the elementary school, and the rest is history."

"Yep," I said, remembering our first meeting. "Well, we're glad you're here. *I'm* glad you're here."

"Me too," Hunt said.

"Anyway, I told this clown a while back," she concluded, pointing to Hunt. I thought he would have told you," she said, eyeing me curiously. "Maybe you guys don't talk about *serious* stuff anymore," she said with a smile.

With that little passing comment, Charlie had no idea what kind of well she had just tapped.

I smiled back at her, but my brow furrowed as a sudden unwelcome swell of jealousy arose in me. I had never felt that before, at least not to that degree. "You told Hunter your story?" I squinted my eyes at Hunter. He was smiling appreciatively at Charlie, and then his eyes moved over to meet mine. His smile faded. Now it was his turn. He tilted his head as if to ask, "What?"

I don't know why it bugged me so much, her confiding in him and not me with her story. It shouldn't bother me, but it did. So, I turned the tables on him.

"What about you, buddy? Tell Charlie *your* story, hmm?" I threw down a challenge. I thought better about it for a second as a heatwave passed through me. Hunter's story wasn't pleasant, and I knew. Furthermore, he knew that I knew.

"Dude, really?" he asked me.

"Yeah, seriously," I maintained. "I've already shared my story with her, and you know it too. Only fair, right?"

Charlie's eyes ping-ponged back and forth between us, sensing something was afoot. "No, it's alright; he doesn't have to. It's all good."

Hunter watched me. I think he understood that I was jealous, but his eyes told me that I had crossed a line. In truth, I had. I wasn't exactly okay with it, but I had gone too far now, and I was *trying* to be okay with it.

"No, no, it's fine, Charlie," Hunt said. "*Okay,* Sage. You wanna hear my story again? You want me to tell it to Charlie?"

"Seriously, guys, it's-" she started.

"No!" he hollered, and we could feel others staring at us, abandoning their own conversations. "It's a *great* story, right, Sage?"

There was a tense moment as Hunter glared at me. In the dim light of the boiler room, his eyes flashed. The light of the pool above us flickering and wavering through to our room below sent ripples of teal light across his face that mixed strangely with the amber hues.

"Sage knows all about it, Charlie," he began, and I clenched my lip, regretting asking him. "It's a great story. See, once upon a time, there was this little boy who had a family. He and his family were in hiding from the big, bad monsters that had taken over the world. And one day they came a'knockin' on the door, right?" He laughed theatrically, but his eyes were shining. "Well, who answers the door but little Hunter Preston! Yep, in his little jammies and ready for bed. There were the bad men on the front porch of a nice little picturesque house on the outskirts of Genoa. Except that nice little picturesque house had *Christians* inside it. *Uh-oh,* right?

"Anyway, it just gets better, Charlie," he said. "Right, Sage?"

"Dude, I didn't mean to-"

He didn't hear me. "See, the big bad men asked if we were Christians, and the little boy in his jammies was happy to volunteer information on his parents because they had told him to always tell the truth, right? The truth is *so* very important. *It's what separates us from them,* little Hunter's parents had said. So he told them, 'No, I'm not, but my Mommy and Daddy are. They love Jesus. Do *you* love Jesus?' the boy asked them."

By now Hunter was tense, and his eyes were filling up. He had risen into a sitting position, waving his arms about as his voice and volume intensified.

"Oh yeah! That little boy was *so* helpful! He even told them that the neighbors across the street, his parents' best friends, were Christians as well! The big bad men found him so helpful that they asked him to tell them who *else* was Christians! And little Hunter, that innocent little boy who told the truth, well, he was able to rat out a *bunch* of families! He was *so* helpful, because he remembered that the truth is what separates us from them! What a good little boy!"

Hunter was staring at me intently, his eyes aflame with rage. "And did you know, Charlie, that the officer on the front porch gave him a lollipop and carried him outside while his forces ran in and executed his mommy and daddy? And did you know that that little boy was sucking on that lollipop on the trunk of a Guardian convoy vehicle while his house exploded, and he wet his pants, Charlie? And did you know that that little boy ran and hid in an outhouse on the neighbor's farm and hid in the crap while his neighborhood exploded around him, Charlie?"

Charlie was crying now. In truth, so was I.

Hunter stood. "Yeah! And he counted the explosions too, because he had learned how to count, and his Dad – the dead one, remember, that the little boy got killed? – had worked on his numbers with him, so he got pretty good! He counted all the way to eight, Charlie! *Eight!* Eight explosions, Charlie! Because that little boy named Hunter was *so* helpful and told the truth! What a great story, huh, Charlie? Aren't you glad I got to share it?"

He erupted into tears and panted angrily.

I felt like a giant loser. "Hunt, I'm sorry, I-"

Hunter wiped his face with a frenzy and then tore himself away from us.

"Hunter!" I called after him in desperation.

He thrust people aside and dashed out of the mechanical room. Swifty followed him.

Charlie turned to me. "You're a punk. That was *so* mean, Sage. I can't believe you asked him to do that when you knew his story all along."

I didn't even look at her. Hunter had told the truth. But the new truth was that I *did* know his story, and that I *was* a punk.

Ξ   Ξ   Ξ

I found Hunter and Swifty up above, in the very hall where we had met Tito, Jenkins and Foster when we first arrived. There were two Camp sentries in the corner of the room, talking lightly amongst themselves.

Hunter was bawling. Swifty was to his right, with his arm over his shoulder. Andréa was sitting to his left with her hand upon his knee. Hunter waved me away to give him space, but I couldn't.

"Hunter," I pleaded.

Hunter's crying abated, and his breath slowed.

"Hunt," I breathed again. "Can I talk to you? Please."

Hunter composed himself and took a deep breath, slowly lifting his head and regarding me. "Great story, huh?"

My heart sank.

"Hunter, I was wrong. I'm *sorry*. I shouldn't have pushed you. I just-" My arms went up defensively as I searched for a way to say it. "I was jealous, okay? I like Charlie. You know that. I was just jealous that she shared that with you first. But I retaliated, and I shouldn't have."

Hunter just glared at me. "Wounds from a friend can be trusted, but an enemy multiplies kisses, right? I mean, you're a friend. I can trust this, right?" he asked accusingly.

I shook my head sadly. "That's not what that verse means. I just… I… took advantage of the situation and I acted out. It wasn't a wound I should have given you, and I wasn't being a friend. Can you please forgive me?"

Hunter looked away. "Sage," he started to say through a heavy sigh…

A loud blast sounded from somewhere on campus. At the same time, radios squawked around us from the sentries in the hall.

We could hear a commotion down below.

Another blast. Something blew a corner off the hall where we were, and chunks of concrete went flying, dropping down to the ground and into the pool below. Mighty splashes lurched up toward the ceiling. The stars sparkled in the black sky beyond, and then large, dark shadows obscured them from sight as they raced by. And finally, *whirring*.

Mayhem ensued everywhere.

People came flying in from all directions, looking for their loved ones and barking orders. Mother and Father raced into the hall, handing out weapons such as they could carry, instructing everyone to take up their assigned positions. Swifty and Andréa yanked Hunter up and grabbed me, pushing us back outside the room and back down below to where our weapons and group members were. Swifty yelled something to Mother – I think he said we'd be right back with a rocket launcher – and then we were racing back down below, sprinting past others. Charlie and Anja were heading up the stairs toward us with weapons. Nicholas was huffing right behind them with his green canvas bag over his shoulder, loaded with RPGs and ammunition. He already had one in his launcher.

"Go!" he screamed at us. "Take the guns and go!" Swifty nodded, grabbing what he could and handing the rest to us. "God protect you!" Nicholas shouted.

"Where's Andréa?" Swifty asked, looking around. She had vanished somewhere in the chaos. The sixty-four

Camp members were all over the place, running in and out, taking up positions, and climbing to fortified points they had erected years before. Just as in countless drills, each Camp member ran to their assigned spot and then radioed the group.

A few more blasts sounded, and we were back down below, hunkered down in the mechanical room.

"We'll hold them here," Swifty said. "Need to protect you," he said to Charlie and me, but he was looking solely at me. I gazed apprehensively at Hunter and Charlie as we followed behind Swifty down the mechanical room corridor to take our stand against the onslaught.

"Hide. Take them out as they come. Charlie, you got medical ready?" She ran to her things and pulled her medic bag, slinging it over her shoulder.

"Ready," she said, hiding and taking aim.

Hunter did the same. A frightening blast of thunder sounded above, followed by answering gunfire. Endless sprays of gunfire traced from multiple directions. Small charges detonated – probably grenades – and then just more gunfire. I glanced in alarm out at the pool and noticed tracers of blasts skirting across the top of it, zipping down into the sides of the concrete. Camp members fell into the water and immediately sank to their death in a red cloud.

A large chunk of concrete dropped from the ceiling into the pool, displacing all the water and sending dead bodies plummeting through the waves and up against the thick observation window. The teal water turned a hauntingly dark crimson.

We heard noises back behind us.

"Be careful!" Swifty urged, whispering. "Watch your marks. Don't hit friendlies!"

Hunter was directly behind me. Charlie was to my right, behind some piping running along the floor in front of her and then bending up into the ceiling. Swifty was ahead of all of us on the same side as Charlie, positioned behind some kind of electrical box.

Suddenly, the door burst open, and we prepared to fire. *They were ours!* Thank God we didn't shoot. My finger flexed on the trigger. Camp members streamed in, retreating from the onslaught above, shouting. Suddenly, one voice rose above the rest. It was Andréa's.

"Sage! Where are you?" She was running and trying to see over the crowd as they forced their way in.

"I'm here, Andréa! Here! We're all back here, hurry!"

She pushed through the crowd, bearing a rifle and taking up position very near to us. Camp members did the same, lining up behind various structures, piping or equipment.

I hated this. It was all so different. We were taught to shoot at machines. But those were humans – *humans!* – running around up there. Could they be young enlistees, as Iris had reported? Young Friends of Nero conscripts? That would be horrible. I wouldn't want to pull my trigger. But if I didn't, they would…

Sounds.

Sounds on the stairs.

They were coming. An army of them!

Once we fired, they would know where we all were. We would be pinned down!

The door burst open in a hail of gunfire!

"Oh no, oh no!" Swifty cried, and he fired. I followed his lead. So did Hunter. So did Charlie. So did all of us. They flooded into the room, firing as they came, and we fired back. Bullets sprayed in all directions, ricocheting off equipment and sounding in horrible retorts throughout the mechanical room. Lightning strobed throughout the corridor and flashed through the smoke of gunfire.

It was horrifyingly loud all around us.

Something burst, and a jet of steam spouted angrily from it, shooting diagonally up into the corridor.

"Kids, stay down!" yelled Swifty. "Andréa, watch them! Where's Nicholas?"

I didn't know. I couldn't see him. The bullets kept coming. Bodies were piling up at the doorway, bottlenecking the entry as the enemy sought to penetrate our defenses.

And then, the infiltration stopped. It grew deathly quiet.

We waited. I didn't dare look over into the pool. More and more bodies had fallen in and were sinking to their final earthly resting place. I could see figures running along the pool edge, figures in uniform; their silhouettes hazy and waving through the pool water.

I didn't know what to do. My heart was pounding through my chest, and the constant drumbeat of my pulse throbbed in my ears as we watched and listened.

My ears picked up a sound, and I looked over. Something small. A round object, set with silver spikes all around the circumference was blinking. I watched in horror as it slowly drifted down through the pool water.

Red digital numbers on the device announced the countdown:

05…

04…

My eyes widened.

03…

02…

A panic tore through me…

01…

"Get out! Move! Get-" I yelled.

And then the blast hit, forcing all of the pool water outward and compressing the concrete walls in an expanding circle. The observation window near the bottom of the pool – seven feet from me – splintered and cracked, fracturing inward. People were shouting and crying.

Glass spilled everywhere, and a rushing, roaring torrent of chlorine water came pouring in, cutting a violent, angry swath down the corridor. It was no respecter of persons, smashing into me and pressing me up against the wall. It trapped Hunter high up toward the ceiling as he climbed, seeking to escape the deluge. Swifty was carried down the narrow corridor. A splinter of glass sliced my arm as the current dragged me down. My gun strap, slung over my shoulder, got hung up on some kind of mechanical wheel on the piping of the wall, a pressure valve, I think, and I struggled to break free. Someone collided with me and was pushed down the passage beyond me. I briefly heard Charlie scream.

I glanced behind me. Hunter was climbing back down, probably preparing to swim out of there before it filled up. We were eye level now.

I turned back the other way. I couldn't see Charlie or Swifty… Nicholas… or the others. Angry foam churned and surged all around me. Machinery sparked and whined.

Andréa called out to me. I could see her across the corridor, desperately clinging to life and machinery as the pool emptied itself into the passage. "Sage!" she called, and she pulled herself along the piping to come my way.

"Andréa! Stop! What are you doing! Get out!" I wailed.

She would not be dissuaded. She pulled herself along the pipes straddling the ceiling, swinging violently through the churning water.

Hunter yelped behind me as the water rose. Someone screamed down the passageway. *Charlie*. She was carried by the current, up ahead with Swifty. Swifty looked back, yelled for me, and then went under. I watched as the water pushed Charlie around a corner, and then out into the stairwell.

I scoured the waters where I had last seen Hunter, and then turned to Andréa. I couldn't see him.

The water still rose, threateningly.

Andréa reached me! "Hang on, kiddo," she said, and she whipped a knife free from her jacket, flipping out the blade with her teeth while she desperately clung to the piping above. In a flash, she let go and grabbed frenetically for my strap to cut me free, but the current was too strong. It pulled her away as she squealed. I reached for her. *Got you!* With all of my might, I pulled her towards me. She gripped my jacket and tugged herself up, grunting. Seconds later she dove under me, found the strap, and slashed it.

In a moment, I was free. *I was free!* But where was everyone? Andréa resurfaced, coughing. She sputtered, choked, and then drew a huge, panicked breath.

"My heart!" she exclaimed, clutching her chest. And then she looked straight at me with sadness in her eyes. "Always do God's will, son. You are a soldier! Never forget, Sage," she choked, amidst gasps. "Never forget that your father and I loved you with all our heart." She placed the knife in my hand.

I just stared at her. My mouth fell open in awe.

"What? *What?*" I screamed at her in horror.

She nodded, fighting against the churning, bubbling water… and it was rising. We had to move. We were running out of time!

"What do you mean?" I cried out to her, my eyes wide with alarm and dismay. My voice rose above the waters and reverberated through that diminishing air. The water roared around us, making conversation nearly impossible.

"Your father's name is," she sputtered, tilting upwards to gasp for air. "Thomas," she breathed. "Thomas Drex-" and she screamed, as someone desperate to anchor themselves to something seized her leg and wouldn't let go. She was pulled under and vanished. I saw a hand grasping for purchase floating downstream, trying desperately to surface.

She never did.

Andréa had drowned, and with her, so had clarity and truth. Questions roared through me, louder than the rushing water. What did she mean? Thomas Drex- something? There was *no way* she could have meant Thomas Drexler, the colonel! Is that what she was saying? Impossible! I knew my mother and father! They were Mark and Tracy Maddox. All my life I had known that. Did Swifty put her up to this? Did Swifty know? And where was Charlie? And Hunter! Where was Hunter? I looked back. I couldn't see him.

The water was rising, ever rising. There was no more time. In a minute I'd be completely submerged. I had to do something, to find a way out. I couldn't go the way everyone else had, or I would be shot on sight, as they most likely were. I had to go out through the observation window into the pool. Maybe the Guardians and the soldiers had all left in prep for that blast.

My eyes were drawn to something in the water. A small ovular rubber surface. It was black, and the tip of it was red.

Hunter's boot!

My skin crawled, I took a deep breath and dove underneath the wave. The water was almost to the ceiling. I kept the knife in my hand.

Underwater, the dim lights along the wall provided some murky visibility. I swam against the stream with all of my might, pulling myself along by the machinery attached to the wall.

There he was!

Hunter was hung up amongst pressure valves and machinery, trapped and tangled with the strap of his satchel, the strap of his gun, his arm sling, and rips in his jacket. He was bleeding from glass punctures.

He saw me and smiled, pointing to something… anything that I might be able to do. I tugged and pulled with all that was in me, but I couldn't free him. I went back up to him and put my hands up, unsure what to do. He made a mime like scissors. Or a knife?

My knife! Of course, what an idiot! I whipped it out hastily, and it dropped to the floor of the corridor, clinking silently. I cursed, swam down, and retrieved it again.

When I reached him again, Hunter looked troubled. Different, somehow. Sleepy. I pulled the knife out and sawed through his rifle sling. I felt him loosen. He looked like he was hiccupping. I had to hurry. *Please, God, let me hurry.* I reached and sawed through his sling. I quickly cut away at his tangled coat pieces. I slashed at his thick rifle strap.

Hunter stopped me. His face was nearly blue, and he shook his head. He looked me in the eyes, and I saw love there. He shook his head once more, and his hand lazily signed not to continue. He thumbed me to get out of there. The water grew remarkably calm around us, and I could see him. My friend smiled, and mouthed three words that I could see plainly and would never forget for as long as I lived.

I forgive you.

My heart leapt into my throat. I watched my best friend drown right in front of me, and then dread, fueled by adrenaline, pushed me on at a fever pace. *No, no, no!* I cried in the water, and my voice gurgled around me. My heart was racing, and I was running out of time. I thought Hunter was smiling at me. I sawed through the strap of his rifle – finally – and he was loose. But his jacket was somehow still tangled up in the machinery, trapping him against it.

I watched his mouth open reflexively and take in water into his lungs. His whole body spasmed, involuntarily coughing. His eyes grew wide…

…and then all was calm.

Hunter was gone. His face was puffy and lifeless.

I felt hot tears mingle with the cold water, all of it flowing around me in a maelstrom of grief.

Hunter was dead.

Charlie was dead.

Swifty was dead.

Andréa was dead.

My parents were never my parents.

There was only one thing I could do. I looked to my left at the yawning aperture blown open by the bomb, jagged shards jutting out from the perimeter.

With the last ounce of energy I had left, I propelled myself through the opening and out into the pool. By this time, it was nearly drained. Concrete chunks, rebar, and Lord knows what else littered the bottom of the pool. The ceiling had caved in and drooped at the corner. No one was up top anymore. They had all run out to kill off the stragglers that had been washed out the other end. There was a service door that led out the far end of the mechanical room, up and outside to the ground level.

Hunter was dead.

Charlie was dead.

Swifty was dead.

Andréa was dead.

My parents were never my parents.

All kinds of warring truths jostled for mastery in my mind as I strove to stop crying, heaving my chest silently so that I wouldn't be detected.

I crawled up the side of the pool using the ladder, dripping noisily and reeking of chlorine. I heaved my beleaguered and grief-stricken form over the edge, out, up, and over, searching. The bleachers on the other side were pulled out from the wall, and into the dark crevices under those long rows I slunk quietly, hiding in the shadows at the far end near the wall. It was utterly black around me.

Hunter was dead.

Charlie was dead.

Swifty was dead.

Andréa was dead.

My parents were never my parents.

As quietly as I could, my chest heaved as I wept, bawling into my wet jacket in silence, attempting to stifle my cries. Hunter was my best friend. Charlie was my love. Swifty was my mentor, fellow soldier and leader.

And apparently my mother and father were not my own. *Andréa... who were you?* I asked in silence.

I was alone. Everyone I loved was either dead, or now dead to me, having never been who I thought they were. I was so confused. I sobbed in anguish as my whole body shook, wracked with heartache and anguish.

There is a quiet grief in isolation.

CHAPTER 15
Drexler

1 . 16 . 2113
Edgewood, KY

Ξ   Ξ   Ξ

This war was growing in intensity.

I feared for my wife and child. Where they were, I had no idea, but Andréa and Sage were out there, somewhere. It killed me not knowing their welfare. If there was even the remotest possibility that Nero had in fact found them...

I swallowed hard.

We had sailed across the Ohio and into Kentucky. None of us wanted to, as only a short time ago there was a mass annihilation of Christians here. We had fled north, and now we were returning to these same dangerous territories.

There, on the other side, waiting for us, was an SUV with its lights off. Someone flashed a tiny LED flashlight at us, and we disembarked the boat and ran up the dock to the vehicle. Parked on the banks was our getaway car. Kent and I hopped in the SUV, driving south through Fort Thomas. I ripped off my mask and cursed, looking back over the Ohio River toward Lunken Field.

Deranged lunatic. There were children in that crowd. Children that Nero had just firebombed. In search of me, and in a fit of desperation, he leveled three city blocks and burned up young children in order to take me out.

I wanted his head. I needed to breathe and cool my jets. Gone was René Angelou. Gone was Hector Vasquez. Thomas Drexler and Kent Cannon were back, and we had to focus.

We took off west toward Crestview Hills. We stopped in Erlanger and met up with Defiance contacts at the former Dixie Heights High School, a few miles away from the 275 and 71 interchange, east of the Cincinnati & Northern Kentucky International Airport. CVG wasn't quite as crawling with Nero worshippers as Lunken Field had been, so that was good for now. We were a comfortable few miles east of it and about 75 miles southeast of Indianapolis.

My mind went back to my wife. I was troubled. For the first time, I was worried. I had heard no word from Andréa or any of the people she was currently traveling with, nor had I received any updates on Sage.

It pained me not knowing where they were, or if they were even alive. But if that information provided to Kent was true, it meant that they were closing in on them. It might even mean that they had them. I didn't think that they were in Minneapolis, however. I had no idea why they would be. The last I had heard, they were west of Chicago somewhere.

Chicago. That was at least 307 miles north by northwest; impossible to travel that far and not encounter Guardians. The risk was too great, and I had no idea where they would even be… *if* they were even there anymore… or *if* they were even alive.

God, protect my wife and child, I prayed silently. I drew strength from Psalm 35, the psalm I had always come to rely on when under siege. The one that spoke truth about my valiant God rising to my defense and protecting me. Kent and I had memorized it together many years ago. I glanced at him on the ride over, confident that he was praying it as well:

Contend, Lord, with those who contend with me; fight against those who fight against me. Take up shield and armor; arise and come to my aid. Brandish spear and javelin against those who pursue me. Say to me, 'I am your salvation.' May those who seek my life be disgraced and put to shame; may those who plot my ruin be turned back in dismay. May they be like chaff before the wind, with the angel of the Lord driving them away; may their path be dark and slippery, with the angel of the Lord pursuing them. Since they hid their net for me without cause and without cause dug a pit for me, may ruin overtake them by surprise - may the net they hid entangle them, may they fall into the pit, to their ruin. Then my soul will rejoice in the Lord and delight in his salvation. My whole being will exclaim, 'Who is like you, Lord? You rescue the poor from those too strong for them, the poor and needy from those who rob them.' Ruthless witnesses come forward; they question me on things I know nothing about. They repay me evil for good and leave me like one bereaved. Yet when they were ill, I put on sackcloth and humbled myself with fasting. When my prayers returned to me unanswered, I went about mourning as though for my friend or brother. I bowed my head in grief as though weeping for my mother. But when I stumbled, they gathered in glee; assailants gathered against me without my knowledge. They slandered me without ceasing. Like the ungodly they maliciously mocked; they gnashed their teeth at me. How long, Lord, will you look on? Rescue me from their ravages, my precious life from these lions. I will give you thanks in the great assembly; among the throngs I will praise you. Do not let those gloat over me who are my enemies without cause; do not let those who hate me without reason maliciously wink the eye. They do not speak peaceably, but devise false accusations against those who live quietly in the land. They sneer at me and say, 'Aha! Aha! With our own eyes we have seen it.' Lord, you have seen this; do not be silent. Do not be far from me, Lord. Awake, and rise to my defense! Contend for me, my God and Lord. Vindicate me in your righteousness, Lord my God; do not let them gloat over me. Do not let them think, 'Aha, just what we wanted!' or say, 'We have swallowed him up.' May all who gloat over my distress be put to shame and confusion; may all who exalt themselves over me be clothed with shame and disgrace. May those who delight in my vindication shout for joy and gladness; may they always say, 'The Lord be exalted, who delights in the well-being of his servant.' My tongue will proclaim your righteousness, your praises all day long.

It was a psalm that David wrote when King Saul was threatening to kill him. He was on the run, in hiding, fearing for his life, for his family, for his country, for his world. A deranged and jealous lunatic was out to get him, and he had to continually flee, living a life on the run in caves and worse. Yet David found his peace and strength knowing that God was in control.

I loved that psalm.

As much as I treasured it, however, I had to reconcile that David found his peace and strength knowing that God was in control. David prayed for Saul, and I was sure that in those prayers he sought the Lord for not only deliverance from him but also deliverance *for* him. That is what I continually needed to do for Nero. That is what we all needed to do. Nero was not the enemy. We had one enemy, and we all knew who that was. It was Satan.

Nero was as delusional as Saul, and was desperately in need of God's healing touch as we all were.

More to the point, he used to be my brother. Brothers in great pursuits, together, we had had lofty dreams and aspirations meant to improve the world.

Dixie Heights High School lay abandoned, as all schools were these days. It had been for some time. However, unbeknownst to Nero and many in the vicinity of the high school, we had purchased the land around it under an LLC, ensuring that no stragglers would wander onto the grounds. There weren't a lot of people living in the houses nearby anyway; many had died off.

Nonetheless, we stuck to the inner parts of the buildings, posted up sentries, and worked as much as possible by candlelight so as to not arouse suspicion or attract any unwanted attention.

We were used to hiding from unfriendly eyes by now.

So, as usual, we started over. We began again. We reconvened and regrouped.

However, each reset button did nothing to lessen the gnawing anguish of not knowing where my wife and son were and not being with them. I entrusted my worry to the Lord, but it remained.

And my worry was growing in intensity.

CHAPTER 16
Maximillian

1 . 16 . 2113
Washington, DC

Ξ   Ξ   Ξ

I was seeing the light now.

"I accept your decision, your worship," I said.

I had to say that after each flogging. Each time the whip lashed across my back and the shock traveled the length of my body, I was required to recite it with sincerity and passion.

And each time, immediately following my recitation, I was flogged again.

My lord was completely silent through the entire beating. I knew in my heart that it hurt him to discipline me more than it actually hurt me. He was loving, kind, and good, and this was for the best.

I would not make the same mistakes again.

Vassal Behmardi was gone. He had been cast out naked and left to fend for himself in the cold, stripped of his robes, his jewelry, his rank… everything. A just consequence from my lord Nero, though I rued the loss of his partnership and his presence. The Emperor told him that he was banished from his 'garden' due to his sin. I suppose I should be grateful that I did not suffer the same fate.

I will miss him, and I wish him well.

After my beating, they let me go, and I was able to put my robes back on. Nero sniffed in between his panting, and his face dripped with sweat from the exertion. He smiled as he put his arm around me – it felt *so* good to be embraced by His Eminence. He breathed into my ear. "There. Better?"

"Oh yes, my lord. *Yes,*" I said, smiling through my tears and sweat, my makeup running in rivulets down my face.

"Good. We must have proper decorum and functionality in the ranks, and there is much expected of a High Vassal. I'm sure you've been reminded sufficiently of that now. Yes?"

"Verily, my lord. Thank you, my precious Emperor Nero! You are wise and just in your discipline, and I accept it," I said, donning my robe once again, and reattaching my brooches. "Thank you, O wise god-king."

He sniffed again and took a deep breath. "Good. Now get yourself cleaned up. We have a broadcast scheduled in an hour." My lord walked out. "My *Gloriosa Revelatio* approaches on January 30th, and we must be ready, yes?" he asked me, turning back.

"Oh, *yes*, my lord," I agreed, blinking demurely at him. The servants who held me during my beating were silent and would not meet my eyes.

I was just glad that Vassal Dubois – I needed to stow my disdain and address him correctly – *High* Vassal Dubois had not been here to witness all of this.

Ξ   Ξ   Ξ

Broadcast time. Everything was set up and ready to go. My lord looked dashing in his regal robes and mitre, perched high atop his throne in His Eminence's chamber. The rainbow of colors adorning his shoulders, the circlets full of opulence, the glittering shroud that draped him overall… he was beautiful and breathtaking. My eyes began to brim with tears. I looked upon my lord in reverence and unbridled worship. In this sacred moment, I could forget my beating, High Vassal Dubois, the casting out of Behmardi, all of it, and focus on all that my lord was and is. If only those watching the broadcast could smell the opulence… could feel the warmth of this room and the radiance that emanated from him high atop his throne in sheer wonder.

Speaking of broadcasts, I had reviewed the footage of the Lunken Field attacks, as well as the catalogued footage uploaded from Guardians patrolling the surrounding areas. Two of those interrogated made me curious: a 35-year-old Frenchman named René Angelou, and a 55-year-old Mexican named Hector Vasquez. They seemed out of place and suspicious. I was almost certain it was Drexler and an associate in disguise; but they were undoubtedly miles from the scene of the crime by now. I made a note to report it to Dubois.

Once more, the light of the setting sun streamed down in golden beams upon him, signifying approval from the Day Star, the thin wisps of incense rising to greet him. The brilliance of the chamber's architecture was matched only by Nero himself. And the cameras were trained on him to cover it all in glorious splendor. I clasped my hands in front of my face, standing below and staring up at him in unceasing reverence.

Quiet was ordered on the set. The media technicians were cueing each other.

The music began. The pre-roll video rolled. A swell of orchestral energy captivated our ears, dancing around us with vibrating vitality.

They cued Nero.

"Citizens of the world!" my lord began. "Greetings and well-met! I trust you are all well. I greet you tonight to announce that soon and very soon I shall be taking my rightful place in a new domain, a deserved sanctum, and upon a throne of high glory. I shall be transferring my throne, as well as my seat of my government, to the Judaic temple mount in Jerusalem, where once stood the ancient temple of the Jewish people. Construction has begun, and we are rebuilding the temple as we speak! Worship shall reconvene, and we shall have one center of worship for the entire planet. One religion through which all of us may commune with the Day Star. And then? We shall reinstitute honorable sacrifices to him!" His voice rose and growled with both intensity and volume.

"We shall be unrestricted and shall all see a new and brighter tomorrow filled with the universalistic hopes and dreams of a thousand generations, where all are united as one, and there is no dissension! No judgment! No condemnation! No retribution! Freedom to worship as we see fit, under one name, one religion, one source of life, and eusexua! Freedom to live and breathe and have our being as you serve me and our mother planet. Freedom from narrow-minded religions and archaic lines of extremist mindsets. And liberty to be governed under one flag, one ruler, one government, and one world! The future!"

Canned, prerecorded cheers blared as my lord pumped his fist in the air.

"The future!"

Even more canned, prerecorded cheers.

"The future!" he shouted once more.

Unrelentingly loud, canned, prerecorded cheers… nonstop and deafening. Thunderous applause was played throughout the chamber from gigantic speakers and piped into the broadcast feed. I'm not sure where the sound effects came from, but they were certainly effective. The media team made sure to splice in footage of gathered crowds in between clips of the Emperor. I just always marveled at how they were able to take people filmed against a green screen and superimpose them onto the floor of the chamber as if they were present with us here and now, watching Nero in adoration.

"Also," my lord said, and he rose up even higher upon his throne, standing fully erect in the glory of the streaming sun, "it gives me great pleasure to announce that the treacherous Defiance leader, Colonel Thomas Drexler, has finally been assassinated!"

My smile faded, and I wondered. Surely I would have heard of this news. I glanced over at High Vassal Dubois, and he could not restrain his look of supreme approval and delight. He hopped on his toes and clapped his hands giddily, his lips pursed in glee; his chin sucked into his neck. His makeup was glistening through his sweat.

I looked back up at the Emperor.

"Yes, you heard correctly!" the Emperor practically yelled. "In an operation at Lunken Field, Cincinnati yesterday, I personally oversaw an operation which took down the enemy of world peace, the treacherous colonel, and over a dozen of his supporters!"

My head tilted slightly. *A dozen of his supporters?* The report that came back from the field was that Colonel Drexler was no longer there, nor were any of his supporters. Some had been taken in for questioning, but none had the mark, and none divulged anything about his whereabouts, even after having been tortured.

Yet the footage now being played was of those in the surrounding area killed in the blast: civilians who happened to unfortunately wander too close to the building we decimated last night. *They were not supporters of Drexler's,* I said to myself, shaking my head. *They were innocent civilians...*

And yet the footage showed otherwise: bodies littering the street, *Friends of Nero* soldiers ripping fake masks off their heads and revealing their true, dead faces. I thought back to the Frenchman and the Mexican I suspected. This footage showed Guardians zeroing in on the dead's wrist IDs, which would then be enlarged and clarified on screen, correlating to a cleaner picture and name of that same deceased person, branded as an infidel for all viewers.

"And yet even in this victory, we are all shorn of gladness. For I bring terrible news! The treacherous, undesirable Colonel Drexler detonated the bomb himself, which brutally killed many of our young soldiers!"

My brow furrowed. I blinked rapidly, trying to clear my eyes as my mind strove desperately to accept what my lord was saying and marry it up to the footage I was viewing.

My jaw dropped slowly as I watched the intercut footage. The truth strove for mastery in me despite what I was watching.

Bodies. Young bodies. Bodies of *children.*

All burning.

The Emperor continued. "This brazen rebel dared to attack one of our government military bases, launching incendiary bombs onto our own troops, knowing full well that there were *Friends of Nero* present, including young children, and now dead! Dead by the hand of Colonel Thomas Drexler himself!" Nero was shouting, and his saliva was raining down onto all of us.

And then I witnessed something I'd never seen before. Right in the middle of the broadcast, Nero started to cry. They were not the genuine tears of remorse at the loss of young life, but tears of staged theatrics, summoned up via other memories – *whatever those might be that could dredge sadness up in him,* I wondered – and played for the viewers. I simply could not deny the truth behind what I saw.

Indeed, many of our own council gathered in here had their hands over their mouths and shook their head at the "audacity of this traitor," as Nero phrased it.

"While Drexler himself looked on, the traitor detonated a large bomb in close proximity to troops who were practicing nearby, training innocent young conscripts in the defense of our proud world. This rebel didn't care to measure or plan what an impact such a bomb would have, and as such, hundreds of young souls paid the price! This despicable Christian, this *un-de-si-ra-ble*" -here he emphasized each syllable methodically, his lips dripping with venom- "showed no mercy and ruthlessly murdered our innocent, young friends!"

But I knew the truth, and that horrified me. I glanced around, knowing that Vassal Behmardi was cast out without honor, and now, also, without credit. It was he who was ordered to drop the bomb and to kill the enemies. He had no choice. All he did was serve his lord faithfully.

And now, here was my lord stating that the bombing was successful. Nero had robbed my compatriot of the credit due him and had, instead, stripped him naked and cast him out in the snow. For what?

I could not control my breathing. I was panting, swallowing hard. Those were *our* people out there, listening to and viewing this broadcast, and the information given to them by my lord – my precious lord, who was *infallible* and could *not* lie – was… *none* of what he was saying was truth! It was propaganda, sure to elicit sympathy for his cause.

I- I *wanted* sympathy for his cause. I *did!* But my head was clouding over, and I suddenly felt ill. I wasn't sure what to do or say.

My vision swam, and my lord's words became obscured and dull, mixing into a swampy, cavernous reverb in my ears and my mind. I shook my head to clear it while he rambled on and on. My eyes couldn't see straight. I had to excuse myself.

I turned to leave. High Vassal Dubois stepped in front of me, fangs bared and eyes squinting. A single tear had traveled down his cheek. He actually believed Nero through all of what the Emperor had said.

"You *dare* to interrupt a live broadcast of the Supreme Emperor, His Eminence!" he hissed at me, not daring to let his own voice rise to the level of Nero's hearing high above his throne.

Think. "I'm- I'm sorry, High Vassal Dubois," I pleaded, panting. "I don't know if it was something I ate or drank, but I really do not feel like myself. My insides are rumbling tremendously. Would you excuse me?"

Dubois donned a sickened expression of revulsion, and then tilted his head back. His chin rose as he surveyed me doubtfully over his decorated nose. He said nothing, just shook his head and flicked his fingers, sending me out of the room with a disgusted click of his tongue.

I clutched my stomach. I truly felt nauseous.

The restroom wasn't far. If I could just make it, I could vomit into a toilet and not on my lord's passageway and thus stain all of these lotus flowers.

I watched them, floating in myriad pools, adorning each side of the hallway, signifying rebirth. They were beautiful. For a moment, however, I questioned: whose rebirth were they signifying?

I made it to the bathroom, threw open a stall door, and emptied the contents of my stomach with an angry purge, choking and coughing through all of it.

My stomach was drained. I leaned over the toilet, panting and staring into the floating crud as all of my servitude to my lord – my precious lord, of whom doubts now swarmed through my mind in a cavalcade of confusing signals – flashed before my eyes.

My mind buzzed.

My body shook and tensed.

From down the hall I heard the muted thunders of my lord, Emperor Nero, continuing to rail. Continuing to yell. Continuing to *deceive.*

In all of my time in his service, all of my medals and my makeup, all of my robes and renown, I had never once doubted. I had never *once* experienced such uncertainty!

Yet here…

Yet now…

My truths were being shaken, and I wasn't sure what to believe.

And there, in the quiet of that lavatory, with the scent of my vomit rising into my nostrils, I heard something.

It wasn't loud. It wasn't showy. It wasn't bellicose. And it didn't lie.

It was a still, small voice.

It quietly urged me, whispering.

What was it saying?

I stopped my breathing and listened.

Peace I leave you, my peace I give to you. Not as the world gives do I give to you. Do not let your heart be troubled, nor let it be afraid.

Somehow, I knew these words spoke truth. I *so* longed for peace.

But I was lost in the dark now.

CHAPTER 17
Sage

1 . 17 . 2113
Kaneville Township, IL

Ξ   Ξ   Ξ

I couldn't wait any longer.

I had to get up and find my way out of here.

From the sounds of it, everyone was gone. But that didn't mean that everyone was taken. Nor did it mean that they killed everyone. It just meant that I was alone.

The heat of the pool room remained for a while but eventually found its way up through the hole in the roof and the caved-in corner.

Two sentries had come into the pool hall, shining flashlights. An AirGuard hovered above; its searchlight reached threateningly into the building but apparently did not find anyone or anything that it deemed of interest.

Gunfire sounded in random bursts outside the gym and swimming pool complex, followed by a few shouts. Eventually, the AirGuard took off into the heavens, and the stars returned. The soldiers retreated. The din of the troops and the cacophony of screams and pleas faded into silence.

I had been under these bleachers for nearly a day. I needed to get somewhere safe. I needed to find Charlie and Swifty and the rest of the gang. Were they dead? In hiding? Had they been executed? What about Mother and Father? Did any of them proclaim Jesus proudly when they died? Or did they whimper in misery and plead for their lives, going quietly into the night as they renounced Him?

If anything, I felt sure that Swifty would not have. No – *none* of them would have. Luca's memory, and his example, would still have been fresh in all of their minds.

Andréa. All the memories I'd had with her came flooding back like that tidal wave that smashed through the mechanical room.

Memories of how she had protected me and watched over me through the years. Memories of playing card games together; of her asking me – only me – if I needed anything else to eat. Of being teased by some from our group that she favored me.

Because she did.

I wept, my mind warring against this new knowledge. But in my heart, I felt at least that it *might* be true. And if it was, I needed answers.

I needed to know why I could suddenly see my face in hers now, whereas I had never seen a resemblance before. This new revelation had a keen bite to it, like I had been slapped into awareness or ripped out of blindness. *Hindsight is 20/20,* they say

Hunter. My best friend had drowned. Such an awful way to go! I just couldn't cut him free fast enough. One minute he was alive, and the next, just… *gone.* Charlie. And Swifty! Carried downstream just as my Andréa was… as my *mother* was? Was she really my mother? And where were Anja and Asher? Nicholas? Were they all gone?

We had brought this upon The Camp. Upon Atticus Flansburg and Miranda Gable. Upon Tito Eldridge and his buddies: Mason Jenkins, Sarah Foster, and Parker, the scout in the red sweater with no last name…who would *never* have a last name. And every other Camp member. They had hidden here for five long years, and now they were all casualties, their lives snuffed out.

How awful!

We should have stayed with Iris.

Ξ   Ξ   Ξ

It took me forever to summon up the courage to inch my way to the outer door and make for the outside. I had no weapons, absolutely nothing to defend myself with other than my fists. I squeezed them tight. If that was all I had, that's what I would use, and the Guardians would taste my wrath before they shot me down.

The entrance was blocked by fallen concrete and bits of plaster. There was rubble everywhere. Maybe that's why there weren't any more soldiers who had entered in this way. They had all been waiting to pick us off as the current carried many to the other end.

I peered over the rubble and didn't see anyone directly outside, but I could only see straight through the corner of the building that had been demolished.

My heart began to thud, skipping a beat. The cold night air bit at me, and I wasn't dry; on the contrary, I was still a bedraggled rat in all of my wet clothes. I briefly thanked Arnold for the short time I had them, but nonetheless they were now all in need of a dryer.

Unable to hear anything, I slowly scaled my way through the rubble, testing each block to ensure it wouldn't tilt and throw me down into a pit.

I had no idea what I would do once I exited. There were plenty of buildings in this school complex, but I didn't know which ones might be locked, might be concealing others seeking refuge, or might be, God forbid, housing informants.

I had no idea at all. The sad truth is that I doubted, since our attack, if anyone would have been so bold as to stay so close to the assault perimeter. Nero's forces would have certainly searched the rest of the school grounds.

I wrung myself out as best I could, pressing my hands firmly against my legs and squeezing the water down and out. I did the same with my shirt and coat before resuming my trek.

In a few minutes, I was finally on the other side. As I crossed the rocks, I kept my eyes focused up toward the ceiling, fearing another collapse of that roof corner, which might drop loose concrete and kill me right before I had a chance to reach safety.

I exhaled and thanked God, turning my head west.

What greeted me there was a sight I never thought I would see. My heart thudded in my chest, and my mouth went pasty as I tried to swallow.

Bodies. All piled together in a twisted heap, carelessly and thoughtlessly jumbled together with complete disregard for life. In my heart, I knew there were at least sixty-four of them there. In my heart, I knew I would find Charlie… Swifty… I would find Asher and Emma and Anja and Nicholas. But more than that, I knew the grisly task that lay before me. I had to search.

My stomach crawled as I inched closer, and then I realized something to my horror.

All of their necks had gone dark.

Their body heat extinguished, none of their amber insignias – none of their Christian marks – burned anymore. They were snuffed out, deprived of temperature warm enough to radiate the signal. They had kept their faith and bore the mark of their Savior to the very end.

I stifled a cry, realizing, perhaps finally, that they were really all dead, and that the Guardians and troops had moved on after this mass murder. These were my friends, my family. I looked briefly back at the building in yearning, wondering if the waters had receded and if I would find Hunter's dead form still entangled in the wall.

I swallowed hard and steeled myself to just move on.

I didn't recognize anyone. No one looked familiar.

Then I saw Mother and Father. And then, a little further into the pile, there was Parker. And Tito, Foster and Jenkins. All of them, dead.

In a macabre sense of comfort, I thanked God that I didn't find any of my own group, but I swiftly ceded that thought to Him in surrender, as it felt utterly selfish. All these dead souls had been a family unto themselves. I wondered how many of them were executed while the others had to watch.

Had they cried out Jesus' Name before they were shot? I wouldn't have heard anything above the roar of the water. It had been utter terrifying madness: the relief of being rescued by Andréa mixed with the panic and pain of trying in vain to save Hunter. On the ground, lying next to one of the bodies, was a choker. It would still work, hopefully, and perhaps the Guardians and troops didn't know what it was. I picked it up as well as another one nearby, stuffing one in my pocket and applying the other. I wrung out the collar of my still wet shirt and pulled it up over the choker.

I silently thanked the donor of the choker, whoever it was. I bowed my head and raised my hands, surrendering them to the Lord and thanking God for their service, their hospitality, and their fidelity to Him. I prayed for vindication and deliverance. They were with Him now. Their troubles were over.

Mine were just beginning all over again.

Ξ   Ξ   Ξ

I moved on to the shadows, with no clear sense of destination. I knew south of Keslinger there were a lot of crops and fields, and we had already been there, so I doubled back that way, trying desperately to think as I burrowed into the fields.

What was it that Iris had said? Something about farther east and the city of Elburn?

And yet someone – one of the Camp members – had mentioned something about the sportsmen's club and the manager there just south of that church off Keslinger; what was his name?

Think, Sage Maddox, think, I said to myself, and then stopped short, shuddering at the revelation. *What if I'm supposed to be saying, 'Think, Sage Drexler, think'?* The very notion unraveled me for a moment. I had to calm myself and breathe. I could sit down and quietly reason later, once I was safe.

Jasper. That was it. It came to me, suddenly. I would make for the sportsmen's club and see if he was there. And then, on to Elburn maybe?

After that, who knows?

Ξ   Ξ   Ξ

It was probably getting close to dawn as I threaded my way through the fields.

At one point, I got the same sensation that I had experienced once we had left Iris' house, and I needed to duck down low. Something was up there in the sky: some dark and silent craft, thriving on stealth, sleuthing like a fox in the night. A logical guess would be an AirGuard. Some kind of new and improved ship was up there, and maybe more than one.

The feeling passed, and I moved on. I had to stop again and take cover at the sound of another convoy driving up the road, escorted by Guardians.

I crouched low, and at one point dang near broke a twig underfoot. The last Guardian stopped, whirling my way just after I hit the deck. I held my breath as those dreaded searchlights illuminated a large swath of the field. I was glad I was amongst the organic.

Foiled, they finally moved on after one of their troops urged expediency, chalking me up to wildlife. "There are a lot of deer in these parts, sir," he had said to the mechanoid.

'Sir.' *What a strange way to address a Guardian.*

In my heart, once more I thanked the donor of the choker… that was the only reason they couldn't scan me since it still repelled the signal.

They finally moved on, but I waited a good twenty minutes before I was ready to move again. I was shivering the whole time as winter's chill still clawed at me.

I crossed a creek that served as a dividing line before some of the further fields, but thankfully, it was narrow and not too deep. Nonetheless, I slipped in my attempt to jump across, and my feet landed in the wet, freezing muck. I wasn't going to make it much longer unless I got into some new clothes and found a place to shelter in that had four walls, no pool, and an intact roof.

I trudged through the fields in a more or less northwestern direction, eventually crossing through a patch of trees. Upon emerging through the far side, I noticed a small building that looked like a church. It was easy enough to stick to the tree line and cross around it, whereupon I saw the sign. *Family Life Church Assembly of God.* That was the church that Iris had mentioned! South of there would be the sportsmen's club!

With renewed hope, my feet felt less frigid, and I reversed course, heading south. I didn't dare travel along the road. I stuck to the fields, even though they didn't provide much cover since the crops were shorter and the field had been partially razed.

In another five minutes I finally reached a turnoff to the east, and there was the sign I was hoping for: the sportsmen's club.

I would have to wait here until someone arrived. It was the thick of the night, and dawn might still be a long way off. I had to find somewhere I could hide out and wait for someone who looked like a 'Jasper.' A kindly old African-American man, so they had said. Easy enough.

I had barely made it into the drive when a door opened on a building at the south lip of the entrance.

"Help you, son?" asked a voice.

I turned in alarm, and couldn't see him because the building light was behind him. I shielded my eyes.

"Oh, I don't mean to disturb you, sir… sorry… I-" I faltered, wanting to be safe, yet struggling with not caring anymore if whoever he was knew the truth about me, "I was part of a caravan of friends going to see a concert, and I, uh, fell out of the truck. I don't think anyone saw."

I began to inch my way toward him, shielding my eyes with my hand.

"Concert, huh? Ain't no concerts around here, kid. Which band was it now?"

"Uh, the White Knights. Up at, uh, United Center."

"Hmm, now that be a long way to go for that this time of night, sure. You be livin' 'round here?"

My head was swooning from fatigue, from the cold, and from deception. "Yeah. I mean no! No. I live in…" I don't know why I paused. I shouldn't have paused. But I was so tired. "Aurora," I said, remembering Charlie's hometown. I was almost to him.

"You all wet."

"I am. I, uh, I fell out of our van into a puddle." I was breathing hard now, and my heart was thudding in my ears.

"Hmm, now I thought you done said it was a truck," he said, feigning confusion. "Isn't that strange now?"

"It was! Sorry. I'm just tired, I-"

The old man caught me as I swayed, and started to fall. Just before I passed out, I caught the whiff of some kind of coffee, and a glimpse of an old flannel button-up sweatshirt. Glowing against the back of that sweatshirt was a faint amber hue, and at the sight of it, I knew I was safe. His thick mutton chops scraped against me as he grabbed me and pulled me up.

Darkness took me, and I passed out.

I just couldn't last any longer.

CHAPTER 18
Maximillian

1 . 18 . 2113
Washington, DC

Ξ   Ξ   Ξ

All of this had to be wrong.

I was still struggling, reproaching myself for having such thoughts. I had served Nero faithfully, and he was my liege and god-king. Who was I, pathetic worm that I was? I was *nothing*. Nero, the Emperor, His Eminence, was *everything*.

Over the past two days I had wrestled. I wrestled and strove with myself over what I truly believed, and I willed myself to abandon these evil doubts that crept over my heart. For that is what they were: evil. Deluded. *Sinful!* I had no cause, no right, to question my divine lord. His will was inviolable, his motive pure, and his cause righteous. And I was so privileged, *so* privileged…*beyond* privileged to serve him in such close proximity as his High Vassal.

I may detest High Vassal Dubois, and I may miss Vassal Behmardi – the fondness that we shared for each other, the sweetness of his soul, and the maddeningly broad reach of his talents – but change is the only constant, and time marches on. It was time for me to get on with it and put these foolish and immature feelings of doubt aside.

However, I must admit I had been hearing whisperings over the past few days. A quiet voice: gently unnerving in its tender urgings; sweetly calming in its uninvited beckoning that had sporadically infiltrated my mind. I passed them off as perhaps part of a gathering flu.

But I had experienced no other symptoms…

I gathered myself for my morning meeting with my fellow High Vassal. We were to meet before the Emperor.

I arrived at the old Senate chamber. It was still just as unkempt as ever, littered with papers and folders, memoranda, charts and graphs. How he pretended to pore over all of those things was not my aff-

I stopped myself. *Careful, Maximillian. It's that kind of immature thinking that will get you in trouble. Go with the flow. Respect him. Try.*

"Ah! Greetings, my dear High Vassal Maximillian! So glad to see you up and around again and feeling better. I was alarmed for you," he said to me sidelong, striding toward me in suspicion. But he quickly shifted. "What a pleasure, another High Vassal in my chamber!"

He greeted me with serpentine sways and bobs of his head, his face awash with a rainbow of colors, his long eyelashes thick with hardening oil and sticking out from his face like a porcupine. *A* beautiful *porcupine,* I corrected myself.

"My dearest co-High Vassal Dubois!" I addressed him in return, and we snickered together, laughing jovially at the silliness of it all. We were equals, and it was high time for me to put away my nonsensical jealousy.

I chortled with him, and he clutched his abdomen as if he was in pain. His laughter took on a pubertically high timbre, and he batted his eyelashes at me. "You stop that, you silly *co*-High Vassal, you!"

"No, *you* stop that, *co*-High Vassal!" I protested theatrically.

See? I can do this.

"What say we get started, yes?" he said suddenly, snapping himself out of his giddiness and looking at me sidelong with a fiendish flare before breaking out into renewed tittering while flitting over to a lateral file cabinet to extract some overly large scrolls.

"Indulge me, for a moment, if you will, my good Maximillian," he said, spreading them out before our eyes. "Our lord plans to relocate, and it will be *marvelous*," he crooned in a breathy, low purr, his hand extended toward me. "No one will ever stop talking about it."

"Indeed, no!" I said, genuinely gleeful. "Not for a thousand generations, not as long as the flames leap up from the temple mount and consume the sacrifices to our god-king and the Day Star!"

Dubois purred with delight. "Yes! But before that, we must be ready for his *Gloriosa Revelatio* on January 30th. Where the entire world will behold the power of his tremendous might, and none will ever dare oppose him again! Our lord reigns supreme, and every eye shall see him!" he exclaimed, practically yelling. "It will be so wonderful, Maximillian. Do you know, I used to be a knight in his army before my promotion to my current esteem?"

"No. Do tell!"

"Yes! Quite true. I charged the ranks with my fellow soldiers, and I ran down the enemy with the power and might of our beloved Emperor. And," he said, recoiling somewhat, as if he was ashamed, "though I may not have been as spry as those gallant soldiers to my right and left – I'm still a million undesirables shy of being a million-undesirable-killer after all, ha! – I did my part." He laughed, as if this was a score he would have liked to have attained. Dubois bowed demurely.

"Of course you did! It must have been glorious."

"Indeed. Nerve-wracking, yes," he said. "But glorious. Alas, I was never made for the battlefield. These bones were meant for striding in high courts among His Majesty in robes like these." He threw his head back and spread his arms out wide theatrically, displaying his gaudy robe of many colors. It was dazzling as it sparkled and shimmered underneath through hues of purple, crimson, and pure white.

"Beautiful, just beautiful!" I said, clapping my hands.

"Yes! And the event on the 30th promises to put the world on notice that the armies of Nero are spry and gallant and a force to be reckoned with! It shall reveal his glory!"

And then I heard the voice again.

You will know the truth and the truth will set you free.

I stopped, listening with my eyes, looking around. It was a gentle whisper, as in the lavatory two days ago. My eyes darted across the room. Was someone playing a practical joke on me? Was the voice real? It was so hard to be sure.

High Vassal Dubois noticed my pause, and my darting eyes. "High Vassal Maximillian, are you alright? Is something the matter?"

I whipped back to Dubois. "Hmm? No. Certainly not. I-" I stopped, listening once more. "I'm sorry, High Vassal Dubois. Have you ever heard voices?"

Dubois threw his head back and laughed mockingly. "Have I ever heard voices? Well, of course, Maximillian! I hear the voices of angels sing each and every day in the presence of our lord *Nero!*" He danced around. He was filled with mirth, twirling like a schoolgirl's braided hair, dancing freely on a glorious stage.

We still hadn't even looked at his schematics yet. All of these pleasantries were sweet, and they were welcome, because I had erroneously and childishly allowed a wedge between myself and High Vassal Dubois. It was time to put childish ways behind me. But we also had business to attend to. I wasn't sure what he wanted to show me, and now, yet again, I was hearing voices.

"Of course…yes, you're right. Perhaps that's what I'm hearing: angels! Sweet whisperings of our beautiful lord. Certainly! Oh, that's it! And how honored and esteemed I must be, so graced with his praise!"

Dubois clapped his hands and cooed.

"Go on, show me what you have planned, my good High Vassal Dubois!" I urged him.

"Yes! Indeed. Well, it's all right here. I have devised a *schematic*," he said, turning to me and overloading the word with gravitas, "and this shows the timeline for His Eminence's departure from our current whereabouts. Excavation crews have begun to outline the old foundations of the Jewish temple, being sure to eradicate any trace of caustic religious underpinnings for our lord's new domain, and then we shall-"

I tried to follow him, but this was his purview, not mine, and in the back of my mind I was bracing myself for more voices… more urgings… more whisperings. I had heard this last one loud and clear, unmistakable.

You will know the truth and the truth will set you free.

For some reason, this last one registered more with me. I had heard that line somewhere before, but couldn't remember where nor when. Yet it held an inexplicable and alien comfort that I had never before experienced: a tenderness that churned up warm emotion in me.

High Vassal Dubois was rambling on – *forgive me,* he was fully immersed in these glorious new plans that were sure to usher our lord into Jerusalem victoriously – and I just tried to keep up. This was his affair, his domain, and it was going to be a spectacle; that much was clear.

You will know the truth and the truth will set you free.

The rest would be left up to me, and that entailed tending to my lord Nero's every need, ensuring he was well taken care of.

I couldn't let these whisperings distract me from what lay ahead. If the Emperor was to take the throne that was rightfully his and fulfill all the prophecies that he had told us were about himself, then I needed to be on my A-game to see all of it through.

You will know the truth and the truth will set you free.
Another mistake could be costly.
You will know the truth and the truth will set you free.

Another mistake could see *me* cast out naked in the snow.

You will know the truth and the truth will set you free.

I couldn't afford any mistakes!

You will know the truth and the truth will set you free.

All of it had to be right.

CHAPTER 19
Sage

1 . 19 . 2113
Elburn, IL

Ξ   Ξ   Ξ

I awoke with a start.

There was Jasper, leaning over me, a mug of something hot in his hands. I sat upright and looked around in fear.

"S'alright, you alright, kid," he said calmly, placing his hand on my foot.

I looked down. I was under a heavy blanket, and I could instantly tell that I was naked, at least down to my boxers.

"Where the heck are my clothes?" I asked in fright.

He snickered. "Relax. They be dryin'," he said, thumbing a finger behind him down the hall. "Washer and dryer down that way. Shower, too, when you's ready. You was filthy. You was a soppin' mess when you came here, when I finds ya. Ya don't 'member? You's feet was almost frostbitten, my man." He chuckled.

My toes wiggled in answer. They felt warm. I looked around. We must be in the building that I saw this man come out of, south of the sportsmen's club. It was some kind of lodge, or at least the man had made it so. This must be where he lived and stayed when he wasn't during working hours across the drive at the club.

"Who are you? How long have I been here? Are you… Jasper? What day is it?"

He nodded with a smile and laughed. "Which question does I answer first? The very one. I reckon you heard o' me, now. And it be the morning of the 19th. You done slept a long time, child. You musta been plum exhausted, young'n. How you found me?" he asked, with a cock of his head.

"The Camp at the high school said-" I started, and then feared that I had outed myself *and* them. "I mean, some people, they said… said that you-" I ended lamely.

"Hey, juss relax a bit, now. I be on *your* side, 'member?" he said, and he tugged his collar away from his neck, allowing the amber glow of his mark to illuminate his grip. "We both be marked, friend. I knows all about The Camp. I done met Atticus and Miranda. Fine folks. I be on your side. And," he said, pausing, and his face growing pale, "I knows what happened. I be *truly* sorry, son. I watched it from all the way here." He stopped and studied me. "Your name's Mr. Sage?"

I startled. "Yeah. Just Sage. How did you know?"

He held up his left arm, revealing his ID brand on the underside of his wrist through his skin.

I nodded. "Of course." The sad truth, however, was that I couldn't be completely sure that was my actual name. On top of that, I didn't know what to say in response to everything else. An apology of equal measure might do.

"I'm sorry too. We might have led the Guardians to them. I don't know. It's hard to be sure. I… I saw so many dead bodies, Jasper," I said, pulling the blanket up toward my chin, feeling the fright and the horror of that night again. "I lost all my friends and family in the attack."

Family. That took on a whole new meaning now. I had literally lost family, if what Andréa had said was true. The only problem was, I had no one left to verify it with. Swifty is who I would have asked, and Swifty was gone. At least, I felt he was gone. I shuddered as I thought back to that pile of bodies again… but I hadn't found any members of my own group in it.

"Well, Mr. Sage, I is so sorry. I could see them God-forsaken AirGuard ships from here. That and a few convoys done swept by after the raid on that po' school. For shame. Yep, it be impossible to know who tipped 'em off this time, but that ain't important right now. What *is* important is figuring out where you s'posa go, and keeping you safe, hear? These marks don't tend to elicit no sympathy," he murmured, getting up and walking to a stove on the far wall. His neck glowed amber at the nape.

"No, they don't. Have you seen anyone else from the raid? The Camp guys said that they would come here now and then and that you would help them."

He poured himself some coffee, and shook his head slowly, sighing. "Regrets, no. No one done left that place, at least not as I could tell. When them *Guardians*" -here he wiggled theatrically in mockery- "attack, they don't spare nobody. At least, not as I've ever seen. Coffee?" he said, turning and extending the pot toward me.

"Sure."

"Cream and sugar?"

I tilted my head.

"With your coffee, boy! You take it with cream and sugar in it, or does you like it nekkid?"

I had to laugh. "Uh, I- I guess I've never had it that way. Is it good?"

"You never had no cream and sugar in your coffee? Man, we undesirables gotta stick together, mm-hmm! You 'bout to have yo mind blown, son. Boy, there was a day when I would stick tiny marshmallows, creamer, artificial sweetener, *and* egg nog in mine, all together. Mmm-mmmm!" he said, licking his lips. "So thick and dee-licious. This one's a bit skimpy, but still good. Hold tight now."

"When will my clothes be done?"

"I reckon they might be done now," he said, finishing up and bringing a hot, steaming mug to me. "You drink that, and I'll go fetch 'em for you. Then you can get all dressed up private-like and call me when you's through."

"Thanks, Jasper."

I gratefully accepted the mug from him. What I then poured down my gullet defied belief. It was coffee such as I had never experienced before. My mind was blown. It was a sensory escape beyond this world: a flavor that I couldn't quite identify with my tongue.

"Jasper, what *is* this in here? This is *awesome*. What's the flavor?"

"Hazelnut!" came the answer from down the hall.

"Hazelnut," I whispered to myself, thoughtfully.

God bless you, hazelnut.

"Yessir! You can take everything away from him, but as long as he gots his coffee, old Mr. Jasper, well, he gonna be juss fine."

Ξ   Ξ   Ξ

We sat and talked for a while in comfort and ease. Jasper was the sweetest old man. He shared his story with the grace that comes from being on the back curve of life.

"When they done came for us, I was not prepared, like none o' the rest of us was. No one was prepared for them *Guardians*." Distaste blanketed his words.

I was now sitting in a comfy chair in dry, clean clothes and sipping a hot, delicious drink. I felt I could fall asleep again.

Jasper spoke slowly, cradling his coffee in his hands – his second cup – and I was ready for my third – while we both stared at the imitation fireplace emitting a quiet orange glow and artificial crackle throughout the room.

It was still early, and he and I were sitting in the matching plush chairs facing the fire. His brown eyes twinkled, and I couldn't help but sigh, remembering my conversation with Hunter on New Year's Day as we held our Remembrance in front of our own artificial fireplace. That seemed a memory out of a distant time now, far away and remote; fictional and hazy. Less clear than the stark imagery of a best friend drowning right before my very eyes.

I shook it off and listened to Jasper.

"My wife is named Delores. She be out there somewhere, mm-hmm. I don't rightly know where, but I do believe she still alive. You'll get there one day, kid. You just know thatcha know. Thousands of miles be separatin' us now, but I'd know if the Lord done took her home and she was gone from this place. There be a spiritual tether that we have. Much like what we have with Jesus, son. You can't see Him now, but you *know* He's there. And you know fo sho that He's alive."

"And reigns forevermore," I added. The words sounded robotic through my teeth as I fixed my gaze on the fire.

"Yes, indeed," he said, and he turned to me, slapping me in the shoulder lightly. "That be the one thing we all gotta remember through all of this here madness. Jesus Christ, the Lord Almighty, He reigns forevermore. This *Em-pe-roar Nee-ro,* shoot. He done lost his mind! Guy's an imposter. A nobody. A bum. A pretender. A deluded dreamer. But The Lord God and His Son? They be the real deal now! And they not gonna let this here go unpunished. You mark my words now, Mr. Sage: justice is a'comin' someday. And until that time, well, we just gotta hold on and trust, now. Faith be the substance of things hoped for, the evidence of things-"

"-not yet seen," I finished. "Yep."

"That's right, you got it. And faith without deeds is dead, just like good ol' James say. Our faith, you and me, and all of us in this time, work itself out through perseverance. Holdin' fast and pushin' through, strugglin,' fightin,' yearnin,' and waitin' for that time when blessed dee-liverance come. That be faith in action, sho nuff. We all been through plenty before, and we had to hold on then, same as now. We hold on even when that foo go and say somethin' crazy like he juss did about the good Colonel."

That got my attention. "What?"

"Yessuh! The latest broadcast. He gone and said he done killed off that Colonel Drexler fella. I doesn't believe it for a second, Mr. Sage. Not one second."

I swallowed hard. Could it be true? Coming from Nero, probably not. Probably just more ridiculous propaganda. Nevertheless, concerning. I hoped it wasn't true. If Andréa had told me the truth, then Drexler was my father.

I continued to watch Jasper. He seemed lost in thought. And then it hit me, from everything he had said before the Colonel. "You lived through the gorgon invasion and the war of the forties, didn't you?"

His lip curled up at the end in a faint smile, stirred by old, painful memories. "I sho did, kid." He shook his head and blew out a noisome exhale. "That was somethin.' Hoo! Barely remember them. But I remember what they do, now. They freezes ya. Then they eats ya. Lord Almighty, but those things were scary."

"Did people think that was the end times then?"

"Are you kiddin'?" he asked, turning to me quickly. "Everyone ragin' on and on about how it could only be a pestilence and a plague brought about by God Hisself… from Revelation… on and on. End times stuff. We all just run things through all the filters of what we knows. 'But the foolishness of God is wiser than human wisdom, and the weakness of God is stronger than man's strength,' the Bible say. God? He know everything. And even where it seems like he don't, our highest wisdom still don't even come close.

"Ol' Jasper's seventy-six now, Mr. Sage. This ol' guy was born in the shadows of alien occupation. It wouldn't be another four years until the big war that drove 'em off. My mammy and pappy kept me alive; I don't rightly know how. We holed up in one of them blockades they was called. I growed up listenin' to all kinds of sermons on *Revelation* and *tribulation* and all the other *-ations,* kid. Tense stuff.

"And when we was finally liberated, none of us was sure it was safe to come on out. We finally did, and ya know what? The darned things come on back again in a *second* wave. So we go back to hidin' once more. Oh, we all beat 'em 'ventually, but not before folks started questionin' and preachin' fire and brimstones all over again. My Aunt Bertha, oh my, but she was a headcase fo sho." He chuckled again. "That woman had no 'off' switch, nhh-hhh."

I smiled, listening to him recount the history of years that I had never seen, tensions I had never experienced.

"So this guy all high and mighty callin' hisself *Emperor*" -here he rolled his eyes and pretended to vomit- "shoot," he said, waving his hand dismissively. "He gonna pass away without no memory of his bad self. 'Heaven and earth will pass away, but My Words will never pass away,' the Good Book says. I ain't worried. Matthew 24:35."

"So you think he'll just 'pass away'?" I asked him. "Doesn't God need to use somebody to make that happen? He's not just gonna step down and quit being Emperor. Somebody needs to take him down."

Jasper looked at me with alarm. "And is *you* gonna be that somebody, kid? Ain't no reason to go plottin' somebody's demise. You can't juss take no revenge, kid.

Ain't nobody winnin' with revenge. But justice? Shoot.
That be another matter. Justice belongs to the Lord now."

I swallowed and shook my head. "I get it. But I hope
God uses somebody like Colonel Drexler to take him out.
That would bring an end sooner."

"Would it now? You take somebody out; you just as
bad as them, kid. You can't win with revenge, but you can
lose *you*, fo sho. Vengeance belong to the *Lord*, kid."

We looked at each other, fake flames illuminating the
sides of our faces. Jasper seemed to want to use the silence
to let his words sink in. I understood, but I didn't like it.
God had all kinds of people like Joshua in the Old Testament
lead all kinds of wars. He had the Israelites rout out the
Amalekites and other people He wanted them to displace. I
mean, was Nero any different? He needed to be deposed.
And God was going to use someone to do it. For a passing
second, I hoped it would be me. I thought back to that
conversation with Hunter a few days ago. About being a
jackal. We all wanted him gone. What if it was somebody
like me to get rid of him? Surely, God wouldn't look poorly
on that. After all, His people would then be free.

How long, O Lord? Will we see justice?

Jasper released me from his gaze. "Anyway. He full
of pride. Pride is what did in the devil, kid. Nero's pride?
That'll be his downfall, Mr. Sage. You mark my words now.
Juss wait. He is 'a mist that appears for a little while and
then vanishes.'" He turned and leaned in toward me. "That
one's James 4:14." He winked.

I smiled at him. "You know a lot of Scripture. Is that what you do here when you're not loaning out guns? Memorize the Word of God?"

He smiled gregariously, nodding. "I do. I do. And maybe, sure. Gotta keep at it. Gotta keep hidin' God's Word in yo heart, now. It's the one thing that done keep ya goin' when all else fails. 'The Word of God be livin,' active, sharper than a double-edged sword,' right? I gotta keep livin' and active myself, kid. Ol' Mr. Jasper ain't gettin' younger."

I got up to get myself more coffee, and grinned.

A beep came from somewhere in the kitchen, and I looked around to see what it was. Jasper got up instantly and went to a cupboard behind me. To my surprise, there was a bank of monitors in the tall, vertical cupboard to the left of the stove.

"Well, well, we got company, now. Guardians. Come here, son. Don't waste no time, now. Quick."

A sudden panic spread through me. I downed a big swig of my coffee and set the cup on the countertop. Jasper led me to the couch that was positioned perpendicular to the plush chairs. He reached down under the cushions and pulled upward. I half-expected him to pull out a hide-a-bed. I had stayed on plenty of those.

But no - he revealed a false bottom: a cavity underneath the couch, hidden by cushions, and supported by a long plank. I'd had no idea it was there; it had looked like a regular couch.

"You best be climbin' on in here, and I be dealin' with these guys." He turned over the cushion on my chair so there was no telltale dimple that I had sat there.

"Do you have weapons? What are you gonna do?" I implored him, climbing in and hiding as instructed.

"Don't need 'em." He closed the lid.

The sounds were muffled and muted, but I could hear the knock on the door.

"Who be knockin' at this hour?" he asked.

"Open up in the name of Nero," said a commanding voice, low and firm. Jasper did so.

There was no delay. The Guardians recognized the mark on Jasper's neck. They immediately activated, raising up erect and leaning toward him. Their turrets fanned out as they spoke in their cold, mechanized voice.

Citizen, this is your final warning. Do you recant?

I almost gasped, biting my lip and gritting my teeth. There was no first warning, or second. Only the final one: so threateningly decisive.

"Yes, yes I do," said Jasper. "I do recant."

My mouth dropped.

Do you solemnly state that Jesus is not the Christ, and that His Eminence Emperor Nero is the true Messiah?

"Absolutely," said Jasper, cheerfully. "Ain't no doubt about it. I don't serve no Jesus nor do I call him king," he said forcefully to the machine.

My eyes went wide.

The troops who were with him asked if he had seen anyone else in this area. Jasper played dumb and staved off their questions, denying seeing anyone and denying any knowledge of pretty much anything else whatsoever.

"Step aside," barked one of the men, and Jasper did so. Another nonchalantly uttered "Identification, please."

I could barely make out the searchlights from my lookout under the couch, but I could clearly see booted feet striding then wavering through the light. Heavy treads mixed with barking commands and vibrated the room. Someone barked orders and they filtered into the building.

One of the troopers came and stood toe to toe with Jasper. "Do you always have two different cups of coffee for your morning intake, Mr. Davis?" He had a thick European accent that I couldn't place.

Jasper laughed. "Actually, I do, my man! My wife be out there somewhere, and oh my, I do fret with loneliness sometimes. I likes to think she be burstin' through that door any day now, and she'll be wantin' a fresh cuppa joe!" Jasper gave a silly laugh.

The trooper said nothing in response, but there was a long pause during which I started to squirm; it felt like he was scanning Jasper for deception.

At last, spinning on his heels, he and his battalion left. The Guardians began to whir outside, announcing the convoy was on the move once more. Jasper must have given a friendly wave and wished them well, or something, because I couldn't hear him over the roar of the vehicles and mechanoids.

The din faded into silence.

Jasper closed the door.

It was some time before he came back over to me, and I thought I heard quiet whispers, as if he was talking to himself. Eventually he raised the cover, looked down at me, and let me out without a word. He was sweating. I just stared at him.

"You… recanted," I said to him, incredulous. "You denied Jesus!"

Jasper nodded, and then he opened his mouth to pant.

"And so I did," he muttered feebly.

I looked him up and down. "But-" I started. "But the Bible says, 'So everyone who acknowledges me before men, I also will acknowledge before my Father who is in heaven, but whoever denies me before men, I also will deny before my Father who is in heaven.'"

Jasper raised his head and looked me deep in the eyes. "I know it deep, son. Don't you go thinkin' for one second it don't pain me eternally to play act so," he grumbled, and then started walking back to the kitchen sink as I watched him. He picked up his mug, threw back the rest of his coffee, and then sighed heavily.

He didn't turn around. He just uttered these words over his right shoulder: "Besides, Mr. Sage," he said. "Those ain't no men."

A smile crept across my face. *Loophole.* Jasper had found a creative way to stay alive and not dishonor the Lord. He wasn't denying Jesus before men. He was denying Him to unfeeling, cold machines who could never be won over to salvation. Their fate was sealed, their future irredeemable, and their purpose irretrievably malignant. There was no saving the machines.

I looked down and sighed nervously.

Jasper came and sat back down in the same plush chair opposite me, breathing hard and wiping his brow with a soiled handkerchief he had extracted from his pocket. He dabbed the loose beads of sweat that dotted his brow, and the rivulets that ran down his cheek. Clearly the experience had taxed him.

"You okay?" I asked.

"Don't you fret about me, now," he said. "As long as Ol' Jasper gots his coffee, he be just fine." Jasper smiled.

We reminisced, talking about the early days of my youth, his earlier life, the Cleansing, the virus, the diaspora when we all were scattered and in hiding, Nero's rise, and the appearance of the Guardians. The fire continued to crackle and warm us, and every now and then I felt my eyelids droop as the warmth enveloped me.

But each time, I would take one hearty sip of that delicious hazelnut coffee, and my senses would stir.

I would start to awaken again.

CHAPTER 20
Drexler

1 . 20 . 2113
Edgewood, KY

THE END: ALPHA

Aaron Ryan | Follower of Jes

Ξ   Ξ   Ξ

My heart was growing heavy.

For the past four days, since the night of the 16th, I had felt a weight descend upon me… something I had not experienced before. For the first time, I began to genuinely fear for my wife and child.

The last time I saw Andréa was when I left to pitch *NeroTech* to the government along with Constantine Jedidiah Goodfellow nineteen years ago. Goodfellow and I were partners then; he needed someone to effect change with the American government by providing expendable military machinery. These droids would save many lives by fighting our wars for us. I wholeheartedly supported the idea.

We called it NeroTech because we both thought it a double entendre: 'Nero' would burn up the opposition. And, at the same time, we wouldn't sacrifice our own soldiers. The droids would be on the front lines of future wars. Consequently, our military would save countless lives and ensure victory. It was ingenious.

That was before the virus. Before The Defiance was formed. Before his aspirations matured and deformed. Beyond simply pitching military equipment to the government, Goodfellow aspired to *be* the government. I didn't think he was serious until he decided to run as a senator, leapfrogging both councilmen and representatives who were distinguished politicians long before him. His message was resonant; his charisma was attractive; his resources were limitless. Here was a man people could look up to and follow, and his magnetism held no trace of deceit.

That was nineteen long years ago: Andréa was pregnant with our first child. She did not like me leaving. And I most likely wouldn't even be able to be there for his birth, much less his first year. She was rightfully irate. "He won't even remember you if you bump into each other on the street, Thomas!" she cried.

Oh, how I should have listened.

I watched his birth live via remote conference. It just wasn't the same.

I watched him grow up. Andréa and I had spoken openly after I left, offering heartfelt but uncertain promises that we would be together again soon. She never received my pledges of reunification well. My wife is wise, and she has insight well beyond that of mortal man. She felt something was amiss, and she never fully trusted Goodfellow. He was on the rise, and that meant I would be far too busy to return home.

When our government contract was awarded, bankrolling millions of dollars in funding and grants, I was enamored by the prospect of becoming a multimillionaire.

She wasn't.

When the programming and encryption went online for the first time, I celebrated wholeheartedly.

She didn't.

Then came the virus, mass hysteria and death.

People were dying everywhere. Somehow, Goodfellow survived it all. She cynically replied, "What a surprise." When I told her that he was going to be appointed president by a special vote of Congress and ratified by the Attorney General to restore order, I promised her that I would be buying a house for us in Washington, DC, and that I needed her to move here so she could be safe.

She wouldn't.

And when Goodfellow revealed his true intentions, he began to demonstrate tyrannical behavior and dystopian rule. He pushed me out. I urged her to cut ties with me and go into hiding.

She couldn't.

She stayed out there, waiting for me. Only when I spoke out against Nero and defied him did she realize the grave peril that we were in. She took our baby and ran. It was eight months before I heard from her through highly vetted and confidential channels that I was able to maintain. She received help from a network of other dissenters who never fully trusted Goodfellow and certainly couldn't trust Nero.

They were alive! I remember breathing a long sigh of relief. They were alive, at least for now. But where *were* they now?

Andréa had Sage baptized early on, and she called him a Christian, though he was too young to consciously know anything about it. However, when they went to the census without me, both of them were branded. Sage had been branded under Mark & Tracy Maddox, his adopted parents. Andréa had the wisdom to adopt him out before the census. Before that time I was able to have a trusted confidant reprogram both of their wrist IDs using a software patch; otherwise she and our son would have been snatched up immediately by Nero's forces at the census, and used as leverage to draw me out.

Unfortunately, none of us knew of Nero's true intent with the census or suspected such depraved levels of malice and treachery. We all thought that he and the Council were genuinely trying to stem the tide of the VZV2 virus. We knew he was sinister, but never expected he would brand and hunt down his own countrymen.

And now he was killing his own troops and blaming it on me. He continued to descend to new lows.

I wish I could have been there to prevent my family from being branded, to keep them safe and unmarked, as I was. Yet, now the three of us were targets. Both unmarked *and* marked, all of us were at the top of a very long list of Nero's 'undesirables.'

He was utterly unrecognizable anymore. Beneath the makeup, the pomp and the flamboyancy, lay unbridled repugnance. Malice was eating at him like a canker. He had become a raging narcissist, utterly consumed by self, drawn inward, reclusive… and hell-bent on the eradication of any opposition.

And he possessed the equipment to do it.

It was all The Defiance could do to keep up with him. I thank God in Heaven that I was able to build a backdoor into NeroNet prior to my departure, allowing for the hijacking of the kernel code that controlled all of the

Guardian force. But now, he was building a new force with an engineer I didn't know. I shuddered every time I thought of it. If Nero rebuilds from the ground up, then he could have – *would* have – designed them completely independent of the control matrix. The Defiance would be powerless to stop him. All we could do was pray and keep up our own network of hackers, scattered abroad. Nero tried his best to thwart our attempts at remote shutdown by rebooting, allowing a kernel refresh, and forcing us to start over.

But at least he would have to start over as well.

Andréa and I had spoken intermittently over the years, briefly and over an encrypted line. She had wisely kept the truth of my paternity from Sage in order to afford him plausible deniability. In the early years, to keep them separate and thus increase the chance of survival, Andréa adopted Sage out to her sister, Tracy, and her husband, Mark. He was just two then.

Andréa was able to keep tabs on Sage. Their forced separation offered protection against being apprehended together.

But then came The Cleansing. I called my wife soon after the decree went out. The news she delivered tore up my soul. Mark and Tracy, along with their daughter Heather, had been murdered.

And Sage was missing.

For a while I lost all hope. How long before my wife was 'cleansed' as well?

Nero, I thought. *Just like the Emperor of old, all you do is burn things to the ground. If I ever get my hands on you, I'll kill you slowly. I'll roast you over a long fire.* It was all I could do not to fly to Washington hell-bent on disabling the whole defense system, penetrating his lair… and killing him myself.

But God is faithful. The Scripture says that He will not let us be tempted beyond what we can handle, but that He will also provide a way out, so that we can stand up under it.

My way out came with a phone call from Andréa.

She was holding Sage in her arms. My four-year-old son was alive and unharmed! The group that my wife had joined, somewhere up near Minneapolis, was planning to leave soon, as there were too many informants and D.I.s concentrated in that area. The risk of sitting still was always a grave one. The life of an 'undesirable' was one of always being on the move. So, she moved, and found him in another cell in Illinois.

I was overjoyed and relieved to hear that they were both alive. I slept for the first time in weeks the night that call came in. The news: my innocent, 4-year-old son fled on his own, the sole survivor of a massacre, only to run straight into a Christian group who took him in and gave him refuge.

One thing about the mark: it makes you an easy target for Nero's forces, but it also affords you an easily identifiable sympathy pool of Christians. They knew you when they spotted you. That poor little guy was wandering for a while. I had never met my son, but he was proving hardy and resilient. Street-smart. A survivor. I hoped to meet him someday.

Andréa told me many times over the years that she forgave me for "running off with Nero," as she put it. It was an easy joke for an uneasy scenario. She truly did; I knew it in my heart. I wished I could undo all those years of separation. I'd give anything to be with her.

All the while, The Defiance was determined to find a way to beat the mark. One of our guys in Tuscaloosa first conceptualized the idea of the chokers. They weren't hard to mass-produce; it would be the *dissemination* that would be difficult. That took time: three solid years, in fact. And getting them across the oceans would be especially arduous; I don't know how they're faring over there. International commerce has proven more complicated these days with the rise of tech scanners to root out smuggled contraband disguised as perfectly innocent shipments of goods and merchandise.

Still, we had survived to this day, though we were no nearer to deposing Nero and no nearer to unifying our people. Whether in the United States or anywhere else, Christians were largely despised and routinely handed over to the authorities. Rooted out, persecuted and hunted down, our numbers were growing thin. And not all of those converts were part of The Defiance… *yet.*

We had to find a way to unite all of them if we were going to fight back against Nero.

The rest, as they say, was history.

And now I was apparently dead. We all saw Nero's broadcast announcing my demise. A foolish move on his part. All I had to do was reveal that I was alive, and that would send ripples of uncertainty through his flood of deluded followers. But our timing would have to be right, and I began to strategize to that end.

In other news, my Lieutenant Colonel Kent Cannon informed me that The Defiance here had a shipment of the new signal-blocking patches, which had been successfully deployed and tested out in the field. So, our forces were now more protected than they had ever been before. That gave me some comfort knowing that our troops would have more freedom of movement out in the open.

But where were my wife and son?

For the past four days, I had been unnerved and unable to sleep. I had no appetite, and stress had consumed me. I could not focus as easily. I was distracted.

Something had happened. Something was amiss. Last I had heard, Andréa's cell was somewhere around Maple Park, Illinois. Directly west of Chicago, about sixty miles, give or take.

It was an unwritten rule that she had to call me. I could never call her. I wouldn't know where to call anyway. Phone calls could be tracked, and many of the networks were down anyway. Nero's satellites still worked, and he has been actively increasing surveillance.

A final reckoning was coming. Forces were massing. New equipment was inbound. Recruits were signing up in defiance of this corrupt tyrant. We had a few people on a fifth column on the inside, but not enough. Sooner or later, we would have our chance. I prayed that day would come soon. Even more, however, I prayed that Jesus would return soon. He would end all of it. He would bring justice.

In the meantime, something told me that either Andréa or Sage – or *both* – were in danger. I couldn't shake the uneasy feeling. We had a spiritual tether, my wife and I, and we always had, despite the miles and the years. But now – I couldn't feel her. It felt strangely like the tether had suddenly been *un*-tethered, and the line was now unsecured from only one end, blowing lightly in the wind.

My heart was growing heavy indeed.

CHAPTER 21
Sage

1 . 21 . 2113
Elburn, IL

Ξ   Ξ   Ξ

As for most of them, I had lost them forever.

Be that as it may, I needed to try to find them. Like Jasper said, there was a spiritual tether. They didn't feel dead to me. I had to at least *try* to find them. I didn't think Aurora was all that far away. It had been mentioned in conversation with Mother and Father. Maybe Charlie, if she were still alive, would make for her old hometown.

And if I couldn't find them? Well, I was needed out there anyway to run for supplies or use these good ears to listen for Nero's forces and other dangers.

Charlie. Did I have a spiritual tether with Charlie? I wasn't married to her, of course, but I loved her. I had felt no such tether to Andréa. Maybe it wasn't a thing between families, but rather between lovers. In any event, I never even knew Andréa was my mom. Maybe someday I'd feel it and convulse with memories and tears over a life I never knew.

I tried to think of my mother, Tracy Maddox. I barely remembered her anyway; she was killed fourteen years ago. Some of my earliest memories were still there, but they had receded into the past like a dim echo, and I could no longer see her face. The face that I *could* see, however, with much more clarity, was Andréa's.

What a mind job. It called into question who Auntie Leah and Uncle Ethan even were. They had died from VZV2, when I was even younger; I knew them even less. But were they really my aunt and uncle? Were they tied to Mark and Tracy? Or to Andréa? Or *nobody*?

I couldn't think about my old life right now. I needed to focus on the new.

In my heart, I had to believe that Charlie was still alive. And maybe, just maybe, some of the others were as well. They would have stuck together.

Elburn Central wasn't that far east. Aurora wasn't that much further southeast beyond that. Aurora was about twelve miles away, Jasper said.

I gave Jasper the longest hug. He had given me warmth, love, protection, grace, warm clothes, and hot coffee that I'll never forget.

"Juss remember," he said to me, holding a finger up, "where ya got good coffee, ya got good folks. Remember I done told you so, Mr. Sage." He grinned warmly and displayed two rows of brilliantly white chompers, unstained by coffee. I'm guessing he had drunk so much that he had stained his original teeth brown and had to have them all replaced.

I gave him one more hug, and was off. My pack was loaded with food, a handgun and ammo, and, perhaps most importantly, the two chokers I had. I was freshly showered and dressed in clean, newly washed attire. It was high time to set out once more.

Let's see what Aurora holds, I thought, and walked out to an unknown sunrise.

Ξ   Ξ   Ξ

I had no idea what – or who – I would expect in Aurora. I didn't know if I would find anyone else there, and if I did, how many of our original group I'd find, nor what horror stories they would share. I only knew that if I ever saw them again, I'd wrap my arms around them so tight and never let them go this time. In hugging them, I would also be wrapping my arms around Hunter… Andréa… Luca… Fritz… Leona… and maybe even more from our original group.

Hopefully somewhere out there were Miles and Reina's teams as well, since none of us had heard from them. We all knew that these groups were itinerant; these cells were never the same. Every day could change our dynamic, split us off, take us elsewhere, or take others to us. It was a sad reality that we had acclimated to long ago.

Jasper cautioned me to head south and then stick to the road. As the sun rose, I'd be more visible, and thus, people would take less kindly to a stranger walking over their land. I'd also look suspicious to anyone who expected wayfarers to be *on* the road and not trespassing across fields.

"You best be headin' to Rowe Road south of here. You take a right, now, and then you'll be seein' a big ol' reservoir on your left. The road next to that? That's Bateman. Take another left there, you just stick to that; let it wind around south onto North Lorand Road and take ya wit it. It'll dump you out onto Main Street, and you take a left there and get y'self east. Keep goin' aways. Pass Blackberry Creek, and then you gonna hit Highway 47. Head straight south, and that'll be takin' ya to Highway 88, sho nuff. Drove that route a thousand times for milk and bread. You ride 88 all the way right into Aurora. I can't promise none o' these blasted Guardians, now, ya see? But iff'n you can get there, why, you's just gonna have you a smoother road, Mr. Sage."

He was kind enough to draw me a map, and I stuck to that. Once I got to the road, there couldn't be much harm in hitching a ride with someone. That would speed me along in my journey and save a lot of walking. So that's what I planned for.

And then he gave me a gift that I would not soon forget. He recited, "Trust in the Lord with all your heart and lean not on your own understanding; in all your ways submit to Him, and He will make your paths straight."

"The Lord make yo paths straight, son," he said, giving me the verse and sending me off with a wink.

With that, I was on the road again.

Ξ   Ξ   Ξ

The golden orb was riding low in the sky, peeking over the tree line to the east. It had been a relatively noiseless walk, but then again, it almost always was. When half of the world's population is killed off, that's the kind of acoustic environment you face: quiet and desolate, yearning for those who have gone before.

In about an hour, I had made it down to Rowe Road and the reservoir Jasper mentioned. I wound around it and then hung a left onto Bateman. There were very few cars on the road this early, and the sun was beating down on me. For that, I was grateful. It brought heat to already warm clothes.

Thank you, Jasper, I said quietly to myself. *Lord, thank you so much for Jasper. Please take care of him and keep him safe. Thank you for all that he taught me, all that he shared with me, and how he protected me. Protect him in turn, Lord.*

A verse came to me out of the past, something Swifty had once shared. 'You will keep in perfect peace those whose minds are steadfast, because they trust in you.' Isaiah 26:3.

Jasper trusts in you, Jesus. Keep him in perfect peace, please. Amen. Oh- I thought, wanting to add on to that- *I trust in you too, and my mind at least* feels *steadfast. Keep me in perfect peace too, please. In Jesus' Name, Amen.*

I had literally just finished my prayer, when I heard the whirring, and the rumble of vehicles. I didn't dare turn around. Let them pass. I rolled my eyes and closed them tight. *Uh, Lord… I was kinda praying to be steadfast just a bit longer…*

I clenched my teeth and took a deep breath. *Lord, keep me in perfect peace. Please.*

They drew closer. I could practically feel the rush of wind from their vehicles.

I trust in you. Please.

They silently rolled by, and I pretended to be surprised while keeping my pace, trying to look as nonchalant as I could.

The convoy passed and continued on down the road toward Main Street.

In another ten minutes, it was warm enough to not be able to see my breath in front of me anymore. My cheeks were cold, but I felt okay, and my legs were still able to carry me on.

Ahead of me loomed a sign for Main Street. I followed Jasper's directions and turned left, heading toward Blackberry Creek and Highway 47. That would be the last leg before I hit Highway 88.

The familiar rumble of a vehicle sounded behind me. The hood of a car slowly crept into view to my left.

I trust in you, Lord.

"Need a ride?" a voice said.

I paused and looked over. A middle-aged man was behind the wheel, staring at me under thick, bristling brows set below a wide-rimmed cowboy hat. His voice sounded like it had been dragged along asphalt and then hung in ribbons on a clothesline to crack in the sun.

"Uh, yeah, sure, that'd be great," I said. "You goin' to Aurora?"

"Ha! And beyond," he said. "Aurora's nothin.' Be there in five minutes," the man chuckled.

"Great," I said, hopping in. "Thanks for the lift. Cold," I finished, rubbing my raisin-like hands together.

He looked at me curiously for a moment, and then he lunged at me. I put my hands up in fright as his fist flew toward me – but all he did was grab for my neck and lurch me forward while peeling my collar back. The choker fell off clumsily at the impact. "Hey!" I yelled. "What are you-"

He slowly retracted, studying me curiously. "Sheesh. Whaddaya wanna cover that up for, kid?" And then he smiled warmly. Our eyes locked for a moment, and then he twisted his head to the left and pulled his own collar out. There, below it, was the familiar choker covering his own mark, blocking the telltale amber glow of a brother in Christ.

I took a slow, steady breath. "Thank God," I breathed out nervously.

"Hey, I'm sayin' the same thing. 'Always vet the hitchhikers,' the wife says. She's been right on more than one occasion. Name's Rex."

"Rex. I like that. I'm Sage. Thank God, brother."

He laughed heartily, and put the car in drive. We picked up speed and headed down 88 into Aurora.

"Whaddaya doin' out here all by yourself?" he asked.

"We, uh," I began, slowly. "We were up at the high school back there. We were attacked."

He threw me a look filled with alarm. "*Kaneland High School?*"

"Yeah," I said curiously, "you know it?"

"Every Christian for miles around here knows what happened there. You survived that attack too?"

"Yeah, somehow. I don't know how. It just sort of happened suddenly. A lot of us tri-" And then I stopped mid-sentence. "Wait – what do you mean 'too'?"

"You survived the attack too? Like the others did."

"*What* others?" I asked him, eagerly.

"There were four or five others who made it outta there, they said. Made it all the way to Elburn and then Aurora from there. I heard they ran all night and the next day. Took the train, I think."

My heart leapt at the thought, but I was simultaneously seized with terror. My jaw dropped as I stared out into the road before us: a road now fraught with uncertainty.

"What's the matter?"

I couldn't hold back a tear. "Where are they now, do you know? Someone *has* to know. Do you know anyone who might know? I have to find them!" I sniffed.

"Whoa, whoa, ease down, boy. First of all, I'm glad you're safe. Those accursed Guardians killed a lot of good Christians. *Young* Christians. They didn't stand a chance. I'm glad you're okay." He studied me for a moment.

"Sage, there's a brother in Aurora who might know. Knows practically all the believers in Aurora. He runs an unofficial underground church, and they have daily prayer times for whoever can make it. I can take you there, but I can't make any promises that he knows *them*. But he may know someone who does. His name's Mackenzie Allen. You tell him Rex sent you. He'll ask you what my favorite verse is. You tell him Galatians 2:20."

I nodded, swallowing hard. I could remember all that better than Jasper's directions and would need no map.

Charlie. Swifty. Asher. Anja. Emma. Nicholas. They might be *alive*. I would soon know.

Time to trust that tether.

Ξ   Ξ   Ξ

"You keep that choker attached, kid," Rex said. "Plenty of Guardians in and around Aurora. Don't ever forget it. You lose it, you're history."

I nodded. "You too, Brother Rex."

He offered a weak smile. "Alright, this is it right here. We just passed Fox River and Stolp Island. It's a community center. We're at 4th and Downer. Remember that. That's the hub of all of us that are left. I imagine you've seen your share of hideouts. This one ain't no different. You go in there and tell the front desk lady, 'it's a hot day out.'"

I looked at him quizzically. "It's *freezing*."

Rex smiled. "You tell her that. You say, 'It's a hot day out.' She'll say exactly what you just said. And then you say, 'Nah, it's hot… if you got eyes to see it.' And then you just don't say anything at all. You got it?"

At last, I understood. "Got it."

"Good luck, kid. I hope you find who you're looking for." He tipped his hat and I made ready to hop out.

"Thank you, Rex. For the ride, and so much more, brother." I pretended like I was going to throw him a return punch, but then stretched his collar back as he had done to me.

Surprisingly, he yelped just as I had done. "Hey!" And then, seeing my jest, he said, "Oh, I get it. Nice one, kid. Vaya con Dios."

Ξ   Ξ   Ξ

"Hey there," I said to the woman behind the desk as the bell attached to the door gling-glinged. She was a bit older than me, and appeared to be busying herself with paperwork. She had a turtleneck on, and was chewing noisily on a big wad of gum.

There was a pot of coffee brewing on a table behind her, and the aroma filled the front office. I thought back to Jasper's words about good people, and hoped it would be true here.

"Morning," she greeted. "Can I help you?"

I looked at her turtleneck. "Why are you wearing that today? Sure is a hot day out," I said, feeling like I was overacting.

She raised an eyebrow at me and smacked her gums. *"Huh?"*

My mouth suddenly felt pasty. Fearing that the code had failed or I had screwed it up, I stammered. "Uh, I mean, it's, ya know, it's hotter today. Hot. More than… I mean, than yesterday. A bit hotter out. Yeah." I shuffled my feet and looked around.

A smile teased at her lips, and she leaned forward over the top of her counter at me, her eyebrows up but her chin cocked down. "No, it ain't. It's freezing."

I raised my hands up in protest. "No, not really. I mean, it's hot… if, ya know, if you got eyes to see it." She watched me intensely, as if I was really overacting. Made me nervous.

I just nodded my head wordlessly.

"If you got eyes to see it, huh," she eventually repeated. She blew a massive bubble that popped obnoxiously before she sucked it back into the vortex of her gawking mouth.

She smiled at me wholeheartedly, breaking the tension. "It *is* hot," she agreed, tugging at the choker cleverly concealed beneath her turtleneck. "Do you see it?"

"I see it," I said, tugging at my own. I smiled back at her. The cloak-and-dagger nature of it all was amusing. I had to admit, though, that I was now very eager to meet this Mackenzie Allen Rex had spoken of.

"Lemme guess," she said. "Brother Mackenzie?"

I nodded. "Yes, please. Thank you."

"Mmm-hmmm," she said, rising and turning to her phone. She punched a number into the keypad. "Mack. Wendy Jo. Visitor here for you."

In less than a minute, the office door at the end of the lobby opened, and a tall and fairly elderly man with solid black frames came striding toward me. If I didn't know any better, I would think he was eyeing me suspiciously. But suspicion is probably what had kept them alive.

"Thanks, Wendy Jo," he said to the receptionist.

"Yep. This one," said Wendy Jo. "Using *Rex's* greeting, no less."

The man looked me up and down. "Rex, huh. Show me your neck, son."

I did so, revealing my choker underneath my jacket collar. He continued to eye me.

"He tell you anything else to say?"

I thought back to that great guy with the cowboy hat who came in the nick of time in the middle of nowhere, and it brought a smile to my face. I knew Galatians 2:20, sure enough, and rather than just give Mackenzie the address, I spelled it out for him.

"I have been crucified with Christ, and I no longer live, but Christ lives in me," I spoke proudly.

Wendy Jo shifted her gaze from me to Mackenzie. "The kid knows it, Mack." He turned to her. A smile crept across his face as he remained facing her but slowly moved his eyes back to me.

"Mackenzie Allen. Call me Mack. Welcome."

I breathed a sigh of relief.

"Thank you, sir. Thank you, Wendy Jo."

She batted her eyes at me and grinned.

Ξ   Ξ   Ξ

I just stared at him, my mouth agape. "You're sure?"

He nodded his head. "I can take you there. I can't promise it's them, though. They gave us names, but they're not *those* names. Given what they've been through, I don't blame them."

It was reasonable to assume that they were now traveling under pseudonyms after the attack.

"But it was an older guy, two girls around my age, and a boy?"

Mack nodded.

"Did they look beat up? Uh, did the girl have dirty blonde hair?"

"One of 'em did."

"What about the older guy? Was he brunette, about yay tall?" I motioned with my hand.

"That sounds about right."

"Was there another guy with them? Another older guy?"

Mack looked confused, like he was searching his memory. "Sage, I'm sorry, I don't think so. I really am sorry."

An older guy, two girls around my age, and a boy. That meant that it could be Swifty – or Nicholas. The boy had to be Asher. And the girls could be any two of the three: Charlie, Anja, or Emma. At this point, I just wanted to take what I could get. I had to see them.

"Can you take me there? Can somebody take me?"

"I can't, but Wendy Jo can take you in a bit. They wouldn't say exactly how they got here, but Burlington Northern is still runnin', and it goes parallel to 88 right into Aurora. They're hiding out in a warehouse off East New York St and Edge Ave. It's just a six or seven minute drive from here." The only problem is that there's a barricade at New York and Ohio Streets. Big Guardian battalion and checkpoint. Everything east of that is Guardian central, and they fan out from there. It's getting closer to the Windy City, and the big city metros are all Guardian strongholds, you know. They leveled Oakhurst Forest. There's a new Guardian base there. AirGuard and everything. Won't be easy, Sage."

"Why would they be hiding out there then, if it's so close?"

"Probably because they wouldn't look there. It's dangerously close to their little frontier," Mack said.

I thought to myself for a moment. Then I looked up at Mack and asked, "Do you think I would be jeopardizing their safety in going to see them?"

"Only you can determine that." He looked at me earnestly. "I want to give you something, though. A gift. These are being disseminated and shipped out as we speak. If you're going into enemy territory, then you should definitely have one of these."

He rose, turning behind himself and rummaging through a box on a corner table. He pulled out a strange rectangular object, flesh-colored and flimsy, the shade of which seemed to adapt to the light.

"We just call 'em patches. They're the next-gen chokers. They blend right into your skin, and the aluminum-glass plate is still in there, but it's pliable. Takes quite an eye to see them against your skin. Let me put this on you. Here, stand up."

I obliged and turned around, removing my choker. He peeled the adhesive backing off the patch and slowly pressed it against my neck, smoothing it out. I didn't feel any different except for a slight tug against my neck hairs, which I was sure I would eventually acclimate to.

"There. Feel that?"

"Feels funny."

"You'll get used to it. You didn't even notice mine, did you?"

I gasped. "You're marked?"

"Can't even tell, can ya? Here. Take these too. I want you to give them to the people you find in there." He stuffed ten or so more of the patches into my pack.

"Why doesn't Wendy Jo have one?"

He scowled. "She says I don't have anything 'in her shade,'" he said, and then shook his head.

Ξ   Ξ   Ξ

Wendy Jo and I climbed into her Ford Explorer, and headed off to our rendezvous. It would only be a short drive, per Mack. He wished me well and said he'd see me soon. It was now 11:42 am.

We were approaching Ohio and New York. I saw the towers well before we got to the intersection. Small dots descended from the air and came in for a landing somewhere in the encampment ahead.

I swallowed, and my stomach fluttered nervously.

"Just relax," Wendy Jo said, popping her gum.

"You sure you don't want one of those patches?" I asked her.

"Whaddaya think I chew the gum for, honey?" she asked me. "So I don't *have* to smoke anymore."

I took her meaning after a moment. "No, no, the signal patch. The one that blocks the mark. Like the one Mack gave me. It blends right into your skin, and you can't even see it, I guess."

She scoffed. "One day, maybe. Until then, I like my chokers and my turtlenecks. Although, *sure is a hot day out,*" she said, winking at me and blowing a bubble.

The street was closed in all directions, with barricade gates lowered. It was a frenzy of activity in there. A trooper came toward us, armed and holding a tablet.

"Identification," he said curtly. Wendy Jo blew a bubble and held up her wrist. "You too, sir. ID," he directed at me, and I extended my wrist toward him so he could check my name. He punched something into his tablet. "What is your destination?"

"Taqueria la Palma. The Mexican joint up the road. Lunch," she spelled out for him. He cast a glance at her, seeming like he was being patronized, and continued punching things into his tablet. Wendy Jo looked at me and rolled her eyes.

"Wendy Jo Hanson?" he asked. She nodded. He studied her for a moment. "Proceed," he finally said, and then blew a whistle, motioning to someone in the tower to raise the barricade arm.

Two Guardians went zipping past ahead of us, heading north. In the distance, we could just make out an AirGuard coming in for a landing at the forest. "You're allowed three hours maximum. If you're not back within that time frame, you'll be reported missing and in violation of proximity code 534."

"Okie-doke," Wendy Jo said nonchalantly. The man shook his head and backed away.

The arm raised, and we were through. Good thing we weren't actually going for Mexican food, because my stomach couldn't have handled it.

Ξ   Ξ   Ξ

In three more minutes, we arrived. Wendy Jo pulled us into the Mexican restaurant parking lot. I was amazed. "Are we actually eating?"

She shook her head. "No, but this is where their satellites and AirGuards are going to look based on what we said, so this is where my car needs to be. Hop out and give me a hug."

I furrowed my brow but did as she requested. I walked around the Explorer. She was all smiles, talking rather loudly, as if she expected to go on record.

"It's right there, honey. O'Reilly's. Just get a bunch of the stuff, you know, car freshener, extended mirror, steering wheel cover. Mmkay?" She pointed over to the auto parts store after handing me her purchase card.

"Okay, got it. See you in a few." I went in to hug her. She drew me close and whispered in my ear.

"Walk like you're going in but keep walking past it. Head around the backside of the used car lot next door. Somebody'll meet you on the grass at the back door."

She pulled away from me. "And make sure the wheel cover is *pink* this time, okay, hon? I'll be right here waiting."

Man, that woman is a good actress, I thought. I wondered how many times she had been put up for these roles, and how many people she had escorted to any Christian refugees in this hideout.

My heart pounded in my chest as I strolled past O'Reilly's and headed around the back end of the used car lot. I wasn't sure where to look or where to go.

I didn't need to know, because suddenly, a back door burst open, and a shadowy figure pointed a gun at me. I stopped in my tracks and raised my hands.

"Who sent you?"

I stammered. "M-Mack. Mackenzie." The voice paused. "It's a hot day out if you got eyes to see it?" I asked him tentatively, trying the code phrase.

I saw him visibly relax, and then he waved me in. I cautiously approached, slowly entering the building. The gunman had a mask on. The door closed behind us.

He led me through the warehouse and down into the bowels. It was cold down here. I thought back briefly to Rex's code phrase. Nothing hot in here, and I had no eyes to see it. I was shivering. Shivering from the temperature, but also from nerves. Would they be my friends? Would they be someone else? Would the whole thing be one giant setup?

I didn't need to wonder long. We rounded a corner, and I heard her voice. That dirty blonde hair and those big brown eyes stared out at me in wonder.

"Sage?"

Ξ   Ξ   Ξ

It was Charlie. And then Swifty. And there were Asher and Emma as well. My friends were alive! They came running to me and embraced me tightly. I never wanted to let them go. The gunman backed off, and I was consumed by tears and racked by memories, good and bad. My friends! Here they were! Reduced in numbers, haggard, wandering, lonely and cut off, and yet here they were. I grabbed Charlie and gently cradled her head at the ears, just drinking in the sight of her. She was beautiful and dirty and she smelled… but she was gorgeous. I pulled her close and squeezed her until all the world bent toward us.

Swifty rubbed my back. I turned to him and buried my face in his chest. He stunk. I pulled away. "You reek, man." Swifty laughed grimly but deeply.

"That's what train life will do to you, brother."

I hugged him again. And then I looked over at Asher and Emma. There was no Anja. Suddenly it hit me.

My smile faded. "Anja?" I looked at Asher, and he shook his head. I turned to Swifty. His face paled for his daughter, and he said nothing. His lip quivered, and his eyes filled. Swifty dropped his head.

Anja, his daughter and Asher's girlfriend, was dead.

I embraced him again. "Oh, Swifty, I'm so, so sorry, man. Asher, come here. I'm *so* sorry, bro."

And we wept for the saints who were lost. It was a horrendous turn, and all I could see was Asher and Swifty's love for Anja.

But as for these, I had found them again.

CHAPTER 22
Maximillian

1 . 21. 2113
Washington, DC

Ξ　　Ξ　　Ξ

Everything I believed would survive.

There were no more doubts. I may be hearing a still, small voice on occasion, but I chalked it up to the stress of being a High Vassal, clasped my fingers together, prayed to Nero and the Day Star, breathed, and moved on. The time for indecisiveness was over!

The lord Nero had summoned High Vassal Dubois and me to his chamber today. He had something very special he wanted to share with us.

It was evening when I reunited with my co-High Vassal – we still snickered at that – and we bowed lightly to each other. We always liked to process quietly and reverently toward His Eminence's sacred chamber. The solemnity of it, the grandiosity of it, the *privilege* of it – ah! – such an exquisite feeling to hold an audience with my lord.

We performed a once-over of each other, noting any possible shortcomings or anything out of place. Our makeup was unsmudged and accentuated our high cheekbones. Our lipstick was radiant. Our high eyebrows were perfection. Our capirotes were secured to our heads, with our short hair pulled back tight beneath it.

Vassal Richards once more opened the gargantuan doors for us, and there was my lord, seated high atop his throne, enshrined in light. He looked to be meditating or deep in prayer to the Day Star.

Once more, the incense.

Once more, the warm rays of the sun.

Once more, the golden beams through the trailing wisps of smoke.

Once more, the brightness and luminosity of all that was my lord Nero.

Draping the stairs were his concubines, relaxing and lying back on the steps, gazing up at him in silent wonder. They wiggled and slithered slowly as they watched us approach, their quasi-nude bodies painted red like blood, their hair gelled back taut, their teeth filed into fangs.

Nero was silent, and therefore, so were we. His head was bowed, and he was never to be disturbed in such a posture. Therefore, our heads mirrored his. We waited patiently, our arms outstretched, our robes fanning outward, our long nails glistening in the light of the shimmering room.

We waited.

It seemed like an eternity, but no duration was too long to wait for my lord.

Finally, he took a deep breath, and exhaled slowly and graciously. *O that some of his breath might descend upon us!* I thought. I know that High Vassal Dubois was thinking the same thing.

We beheld him as he rose slowly from his seat, opening his eyes and gazing down upon us. With his right hand, he grasped a long, elegant sword. Its golden scabbard swung from his waist. With his left, a shining scepter beset with encrusted jewels. He smiled warmly and slowly drew in breath, holding it there for a moment as we waited ourselves with bated breath for whatever gracious words might fall from his lips into our souls.

"Greetings, my most High Vassals. I have been bequeathed a vision by the Day Star," he began, slowly gliding down from his high throne toward us, down the red-carpeted steps beset with lotus flowers. He carefully threaded his way past his concubines as they bowed their heads and stroked his legs lovingly. The train of his shimmering robe extended past him back up the steps, draping over them as he passed.

"It is time for the next step in our evolution together," he said, smiling at both of us and touching us lightly on our shoulders with the scepter and the sword. "Are you both ready?"

We bowed low before him. "O, your grace," I proclaimed solemnly, "we are most ready to follow you, even unto death." Dubois uttered something similar.

"Fascinating," the Emperor said, looking at Dubois intently. "Because it is of death that I would like to speak to the two of you."

"O yes, my lord. Please speak to us. Impart thy wisdom, my lord," chanted Dubois in a high pitch, clapping.

I quickly glanced over at High Vassal Dubois. This was going to be revelatory.

"I will. And I shall start with my most long-suffering servant, my faithful High Vassal Maximillian," Nero said, facing me. I smiled as a wave of warmth passed through my body. "Dearest Maximillian, do you love me more than anyone else?"

"O yes, my lord, you know that I love you," I replied in earnest.

"I do know. My good vassal, do you *truly* love me?"

He asked me the question again, and I confess that I was confused, but a nervous laugh escaped me. "O yes, sire, yes. I truly do love you. I *truly* love you, sire," I said.

"Wonderful," he whispered, looking me deeply in the eye. I felt so connected to him. And then he asked me a third time. "My good High Vassal Maximillian, most faithful servant of mine, do you love me?" He emphasized each word and then fell silent. I sensed Dubois next to me, watching me curiously, his eyebrows raised.

I was confused, and I nervously let my brow furrow before his grace. "Your Eminence, most holy Nero," I stuttered, "forgive me. But, you know *all* things, lord. You know that I love you."

Nero clenched his lips and smiled. He released his grasp on High Vassal Dubois' shoulders and now turned to face me solely, embracing me by both shoulders.

"I do know, Maximillian. I do." He smiled at me. "But…" And with that word, my own eyebrows raised, and I paused. "…I've been hearing some things from your co-High Vassal Dubois here – adorable nickname, by the way – that concern me. Strange things. Troubling things. Perplexing things. Things that ought not to be. You have flinched, have you not? You have questioned me, silently, within your heart, have you not?" His eyes were piercing my soul as he asked, and my stomach was affright with butterflies. "You have *doubted* me, have you not, my good Maximillian?"

My mouth dropped, and I fought for words as I stammered. "M-my lord, O dearest grace, thrice-worthy and potent Emperor, my liege, and my beloved god-king, n-no, sire. I mean… not exactly, sire, I-"

Nero tilted his head. "Maximillian?" He addressed me, questioningly. I was very much on the spot between the two of them, and felt like an AirGuard searchlight was blinding me in the eyes. "Be honest now. It's natural to question, and to occasionally have doubts. You are human, my child. But you are also the closest thing to a son to me. You *are* my son and my child. And you are utterly precious to me. But I must have fidelity and unflinching worship, or there will be cracks in our foundation, our new foundation in Jerusalem, my faithful vassal."

"Y-yes, lord, of course," I agreed, nodding. I was trembling, and he felt it. He clutched me tightly and drew himself in closer.

"You must have complete belief in me as your savior and your lord. You must believe in me and follow me without question. Can you do that, my High Vassal Maximillian? Can I trust you?"

I stared deeply into his eyes, searching my own soul at his request, and inadvertently searching his. Somewhere in that searching, I heard that strange whisper yet again. That voice that had plagued me over the past week. And that same phrase yet again:

You will know the truth and the truth will set you free.

Oh no, not now! I thought. I could feel my Emperor's hot breath on me as he watched me intently. I churned up every ounce of fidelity I could, every bit of belief I had ever developed in servitude of my lord Nero, and breathed out one word.

Yes.

Nero did not reply. He kept searching me. It was almost as if he, too, had heard the whisper. At long last, his grip on my shoulders loosened, and he brought his face to my face and kissed me on the forehead as he bowed my head toward him. I hoped he didn't feel or sense my sweat, for, truly, I was consumed by heat both from his close proximity as well as from this line of questioning.

"Thank you, my good High Vassal. Thank you for pledging to me anew." And then he stopped, glancing briefly over at High Vassal Dubois for a moment. I was breathing hard. "There remains one final thing to do, then."

"Yes, sire, of course," I said.

"You have always been my favorite. But now I require you to *prove* your fidelity to me. Just as in that fictional tale where the bogus god commanded his blind servant Abraham to prove his love for him, I now ask you to do the same. You must prove your love for me."

"Of course, my lord. Anything," I declared while trembling in a cold sweat.

He stepped back. He handed me his sword. With slow, deliberate movements, he placed the hilt in my hand, cupping his hands over mine, and whispered. It was utterly silent. "You must prove your love for me by killing High Vassal Dubois. Right here, right now."

I glanced over at Dubois. His jaw dropped slowly, and his eyes ping-ponged between us. His countenance fell, and his chest began to rise and fall rapidly. He swallowed and stammered. "Of-of course, sire. Your will be done. If I must die in your service as a testament to High Vassal Maximillian's fidelity, so be it, my lord. Your will is just, and your cause is right," he said. "All hail Emperor Nero."

Nero nodded to him. "All hail Emperor Nero."

Was he really asking me to kill Dubois? As much as I had worked to 'like' Dubois, it was sometimes a struggle – but it was never a struggle unto murder. I would never raise a hand against him. Could I do it now, at Nero's request? Could I slay a fellow servant?

"Sire, I-"

"Do it, Maximillian. I will suffer no delays, doubts or questions. Prove your love to me." He stepped back. I looked back and forth between him and Dubois.

High Vassal Dubois turned to face me, and his eyes began to well over. He was breathing hard and trying desperately to form words. "O-oh, that I might have seen your glory displayed in all the earth, my lord," he said, removing his robe. "That I might have seen you ascend your rightful throne in full splendor." He unclasped his shimmering breastplate and many necklaces. A tear streamed down his cheek, carrying his pasty white makeup down with it, revealing a fleshy human underneath it all.

I struggled.

"Do it, High Vassal Maximillian. I await your proof," said Nero, gravely and parentally. I did not turn to him.

Dubois removed his capirote, and his slicked-back hair shimmered. Loosed from the cap trapping in his heat, buckets of sweat ran down his head, face and neck. He was facing down the end of his life and was trying to do it with dignity and courage. He nodded to me.

I swallowed once more, breathing hard, and obediently raised the sword with both hands, placing the point toward Dubois. He opened up his undershirt at the breast, ripping it apart and baring his teeth. His chest was flesh-colored. The white makeup base stopped at his neck. He held his tattered shirt open and stared toward the heavens. Lines of flesh kept appearing on his face as his hair emptied itself of moisture. He urinated on himself.

"I-I'm sorry, sire, I-" Dubois apologized. Nero said nothing to him.

"Maximillian, I await your proof," the Emperor said, quietly urging me on. "Proceed."

I slowly turned toward Nero, his sword in my hand still extended toward Dubois. "Yes, sire," I whimpered, and a bead of my own sweat trickled down into my eye. I blinked at the irritation. "It, uh... it is difficult, my lord. I try to obey."

"I understand, Maximillian," whispered Nero. "Please proceed," he said. He was now standing four feet to my right, hands clasped at his midsection, watching me under his eyebrows.

"Y-yes, sire," I whispered back, and turned to face Dubois for the final time. His panting accelerated, and he raised his head toward the ceiling of the dome above us, his lips straining at the edges. I could hear the nameless and faceless concubines slithering and hissing in approval, leaning toward us in anticipation.

I had to focus.

I placed the point of the sword on Dubois' chest, slowly, careful not to penetrate him.

You will know the truth and the truth will set you free.

The whispers again. I strove for mastery. What truth? What freedom? I tried to focus on the sword. I gripped the hilt. My hands were shaking.

Dubois was hissing and panting in fear. He knew the end was near.

You will know the truth and the truth will set you free.

I shook my head and blinked hard, preparing to thrust the sword into Dubois' chest. He grimaced and whimpered. His fingers flicked out involuntarily, his painted nails drenched in sweat. I tried.

You will know the truth and the truth will set you free.

I tried. I began to push. Dubois shut his eyes.

You will know the truth and the truth will set you free, Darius.

Darius Antone Forrester, whispered the voice gently and in the most intimate way. I had never before heard my name expressed so sweetly, as if someone had loved me from the very beginning of time itself.

No one had called me that name for what seemed an age. That name was dead to me. For time immemorial I had simply been known as High Vassal Maximillian.

My eyes went wide.

I relaxed my grip. Dubois opened his eyes, panting, and slowly brought his gaze down to me.

"I-can't, sire," I said. "I just… can't."

I could see Nero shake his head, with barely concealed rage. He exhaled fiercely. "*Unacceptable*, Maximillian. Do as I bid. Prove your love to me. Now." He spat those last words at me.

My hands stilled. I watched Dubois. He was glancing back and forth in fear and trepidation between Nero, then me, then back to Nero.

"I can't, sire."

"Prove your love to me!" I could feel his anger climaxing. As it did, my will grew stronger, emboldened from some source I didn't understand yet.

Darius Antone Forrester, said the voice again.

A trembling wave of power passed over me, tingling my skin. I gently withdrew the sword from Dubois.

"*Prove your love to your lord, Maximillian!*" he screamed at me.

"I can't, I can't!" I insisted. "You…" -here I dared to say the words that were growing inside of me, unable to prevent them from springing forth from the well of my rising truth- "You… are *not my lord!*"

He lunged at me. His hands went for the sword. He jostled me. I lost focus as my eyes went wide.

Dubois recoiled and stepped away, sniffling. "Maximillian, stop this at once!" he shrieked. "You treacherous rodent, you… *undesirable*! Obey your master, the Emperor!" he hissed.

"Give me the sword, plebeian!" Nero yelled. My anger grew; there was no turning back now. I was no plebeian! I had served him faithfully. I gripped the sword tightly. I would not relinquish it. How on earth was I able to vie with him physically? Should he not be wrenching the sword from my grasp if he truly was a god-king?? Nero continued to try to wrestle the hilt from me. My own fangs shone. My face grimaced in outrage as I witnessed his pathetically desperate attempt to pry my fingers from the hilt. After all, wasn't I struggling with a god-king? Shouldn't he be able to easily overpower me? My thoughts were bathed in incredulity and ire.

Darius Antone Forrester, you will know the truth, and the truth will set you free.

And then, with everything in me, I desperately wanted to know the truth.

I AM The Truth, Darius!

"Relinquish the sword, servant!" Nero howled.

*"*No. No! *NO!"* I screamed. Then with strength I didn't know I had, I ripped the sword from him and sent a defensive swing to my right as I lurched to the left to escape him.

A cry sounded. The concubines hissed. Dubois gasped. I slowly turned around.

There, on the floor, was Nero, on his hands and knees, looking away from me. I turned to Dubois. His face was awash with rage, and his eyes were white with horror. "How could you? How *could* you, vassal!?!" he hissed at me. I turned back to Nero.

This 'god-king' slowly got up, turning to face me. He had a slash on his left cheek, running solidly from his left ear to below his left eye socket. It was coursing with blood. He pressed his hand to his wound in order to stem the tide of red dripping down his face.

Blood.

Blood from a god-king.

I stared at him between horror and burgeoning clarity: every former truth I had known crumbling around me.

You will know the truth and the truth will set you free.

"You can bleed?" I asked him in a stunned whisper. "You can *bleed? You can bleed?!?!?*" I screamed, backing away from him. I was hysterical. It was all I could say! I repeated it over and over through my tears. He *bled!* The god-king *bled!*

Dubois ran to Nero.

I don't know what happened next. Terror consumed me as the deceit of my old life disintegrated beneath me. Nero fell to the ground, and Dubois rushed to assist him. I fled for the doors and threw them open. Vassal Richards was not to enter unless he was called for by Nero; he knew that. He startled in alarm at my sudden exodus from his lord's chambers and stared at my sword, dripping with blood.

Richards looked up at me in horror.

"Blood from your 'emperor,'" I spewed, disgusted and panting. I pointed the sword at him. Richards looked through the door and saw Nero bleeding, then looked back at me in uncertainty. "Choose this day whom you will serve," I seethed at him. I had no idea where the words came from, though they powered through my teeth.

Richard backed away from me and fled into the chamber, the tall doors closing behind him.

I had no time. I dropped the sword and fled from the hall. Loud shouts of anguish came from the Senate chamber behind me. I threw open the main doors of the building and bolted out in a tearaway frenzy, my robes flowing in the wind of my escape.

"The Emperor is under attack! The Emperor is under attack! Help him!" I screamed. The guards at the door fled inside as I continued to bolt toward the AirGuard Epsilon, the newest model, perched like a waiting falcon on the Capitol lawn. I flung myself up the ramp and into the interior of the ship, making my way toward the cockpit. I had been in them on many occasions, performing routine inspections and ensuring their readiness to depart should there be an emergency. I was relatively familiar with the controls and had even taken test flights just in case I was ever needed in an emergency.

There was a lone pilot there, as was protocol, ready at a moment's notice to evacuate. He stood and faced me in alarm. "High Vassal Maximillian! What's the meaning of this, wha-"

"Pilot, take us out at once! The Emperor has fallen to the sword of High Vassal Dubois!" I interrupted him.

He gasped and strapped back into the pilot's chair, exclaiming, "Yessir, right away, sir. I'm so sorry, High Vassal," he said. "Strap yourself in."

"I regret to inform you that I am in charge now. Do you have weapons in here? We may come under further attack. Engage the cloaking system now!"

"Yessir, in the cabinet behind you, sir. Please strap in, High Vassal. Cloaking engaged, we're lifting off." The engines began to thunder, and the ship whined in an ever-rising pitch, throttling to full.

In a moment we were airborne, flying away from the Capitol building with no one to see where we were, much less where we were going.

Adrenaline pounded through me.

I knew what I had to do. First would be to avail myself of a weapon and command the pilot to let central communications eat static. Behmardi had given me enough information to know what to do there.

Second would be to instruct him to leave Sector 1 and fly to a neutral location: a country not under Nero's control yet. I could think of only one: The United Kingdom. Though the USA and the UK had always been allies, Nero had instigated a rift with the surviving UK Prime Minister, and the country was both unsympathetic to his cause, and unsupportive of his rule. They were the sole country that had the firepower and nuclear deterrent to keep the USA, and thus, Nero, at bay.

Thirdly, I now knew that Colonel Thomas Drexler was out there somewhere, completely justified in his 'treachery,' and he would need my help. His last known area was in or around Lunken Field, which we detonated. Poor Behmardi, I said, forsaking his title in a new empowering step to forsake my own.

I removed my signet ring and threw it down onto the floor of the ship. The metal clinks were drowned out by the roar of the ship's engines.

I was no longer High Vassal, much less even a vassal. I was nothing in Nero's kingdom, and now I was on his Most

Wanted list. I had wounded the god-king, who was not a god in any way. My mind was burning with incredulity at the memory, wanting to cling to everything I had come to believe up until ten minutes ago. I had drawn blood from him and revealed him for what he was: a fake, an imposter, and a deluded liar.

I knew the truth, and the truth had set me free.

We flew east, eluding radar.

At some point the pilot would be hailed, and I would pull the gun on him and instruct him to let them eat static and to continue east. We would land in the UK, and Nero would be crazy to defy their sovereign airspace.

My old life lay behind me in tatters; I had never felt more free.

You will know the truth and the truth will set you free.

I now knew whose voice it was, for no one had ever spoken my old name more sweetly, more lovingly, nor more truthfully.

I stared out through the cockpit as the sky rushed past us, heading for a new horizon.

I am no longer High Vassal Maximillian.

My name, I remembered, is Darius Antone Forrester.

Everything I had believed was dead.

CHAPTER 23
Sage

1 . 22. 2113
Aurora, IL

Ξ   Ξ   Ξ

It's a hard thing not knowing what you're supposed to do.

That was the plain truth. And now that I had heard Swifty's tale of what happened when they were all washed down the corridor, my truth became clearer, and my anger more focused.

I was still grieving Hunter and Andréa. I told all of them about her, and what she told me. Then, Swifty dropped the bomb on me. Andréa *was* my mom. She had *not* lied. She had told Swifty upon initially meeting him with me when I was four. I was bitter at first that the two of them kept it from me, but in my heart, I knew it was for the best. I knew that I needed to forgive him. *Plausible deniability*, he had said. My wrist ID had been reprogrammed anyway.

I would grow up believing I was Sage Maddox, when in all reality, I was Sage *Drexler*. And Andréa was Andréa Drexler, though I never knew her alias last name. I wept at not really knowing my mother at all, and especially at not learning the truth until the very end.

I couldn't be angry at Swifty or the other leaders. Nicholas and Fritz knew, Swifty said, but he wasn't sure if Andréa had opened up to Leona. The kids – my friends –

were all blameless; none of them knew. Certainly, Hunter never knew. He would have told me. But neither Charlie, Asher, Emma nor Anja knew, which was some comfort.

I recounted how Hunter had drowned, his last words, losing Andréa, fleeing the school, seeing the bodies, meeting Jasper, his confrontation with the Guardians, Rex, Wendy Jo, and Mackenzie, the checkpoint, and the trip to see all of them. I briefly wondered how long Wendy Jo was planning on waiting for me, if she was even still there. But then, if I didn't come back with her, wouldn't the soldiers demand to know where her passenger went? We had three hours, which meant I only had two left.

The urgency of that thought tugged at me. But then, Swifty told me about how Anja died. I watched Asher the entire time: he was sullen and stone-faced, a slate; he had closed off from his emotions following the loss of his girlfriend. Swifty was more articulate with his feelings, and he shared their account as I sat with my arms wrapped around Charlie. I was afraid to let her go.

"We washed down the corridor and flooded out the other end," Swifty began. "The troops and Guardians were waiting for us as we all poured out. Most tried to flee and were gunned down. Everyone who could, fled, as a hail of bullets blasted the water and the buildings. They took off in every direction, Sage, and all the troops and Guardians pursued them. We stayed near the back and kept our hands up. A Guardian approached and had its guns trained on us. We waited. It inched closer. The others were hunted down and shot on sight, mark or no. Nicholas tried to make a break for it, and, uh…" he trailed off. "Well, he didn't make it."

He paused. He was wrestling with guilt and shame written all over his face. "I, uh," he tried, and then swallowed hard, his eyes filling with tears, "I had t-told these guys quietly, uh…" He couldn't finish.

"What, Swifty?" I asked, leaning forward. "What is it?" Charlie began to quake underneath my arms.

He stared at me, and his lip was quivering. The truth was a somber one indeed. "I whispered to them… I told them to…" he tried again. "I told them to deny Jesus," he said, and then he convulsed and lost all composure, exploding in tears and burying his face in his hands.

My thoughts went back to Jasper. "Swifty, hey man, it's okay. It really is okay. I got some insight on that from Jasper," I tried to offer him, but he would have none of it.

"No, Sage, it's not okay," he said, shooting back up. "At least, it wasn't okay with Anja." Asher visibly tensed, and I stole a glance his way.

"What do you mean?"

"I told them to deny Jesus, Sage, and they did! We all did. The stupid machines asked us that stupid question, and we all recanted. They backed off." He took a deep breath. "Well, that wasn't okay with Anja. My brave baby girl, so stubborn…" It was too much for him. He couldn't continue. Amidst his tears and cries, he mumbled the words, "I'll never be able to undo it; I'll never be able to undo it. I-" Emma put her arm around him, and Asher nudged him reassuringly even as he himself had begun to weep inconsolably.

Emma picked up where he left off. "She exploded in anger. She turned around and pointed her finger at her dad, yelling. She asked, 'How could you?' She was screaming at him, Sage. She said, 'Oh, now that the rubber's finally meeting the road, you just deny Jesus, dad?' Her words were scorching. She shook her head and just tore into him."

Swifty was now a mess, trembling violently. Emma rubbed his back. "Well, that stupid Guardian – I'm so tired of calling them that – told her to get back in line, and asked her once more if she would recant. She had her back to it. She clenched her lip, turned slowly around, and looked it right in its eyes, man. She was *this* close," she said, pinching her fingers. "She summoned up every single ounce of volume she had in her, Sage. She screamed just like Luca, dude. *Jesus Christ reigns! The Son of the Living God reigns!* That thing didn't even let her get the whole phrase out. We didn't have our chokers. It saw her mark. It registered her words. It…" she paused, "blew her whole head off."

Swifty erupted into new tears and could not be consoled. He heaved and retched, and they had him lie back and just breathe.

Awful. I felt a spasm of rage roar through my body, and I trembled from the onslaught. Nero couldn't get away with this. Leona. Fritz. Luca. Hunter. Andréa. Nicholas. Anja. When would it end? When would it *really* end, for him or for us?

I felt Charlie stir. "Anja slumped lifelessly into Swifty's arms, man. Her blood poured out all over him. Well… he looked up, and he was gonna charge at that thing. I dunno how we held him back. The others, they…" she paused, trying to remember, "it was a blur… but they were all over the campus, being hunted down. We didn't know

Asher had a gun. He circled around, took aim and shot it point-blank in the back of the head while it was focused on Anja. Kept pulling the trigger even though he was out of ammo. His expression, it-" she stopped, seized by horror. She turned and stared at Asher, who had his head down. "There was nothing there. There wasn't anything left in him. No feeling, Sage. They had sucked it all out of him. We were fortunate there were no other Guardians around; they were pursuing everyone else."

I looked over at Asher. Still stone-faced.

"We were left alone," Charlie continued. "They were all racing after the others. We just left Anja's body and bolted. That was hard for Swifty, but I think it galvanized him. He was mad, man. We couldn't keep up with him. Well, you know the number one rule: *Keep up with Swifty.* I've never run faster, even when I fled from my aunt's house. We crossed from the school and ran straight south, east, west, I don't even know. I tried to use my ears like you do, Sage," she said. "I thought I heard a train. We made for it and hopped aboard on one of the empty cars. And then… we got here. By God's grace we found Alex. He owns this place. That's who brought you down here. And he knows Mack."

I squeezed Charlie to me. She put her hand on my arm, which I still had wrapped around her. I sighed, glancing over at Swifty. It looked as if he was starting to recover from hyperventilating. I felt like I was just starting to. But I didn't want to hear anymore. I had to collect myself and stand… to get out of there and think what we could do now. What *I* could do. "I need some air. Charlie, come with me?"

She nodded.

"Sage," said a voice. I turned back. It was Swifty. He slowly sat up, and his eyes were red and inflamed. "I'm sorry about Hunter. I'm sorry about your mom. I'm just," he gathered breath into his lungs, "sorry about everything, kid. We couldn't tell you."

"I appreciate it, Swifty. I'm not mad at you. I don't know who exactly I'm mad at. I just need some air, man."

Swifty didn't say anything; he just lay back down. I patted Asher's shoulder and walked out. Charlie followed me into the afternoon air.

Ξ   Ξ   Ξ

I kicked at the clumps of snow outside the building. Charlie stood with her hands in her pockets. I looked over at her. She smiled.

"I'm glad you're okay, Sage."

I nodded. "You too, Charlie. Come here," I said, and then she walked briskly over to me and put her hands in my pockets to keep them warm. I hugged her.

And then, without warning, she pulled away from me, her face an inch from mine. I looked deep into her big, brown eyes, stroking her hair. A moment of rippling uncertainty passed between us. She glanced down at my lips.

Before I knew what was happening, she pulled closer to me, and I to her. She didn't resist, nor did I.

Our lips intertwined, and I came alive inside. I could feel my pulse quicken, and hers too, through my fingers, which were now tracing down her neck. It was the most passionate encounter I had ever experienced. Our moment was beautiful: tense yet calm, sudden yet welcome, passionate yet tender. Her arteries were pounding under my digits.

And then… just like that, it was over. A thousand yearnings culminated in that ten-second kiss. She gazed into my eyes and sunk into my embrace once more. We stared over each other's shoulders for nigh on two minutes, and then headed back together behind the car lot building they were all hiding in, holding hands.

"What do we do now?" she asked me tentatively, brushing her hair behind her ear as the wind whipped it around her face.

I didn't answer at first. She looked at me hard. "Where do we go?"

"I don't know," I said at last as we kept walking.

"Ya know, Swifty said that Mackenzie has heard rumors of something going on around Cincinnati," she said with hope. "Something big. Like, The Defiance. That it probably has something to do with Colonel Drexler."

Something caught my eye on the ground up ahead as she talked, and I angled us toward it. I disregarded that she said his name; as far as I was concerned, I needed to hear from the horse's mouth if he was actually my father. Until that time, I only had a mother, and she had just drowned.

"He thinks we should head that way soon and see if we can connect with the Colonel. After all these recent attacks, he thinks we might be safer there. With them. What do you think?"

We reached a spot on the ground where I saw the yellow object. It was a crumpled-up piece of paper, blowing lightly along the ground from the wind that rushed over the grass south of us.

I released her hand and then crouched down to pick it up. I knew what it was before I even uncrumpled it.

"Sage?"

I pulled it out and read it. From the recesses of my mind, I remembered my best friend. Hunter's words came to me, married to my thought of meeting Nero and taking action against him.

What would you say to him if you ever met him face to face?

I'd look him in the eye and say two things. 'There is a God, and you're not him.' But Hunt, the sad truth is that I might do a lot more than that before I could even calm down to speak to him.

I held that disgusting *Friends of Nero* flyer in my hands, thinking and staring at the ground.

I was to facilitate justice. *I* was the one who was going to depose Nero. I had to. Something in me screamed that this was my calling. It's why I had been protected and sheltered all this time. It's why my father was the Colonel.

It was why I had survived. It's why I was that close to a Guardian only a few days ago, and I was still breathing. God was carrying me through all that – and indeed He had been carrying me all my life – for a purpose!

It was my destiny.

"Sage, you okay? What is it?" Charlie asked again.

I slowly rose. In the distance, I could make out an AirGuard ship flying toward us, presumably heading for that Oakhurst Forest that they had leveled and turned into a new base. I knew what I had to do. Andréa's words came back to me. *Always do God's will, son. You are a soldier! Never forget, Sage…*

I turned abruptly back to Charlie, crumpling the flyer tightly once more. I glanced briefly at her lips. The memory of that kiss still lingered vividly in my mind.

"Time to become a jackal," I said to her, with a thousand-yard stare and a grim smile of determination.

She tilted her head in confusion. "A jackal?"

I took a deep breath, pushing it out methodically. "I'm gonna kill him, Charlie. I'm gonna kill Nero."

She scoffed for a moment, looking at me from under her eyes. "And how're you gonna do that, Sage? You're his enemy. Your *dad* is his *most hated* enemy. You'd never get close to him."

"I *will* get close to him," I said, determined. "And I *am* his enemy, you're right. So? I turn the tables. I become a jackal."

Again, she looked confused, squinting her eyes at me.

"I become a *Friend of Nero*."

Charlie's eyes went wide.

It's an empowering thing knowing precisely what you're supposed to do.

TO BE CONTINUED

The end…is only the beginning.

Nero is coming.

Be sure to visit https://thisisnottheend.com for news about *The End*, or sign up on Aaron's website at https://authoraaronryan.com/blog.

AFTERWORD

When I finished the *Dissonance* alien invasion saga in 2024, I knew there would be something else waiting for me after that: something powerful, compelling, and colossal that would demand my full attention in 2025. It needed to be captivating… enthralling… high-stakes… and Christian.

Wait, what?

That's right, Christian. You see, I'm a Christian: a believer in Christ, and I wanted to write a dystopian series that challenged what I knew of the end times and the tribulation forewarned in Revelation (and elsewhere in the Bible). I wanted to sculpt a conceivable narrative that wouldn't have anything to do with zombies, or aliens, or nuclear meltdowns, or pandemics, but with *people*. The human struggle, at its core, is so gripping and relatable, and were it to involve a Biblical end-times scenario, that would reach like-minded readers who were searching for such material.

I won't ever forget reading Tim LaHaye and Jerry B. Jenkins' *Left Behind* series in the nineties, wondering how close to reality that might be. While my own series is admittedly not the Revelation struggle and is something else entirely, I soon realized that I was at an impasse with something that I would have to find a clever way through. What was that something?

The Bible. The inerrant Word of God, the Holy Scripture, God-breathed and given to mankind, lays out the end-times tribulation in striking detail. I chose to write something that was not in defiance of Scripture but rather complement it as a plausible *additional* scenario that mankind might bring upon itself.

I remain fascinated with post-apocalyptic and dystopian scenarios, as they often draw comparisons with what the apostle John was writing about in Revelation. So many writers of dystopian or post-apocalyptic fiction deal with such a setting (often rife with zombies, *blecchhh!*) but the travesties call to mind what Scripture tells us will happen. These scenarios conflict with Scripture, in fact; there is a discord between the fictional and the coming real: how do they reconcile?

The truth, at least in my humble opinion, is that they do not, in fact, reconcile. One is subservient to another. Even the *Left Behind* series, dealing with the end times and Revelation itself, must bow the knee to the inerrant and infallible Word of God. It's simply a fictional, plausible narrative of what could be. As is mine: a fictional, plausible narrative of what could be. God forbid mine actually *does* happen, and *The End* saga does become a preceding reality to the tribulation. All in all, the writers of the *Left Behind* saga, like myself, are creators: we dreamt up something and put it in print, realizing our own imaginations and conceptions of what could be. The only thing that could possibly reconcile with God's Word… is God's Word itself when it unfolds upon mankind, and all of those end times prophecies actually come true once we find ourselves in the middle of that frightening seven-year period.

For my own series, I've strived to flesh out a story that is compelling, inspiring, and keeps God at the center. Keeps hope at the center. Keeps Jesus at the center. Though everything is blowing apart around us, though our flesh and our hearts may fail, God is the strength of my heart and my portion forever." (Psalm 73:26.)

What I've so loved about this new series is being free to incorporate the most powerful element of my life: *Jesus*. To bring Him into this story – front and center – and to keep Him there, has been so fulfilling. It's Christian fiction with a focus on Christ. Jesus is the Lord of my life. He's my everything, and to write about him in the context of a new series has been utterly fulfilling.

To be able to freely insert Scripture, the Word of God, which is the Sword of the Spirit, so prevalently throughout this story, without shame, without apology, makes my heart sing.

The Word of God is living and active. Sharper than any double-edged sword, it penetrates even to dividing soul and spirit, joints and marrow; it judges the thoughts and attitudes of the heart!" (Hebrews 4:12). Thank you, Lord!

If you, a Christian, have read any of my other works, you'll note that some of them have contained profanity and somewhat objectionable materials. I have *always* struggled with such inclusions. I've always wanted to maintain verisimilitude in what I write, and always longed to present a gritty reality that isn't glossed over.

For example, in the *Dissonance* series, if you're being chased by terrifying gorgons, you don't just say, "Oh, well, fiddlesticks. Shucks. Goldurn it." For this series, however, I desperately wanted clean fiction and to have to apologize for nothing. I trust I accomplished that. Forgive me if I have offended you with anything else I have written.

Thank you to my beloved editor Janine Graves. Thank you to my ARC readers Walker Armstrong, Victoria Richmond, and Laura Vosika. Thank you to my audiobook reviewers Victoria Richmond and Rhonda Davis.

With everything that is in me, *THANK YOU* for reading this series. I hope you've thoroughly enjoyed it and that it has utterly blessed you. May the grace of our Lord be with you, now and always… may you stay blameless until he comes. May the grace of our Lord Jesus Christ, and the love of God, and the fellowship of the Holy Spirit be with you." (2 Corinthians 13:14). *Maranatha, Lord!*

With love,

Aaron Ryan

ABOUT THE AUTHOR

Award-winning and bestselling author Aaron Ryan lives in Washington with his wife and two sons, along with Macy the dog, Winston the cat, and Inky, Pinky, Blinky & Clyde, the finches.

He is the author of the bestselling *Dissonance* 6-book alien invasion saga, the dystopian Christian fiction saga *The End*, the *Talisman* series, the sci-fi thrillers *Forecast* and *The Slide*, *God is Not Santa,* the children's picture books *The Ring of Truth*, *The Sword of Joy* and *The Book of Power*, the business reference books *How to Successfully Self-Publish & Promote Your Self-Published Book* and *The Superhero Anomaly*, 6 business books on voiceovers penned under his former stage name (Joshua Alexander), as well as a previous fictional novel, *The Omega Room.*

When he was in second grade, he was tasked with writing a creative assignment: a fictional book. And thus, *The Electric Boy* was born: a simple novella full of intrigue, fantasy, and 7-year-old wits that electrified Aaron's desire to write. From that point forward, Aaron evolved into a creative soul that desired to create.

He enjoys the arts, media, music, performing, poetry, and being a daddy. In his lifetime he has been an author, voiceover artist, wedding videographer, stage performer, musician, producer, rock/pop artist, executive assistant, service manager, paperboy, CSR, poet, tech support, worship leader, and more. The diversity of his life experiences gives him a unique approach to business, life, ministry, faith, and entertainment.

Aaron's favorite author by far is J.R.R. Tolkien, but he also enjoys Suzanne Collins, James S.A. Corey, Michael Crichton, Marie Lu, Madeleine L'Engle, John Grisham, Tom Clancy, C.S. Lewis, Stephen King and Dave Barry.

Aaron has always had a passion for storytelling. Visit his author website at www.authoraaronryan.com, the Dissonance post-apocalyptic alien invasion website at www.dissonancetheseries.com, or *The End* dystopian saga website at www.thisisnottheend.com.

If you liked this or any of Aaron's books, please visit the Amazon and Goodreads pages for the specific book(s) and leave a positive review. Once it shows up, please email the screenshot of it to me@authoraaronryan.com for a discount on your next book purchase from him! Thank you so much. Reviews really do help a ton.

Visit Aaron's website and sign up at the Blog:

Subscribe to Author Aaron Ryan

Follow Aaron and connect on Social Media:

CONNECT WITH AARON

Feel free to check out the following links for further information on Aaron:

Subscribe to Aaron's blog for free giveaways, news and new releases at **https://authoraaronryan.com/blog**

Join the Author Aaron Ryan exclusive Facebook community at **https://facebook.com/groups/authoraaronryan**

Subscribe to Aaron's YouTube channel at **https://youtube.com/@authoraaronryan**

Visit Aaron's social media links to connect with him at **https://dot.cards/authoraaronryan**

Visit **https://thisisnottheend.com/** for information on the entire epic "The End" saga, or Aaron's website at **https://authoraaronryan.com**

ALSO BY THE AUTHOR

As Aaron Ryan:

The End: Alpha

The End: Omega

The Complete THE END Christian Dystopian Saga

The Talisman Series

The Ring of Truth

The Sword of Joy

The Book of Power

The Christian Kids Values, Identity & Affirmation Series

God Is Not Santa

Examining The Lord of the Rings: An independent critique by Aaron Ryan

Dissonance Volume I: Reality

Dissonance Volume II: Reckoning

Dissonance Volume III: Renegade

Dissonance Volume IV: Relentless

Dissonance Volume Zero: Revelation

Dissonance Volume Up: Rising

The Complete Dissonance Sci-Fi Alien Invasion Saga

Forecast

The Slide

The Phoenix Experiment

The Superhero Anomaly

How to Successfully Self-Publish & Promote Your Independent Book: A Self-Publishing & Business Marketing Guide For The Independent Author

Reflections: A Compilation of Journals and Poetry

The Omega Room (abandoned in the early 90's)

Autobiography (no longer available)

Glimmerings – works of poetry

As his former stage name, Josh Alexander:

Voiceovers: A Super Business, A Super Life

Voiceovers: A Super Fun Pursuit

Voiceovers: A Super Responsibility

Running a Successful Voiceover Business

How do I get started in Voiceovers?

Five T's to Triumph: The Secrets to Getting Cast in Voiceovers